THE HAUNTING OF VELKWOOD

ALSO BY GWENDOLYN KISTE

Reluctant Immortals
Boneset & Feathers
The Invention of Ghosts
The Rust Maidens
Pretty Marys All in a Row
And Her Smile Will Untether the Universe

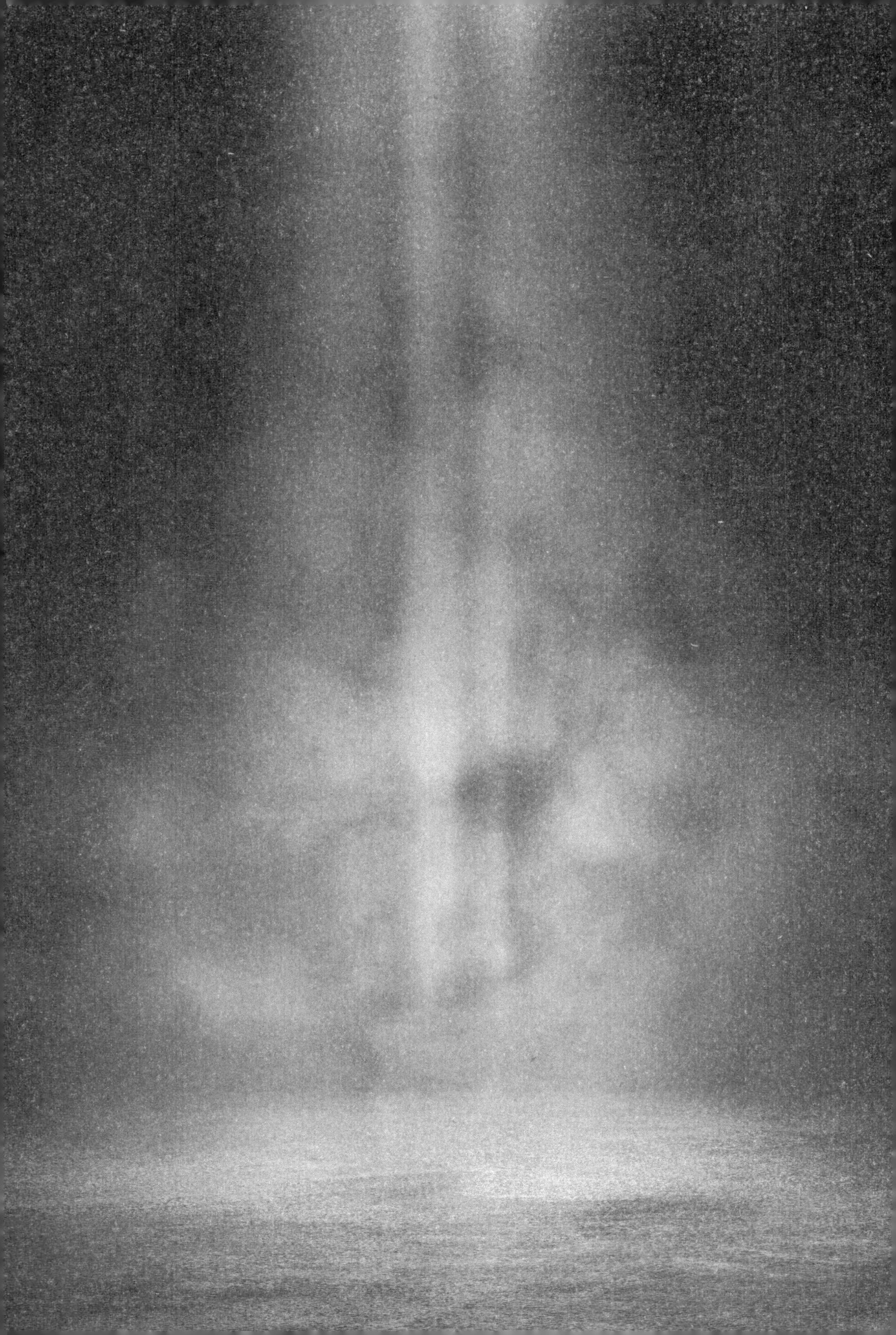

THE HAUNTING OF VELKWOOD

GWENDOLYN KISTE

SAGA PRESS

LONDON SYDNEY NEW YORK TORONTO NEW DELHI

1230 AVENUE OF THE AMERICAS, NEW YORK, NEW YORK 10020

This book is a work of fiction. Any references to historical events, real people, or real places are used fictitiously. Other names, characters, places, and events are products of the author's imagination, and any resemblance to actual events or places or persons, living or dead, is entirely coincidental.

First Saga Press hardcover edition March 2024

SAGA PRESS and colophon are trademarks of Simon & Schuster, LLC

Simon & Schuster: Celebrating 100 Years of Publishing in 2024

Interior design by Lewelin Polanco

Manufactured in the United States of America

3 5 7 9 10 8 6 4 2

Library of Congress Cataloging-in-Publication Data is available.

ISBN 978-1-9821-7237-4
ISBN 978-1-9821-7238-1 (ebook)

For the survivors and the cycle breakers

THE HAUNTING OF VELKWOOD

CHAPTER
1

I'm raking dead leaves in my front yard when a figure with a leather briefcase and a crooked smile appears on the sidewalk.

"Talitha Velkwood?" he asks, as if it's a genuine question, as if he doesn't already know exactly who I am.

I barely look up at him. "You're here to talk about ghosts, right?"

He offers to buy me a cup of coffee at the shop across the street, and with a stack of bills marked *Past Due* stuffed in my mailbox, I'm in no position to turn anyone down.

We sit at a corner table next to a smudged window, fidgeting in our seats.

"Thank you for meeting with me," he says at last, and flashes me that crooked smile again. Up close, he's younger than I expect, maybe even a few years younger than me. These days, it seems everybody's younger than me. He tells me his name is Jack, and on reflex, I introduce myself, even though we've already been over this. He knows my name, knows everything about me. The whole world does. When you survive a tragedy like mine, privacy is suddenly a luxury you can't afford.

"You from the government?" I ask, as I grip my coffee cup in both hands, the heat warming my palms.

He shakes his head. "Foxwell Enterprises," he says, as though that's supposed to mean something to me.

I sit back and stare at him, wondering how long this will take. Those leaves aren't going to rake themselves.

"Foxwell's a nonprofit," he clarifies. "We're interested in the Velkwood Vicinity."

I scoff, turning toward the window. "You and everyone else."

The Velkwood Vicinity. I've always thought how it's a bit of a misnomer since it's not much of a vicinity, not much of anything. It's just a single street, one little block, eight houses in total. A blink-and-miss-it sort of subdivision, smack-dab in the middle of the suburbs.

Or at least it was blink-and-miss-it until something happened, something the world has spent years trying to unravel. A cosmic anomaly, a few people say. Proof of life after death, according to others. Either way, it went from a nothing neighborhood to a literal nothing—you can barely see it now, even when you're looking right at it. Day and night, it wavers in between, there and not there, like some kind of ghoulish Brigadoon.

And because we lived there, me and my mom and my little sister Sophie, it's named after us.

"Why couldn't you choose the Owens or the Spencers down the road?" I asked at the time, but it made sense in its own morbid way. We were the first ones to build a house on the allotment, way back in '88 when Aqua Net and indoor shopping malls were the order of the day, and ghosts were the furthest thing from our minds. That meant the street was christened with our last name. So when reality split in two, and there was suddenly no more neighborhood, only the misty outline where one used to be, the zone ended up named for us, too.

"I've got to tell you," Jack says, leaning forward, cappuccino machines hissing pleasantly in the background. "I've been studying

Velkwood Street for years. Since back when I was still in high school. So this is a real honor to finally meet you."

He's so earnest when he says it that I almost laugh in his face.

I take another sip of coffee instead. "It's been a while since anyone asked me about this."

No matter where I moved, I used to get guys like him sniffing around at least once a month. Cut-rate journalists and eager scientists and more than my fair share of G-men, all of them with lots of questions and very few answers. They expected me to fill in the blanks, like the neighborhood was just a riddle waiting to be solved, and I was their own personal cipher.

But that was a long time ago. It's been twenty years now since it happened, and even ghosts have got a shelf life. Everybody tried to study the phenomenon, tried to get inside and see what had really happened, but the neighborhood would have none of that.

So the government did the next best thing. They blocked it off with pylons like it was a sinkhole and called it a day. Until this afternoon, I thought everyone had abandoned the street.

But Jack's apparently not the type to walk away.

"We just got a grant," he says, a flinty look in his eyes. "For research. You see, I've got a theory."

And with that, he starts in, expounding on his four-part hypothesis. I stare into my coffee cup and wish I was someone else. They all used to have a spiel like this one, everyone so cocksure they knew why the neighborhood vanished off the map, even though they never seemed to be able to prove it.

"I've got pictures," Jack says, and fumbles in his briefcase. "We sent in a drone. It didn't last long inside. They always break down after a few minutes, but we managed to get these."

He slides a small stack of eight-by-tens across the table to me.

They're the same size as acting headshots, as though the neighborhood is an ingenue auditioning for a movie role.

My head down, I thumb through the images, already braced for disappointment. People have tried taking pictures before, but they never come up with anything. And these ones are business as usual—a rusted-out mailbox, a sinuous street draped in shadow, a blur that could be anything at all—until I get to the last one.

It's a grainy photo of a dark gray split-level with red trim, and I recognize it in an instant. That's my house. Or at least it *was* my house back when things like deeds and property taxes and family dinners actually mattered.

I count the windows in the front. The third one over, the one that belonged to my little sister, Sophie. Even from here, I can tell her night-light is on. I always made sure of it. Every evening before bed, I'd tuck her in and flip the tiny switch. Sophie didn't like the dark. She always said it was coming for her.

"Don't go," she'd say, holding tight to her plastic pony named Sam.

I'd just laugh and kiss her forehead. "You know I'll be here in the morning," I promised her. "I'll always come back for you."

"Please don't forget," she'd tell me, her face half-hidden beneath her bedsheet. "Because I'll be waiting, Talitha."

"I haven't forgotten," I whisper and press my fingertips into her window on the photograph, as though I can still feel her there.

Velkwood Street isn't your garden-variety haunting. There are no spectral whispers, no phantoms in chains, at least none that we've seen. Instead, it's the houses and the sidewalk that are ghosts, death leached into the soil, into everything. Or at least that's the official story.

"Are they all dead?" I asked twenty years ago when the government types sat me down at a long, empty table in a long, empty room. But nobody could give me a straight answer. They couldn't tell me who was even still in there. Ghosts aren't keen on roll call, and without a clear aerial view or an eyewitness, it was all guesswork. Sophie might still be inside, haunting her own life. My eight-year-old baby sister, never allowed to grow up. My mom might still be there too, along with everyone else we knew from the neighborhood.

Or maybe they're not. Maybe they've been dead for decades, vanished in whatever disaster turned the street into a ghost in the first place. Nobody knows for sure. That's the problem.

Only I decided long ago what I think: they're gone, plain and simple. After all, ghosts are rarely subtle. If they were still around, somebody would have seen them by now, lingering at the edges of a blurry photo or calling out from within the confines of the street, their ethereal voices ringing out into the night like an eternal curse. But that's never happened, not once, not in twenty years. The only thing left now is the illusion of that neighborhood. A living memory, a vague mirage.

I pass the pictures back to Jack, all except for the shot of my house.

"Can I keep this one?" I ask, holding it close.

He gives me a half smile. "If you'd like," he says, and blushes a little. You can tell he doesn't usually do this, doesn't make chitchat with strangers, doesn't talk much at all. I know what that's like, the way life sneaks up on you. The way you end up alone, one day at a time.

Of course, I'm only assuming he's alone. Maybe I've been on my own for so long that I just figure everyone else is too.

We sit together, the coffee shop bustling all around us, and I hold my breath, waiting for it. For what he's about to do next. What they always do.

"You could help me," he says finally, and I already know where this is going. Or rather, where he wants me to go.

"No," I say, before he can even ask.

I clamber to my feet, my head gone gauzy, because I hate this. The way my past is a spectacle to people, a sideshow curiosity. Somewhere they always want to drag me back to.

I start to move for the door, but Jack is suddenly standing too, something in his face gone frantic.

"Please." He leans closer, his hand on my arm, his touch warm. I should pull away, but I don't. Instead, I ease back into my seat, my eyes on him.

"Why now?" I ask. "After all this time, why would I ever want to go back there?"

"Because," he says, "it would mean so much to us. To everyone. This grant is a real opportunity."

A real opportunity. What a joke. If it were a real opportunity, then they could get somebody else for the job.

"Why don't you ask Brett Hadley?" I say, and for a moment, it takes my breath away. I haven't spoken her name aloud to anyone in years. My once-upon-a-time best friend, someone who's less than a stranger to me now.

Jack shakes his head. "Brett already said no. The same with Grace Spencer. You're our last chance."

It's been a long time since anyone mentioned the three of us together. Me and Brett and Grace. We were the girls who got out, the last ones to escape the neighborhood. We all returned to college on a Sunday night, and the street was gone by Monday morning. Nobody except us called that a coincidence.

I rock back and forth in my seat, my coffee cup gone cold. "There's no reason to return," I say. "Nobody's left over there."

"Maybe not." Jack goes quiet, as if genuinely considering this, the pointlessness of it all. "But if that's true, it couldn't hurt, right?"

He watches me across the table, his gaze sliding slowly over me in a way I like more than I should. He wants me to be thinking about his proposition, about me returning to my old neighborhood, but here I am with my free cup of coffee, thinking of a different proposition altogether. Me and him and whatever fleabag motel room his nonprofit could afford. A distraction from my day, from my life. He's cute enough, and a little desperate too, that spark of hopefulness brimming in his eyes.

I smile at him, the first time I've smiled all day, maybe all week. He grins back, blushing again. I'm practically a celebrity to him, some girl he's studied for years, and I think how easy this would be. I probably wouldn't even have to ask the question before he'd be more than eager to answer.

I start to say something to him, maybe something I'll regret, but that's when I hear her voice in my head, echoing like she never went away at all.

You're not a very nice girl, are you?

My mother, her words like a switchblade in my back. I remember when she said that to me, the two of us alone in the rec room, the rage boiling in her eyes, everything about her looking too disappointed to bear. That was me, the daughter who was only good at not being good enough. And hell, she might have been right. I'm probably not very nice, not the right kind of girl. But if you look at the others in my neighborhood, some of them never got to leave. They're less than air now, less than nothing. So maybe being a nice girl doesn't have the perks everyone tells you it does.

But I'll try to be a nice girl today. I'll try to make my mother proud, even though she's probably dead and would probably be ashamed of me either way.

I finish off the last of my coffee. "I need to get back."

I head out the door, but Jack follows me onto the sidewalk, the November air crisp and unforgiving. "We could pay you," he says, and I can't help but turn back, my heart as empty as my bank account.

"How much?" I ask.

"Five thousand."

"That's it?" I curl up my nose. "One of those sleazy paranormal reality shows could pay me twice that."

"I told you we're a charity," he says, his voice wavering, because he already knows he's losing this fight. I'm already walking away. "Plus, we can get the permits. Those reality shows can't."

He's right about that. You can't visit the Velkwood Vicinity without approval, and most of the time, you can't visit even then. The area isn't very welcoming to visitors, and I don't just mean the government. The land doesn't let you in. You can't get close, even if you try.

Or at least most people can't get close. That's why Jack is here talking to me.

"I already told you," I say, still gripping the picture of my house. "There's nobody left in there."

"That's all right," he says. "You'd get the money either way."

"And what if it's not safe?" I inspect the cracks in the sidewalk, the way the dead grass sprouts up in the negative space. "Almost nobody's been inside since it happened."

Almost nobody. We both know someone has.

"But you could make it inside," he says. "I'm sure of it. The street would let you in."

My eyes flick up at him. "But would it let me out?"

Maybe that hasn't occurred to him. Or maybe it has. A risk is always easier to take when it doesn't belong to you.

I start down the sidewalk again but glance back suddenly. "You knew me by sight," I say. "You've seen my picture before?"

He blushes again, like a guilty child. "I've seen a few of them."

I can already guess which ones. The smiley yearbook portrait taken back when I didn't know any better, and the shell-shocked aftermath photos when I did, and a smattering of tabloid snapshots from over the years—*Talitha Velkwood graduates college! Talitha Velkwood fails at a series of dead-end jobs! Talitha Velkwood takes out the garbage at her shitty rental house where she'll probably die before age fifty and have her face eaten off by her neighbor's cat!*

Fortunately, the tabloids have more or less given up on me now. A small mercy. The one thing I don't want is anyone's pity.

But Jack's not looking at me like he pities me. He's looking at me like an opportunity. He wants me to say yes, and he wants it very badly. One word from me could justify years of fastidious research and fastidious obsession and enough grant money that could pay the bills for months. His and mine.

I breathe deep, the words tumbling out before I can stop myself. "Let me think about it."

With a grin, Jack gives me his business card. Then he turns, briefcase in hand, and walks away. Because everyone can walk away from this except me.

I never finish raking the leaves. I never finish anything. It gets dark early, and inside my empty house, I wait out the rest of the evening. TV tray, TV dinner, TV shows until my eyes go numb. This is my life, the remnants of it anyhow.

But now of course I'm thinking about my other life, the one I left behind. The one that left me behind. All the things I've tried to forget flashing through my head, memories tucked away like a yellowed photo in a family album.

Like the last time I visited the neighborhood. It was two months after everything happened. I went at midnight, dodging the meager patrol, edging toward the precipice where reality ended and something else began.

The news reports always said not to get too close. They said it would make your head hum and your nose bleed and your skin tighten on your bones until you couldn't bear it any longer. Until it felt like you were being sliced apart from the inside out, your guts carved up like prosciutto. That's why they've never needed a chain-link fence around the neighborhood. Nobody can trespass even if they want to.

Except I could. With my entire body quivering, I stood there at the edge of the perimeter, staring down the street that used to be mine. Somehow, I knew I could go whatever way I pleased—back into the real world or back into their world. It felt like I had a choice then.

So I made that choice. I ran far from the memory, far from home, and I never went back. I told myself it would be better that way.

But now all these years later, I have to wonder what's really better about this. I'm forty years old and none the wiser for it. I'm living in a house that isn't my own, still saddled with student loans from two decades ago and a bevy of ghosts even older than that. There's no escaping the past. It's everywhere. It's unrelenting.

I curl up in bed, still holding the grainy picture of my old street. This is the closest I've been in a long time, closer than I ever thought I'd be again. Most people don't know what this is like. They don't know how it feels to know you'll never go home again.

Except there's someone else who does understand. I grab my phone and scroll through my contacts until I see her. Brett. I stare at her name, at the gentle curve of the letters, debating if I should bother her. We're not friends anymore, that's for sure, though we still try to put on the pretense. Every year, she sends me a Christmas card, and I send her one, and that's about it. I'm not even positive this is still her number until I dial it and she picks up, that familiar voice breathless and earthy on the other end.

"Talitha." She says my name like it's a sermon, like something to cherish, and I wonder for a moment why we don't talk much these days.

"Hi, Brett," I say, and then seize up, already knowing what I should do next. I should try to make chitchat. Ask her about her day, her job, herself. That's the right thing to do, the thing a real friend would do. I blurt out something else instead. "Did that guy from the nonprofit come and see you?"

She hesitates. "You mean Jack? The cute one?"

I roll over in bed, still holding the picture, still holding the past. "That's him."

"He stopped by last week," she says, and I imagine her running her fingers through her long hair, bored with the very thought of boys. "I turned him down."

"You must have wondered if he'd come to me next."

"I did wonder that. I also wondered if he was your type." A long pause before she asks, "Did you sleep with him?"

"No," I say and snap my tongue, pretending the notion never crossed my mind.

Even through the phone, I can tell she doesn't believe me. "So," she says, "are you going to take him up on his offer?"

I scoff. "Of course not."

"Then why are you calling me?" The question is all steel and defiance. Brett, the only one who really knew me back then. The only one who knows me now.

"Maybe I just wanted to hear your voice," I say.

"That's not it." She lets out a defeated laugh. "You'd never call me for that."

Shame washes over me, and we don't say anything for a long time.

"I'm not going back," I say, and I'm not sure if I'm trying to convince her or me. "We were dying to get out of that neighborhood, remember?"

"You know I remember," she says, her voice sharp as nails, and instantly, I realize the conversation is over.

"Good talking to you, Brett."

"You too, Talitha."

The line clicks, and regret oozes through me. I want to call her back. I want to try again. Ask her about her day, ask her anything. If nothing else, now I remember why we don't talk more. Because it always turns out this way.

We used to do everything together, the three of us on Velkwood Street. Now Brett and I barely speak to each other, and neither of us ever talks to Grace. That's because she won't talk to us. Not for years, not since she went back to the neighborhood. Grace is the only one who ever made it past the perimeter, and she lasted no more than a night. Longer than anybody else, but too long for comfort. Ten minutes to sunrise, she wandered out, mumbling and barefoot, refusing to speak a word about what she saw over there. Maybe even she doesn't know. Maybe there isn't a word for it yet. All that matters now is that she moved away and locked herself up in a little blue shotgun house on the other side of the state. She's been a shut-in ever since.

I don't want to end up like her. I don't want to end up worse than I am now.

My hands shaking, I look again at the picture of my house, holding it up to the light this time, squinting at the third window from the left. There's a blur I didn't notice before. A shadow almost too slight to see.

Then my heart holds tight in my chest as I realize it's not a shadow at all.

I dart across the room, fumbling through my purse for Jack's business card. It's past midnight, but he answers on the first ring.

"Talitha? Are you all right?"

"I'll go back," I wheeze, still clutching the picture, still staring at that upstairs window.

Right into my little sister's wide and vacant eyes.

CHAPTER 2

I expect the permit to take a month, maybe more, a hopeless tangle of paperwork and bureaucracy, but it gets approved in less than twelve hours.

"I'll pick you up tomorrow morning," Jack says, the phone line crackling between us, and I don't have time to argue. I don't have time for questions either, not that I have any idea what someone is supposed to ask in a situation like this. Maybe what they're expecting of me or when we'll start or how exactly I'm going to cross over to the great beyond and return to tell the story.

But right now, I don't care about the specifics. All I want is to go back. To go home. That's where she'll be. I haven't stopped looking at the picture, not since last night, not since I spotted her there. Sophie's blurry face, gazing back at me.

"I'm coming," I keep whispering. "I promise I didn't forget you."

In the afternoon, my landlord stops by, unannounced as always, with his greasy fingers and greasy smile. He demands to come inside, something about a leaky pipe he's just been dying to work on in my bedroom, but I block the doorway, my jaw set.

"You can fix it tomorrow," I say. "I'll be gone for a few days."

He starts to argue, as if I owe it to him to be around, his captive audience, but I remind him the only thing I ever owe him is rent, and I'm paid up until the end of the month. At this, I can practically see the dollar signs flashing in his eyes.

"If you're not back by the first," he tells me blithely, "I'm selling your furniture to the pawnshop downtown."

I shrug. "That's fine," I say, figuring if I haven't returned by then, I'm probably not coming back anyhow, and I'd hate for my La-Z-Boy couch to go to waste.

After he's gone, already counting down the days until he can sell off my remains, I call my jobs, all three of them, part-time gigs doing medical transcription and tutoring and customer service from home. When they answer, I let them know I won't be around for at least a week, possibly longer. One job fires me on the spot, the second tells me to call when I get back in town, and the third doesn't even seem to know who I am.

"Tabitha?" they ask. "You said your name was Tabitha?"

"It's Talitha," I say over and over, until my skin buzzes and my head throbs and I finally just grit my teeth and hang up.

The rest of the day dissolves around me, the television no more than white noise in the background, as I pack a bag, the picture of Sophie nestled on top.

"What's it like over there?" I whisper to her, but no matter how long I stare at the image, nothing ever changes.

The next morning, Jack arrives at eight o'clock on the dot, driving a beat-up Toyota Camry, a chip out of the windshield, the bumper held on with zip ties. But the junker doesn't seem to bother him. He pretends it's a most glorious carriage, rushing out of the car to open my door and even putting my bag in the trunk for me, the pretense of a gentleman.

"Thanks," I say, though part of me wishes I'd held on to the bag. I hate to think of Sophie being lonely back there.

The inside of his car is warm and clean, the pale gray seats recently vacuumed, a pine tree air freshener dangling from the rear-view mirror. No doubt he's fancied up the ride just for me, like he's taking me on a date rather than to my doom.

"I was worried you might change your mind," he says, as we pull away from my house, the shape of it growing smaller and smaller behind us until it's nothing at all.

"I've got nowhere else to be," I say, and it's true. Overnight, I've shed my life like a useless skin, and nobody's really noticed, not even me.

We drive awhile in silence, shiny rows of station wagons and minivans and coupes clogging up the highway, the morning awakening around us. It's a six-hour trip, half of it by interstate, the other half by sinuous backroads where the pavement's as spotty as the cell reception. A no-man's-land. The perfect domain for ghosts.

"Are you nervous?" Jack peers over at me, curiosity sparking in his eyes. "About going home?"

"I guess." I'm doing my best not to think about it, not to notice the dull ache in the hollow of my gut.

"You lived there for a long time," he says, as though I don't remember, as though he isn't recounting my own life story to me. "Your family moved there when you were six years old, right?"

He spouts this off like it's a piece of barroom trivia, and I'm both impressed and unnerved.

"You've certainly done your research."

"I've tried," he says, and gives me that crooked smile. "So you've never gone back before now?"

"No," I say, and the lie tastes like ash.

"And you didn't keep in touch with Grace or Brett?"

I stare out the window, the skeletal outlines of bare oak trees smearing past us. "Not really."

That wasn't by choice, not my choice anyhow. Grace was the first to go, only a couple weeks after it happened. Dropped out of college and dropped off the map.

Can't take the strain, she scrawled on her withdrawal form, and left everything behind in our shared dorm room.

But it wasn't the last we heard from her. For the next decade, she'd resurface like flotsam, demanding Brett and I meet her for a dubious dinner where she'd lean across the table, one eye on the servers like they were all KGB sleeper agents.

"It's not finished yet," she'd tell us over tense plates of charcuterie and pub pretzels. "The ghosts aren't finished with us, and we all damn well know it."

For what it was worth, Brett and I didn't know any such thing, and we told her so.

"They're dead, honey," Brett would say. "And the dead don't give a fuck about us."

"And even if they did," I'd offer, "they'd want us to be happy."

But nothing we said could assuage Grace's paranoia. So ten years ago, when I heard she tried to go back, I wasn't surprised. I also wasn't surprised that it didn't work out. Grace, with her wide eyes and nail-biting, unraveling one thread at a time, ever since we were girls with skinned knees and pigtails. Life was liable to be hard for her, even under ideal circumstances. Add in the ghosts, and she didn't stand a chance.

Brett, on the other hand, could survive anything.

"Like a cockroach," she used to say, and then she'd let out that unmistakable laugh of hers, sharp as razorblades, sweet as candy floss.

Our neighborhood's tragedy barely slowed her down. She finished her degree, finished her internship, and finished with our street, refusing interviews, refusing all things related to who we'd been. She and I both ended up in the city—I can't remember who followed whom anymore—and within two years of graduation, Brett became the toast of the town. You couldn't escape her, the ultimate entrepreneur, her finger on the pulse of whomever and whatever fascinated her. Featured again and again in every 30 Under 30 list, and then in all the 40 Under 40 ones, always with a glossy, perfect picture of her glossy, perfect face.

"Are you proud of me, Talitha?" she'd ask each time, and I never understood why it mattered. She had the whole world at her feet. I don't know why she needed me there as well.

Brett did other things too. She got married and divorced in short order, as if she was ticking off a box on a to-do list and was just glad to have it over with. That was more than a decade ago, and I don't remember his name anymore. Gerald maybe? Joseph?

What I do remember: she sent me an invitation to the wedding, embossed ivory with gold leaf print, and then she invited me out for tea the very next week to get my RSVP in person. Over a pot of Earl Grey, I made up some reason why I couldn't be there. A lie about leaving town for a business trip to Chicago, the kind of flimsy excuse Brett could see through in an instant.

"Why don't you just tell me not to get married?" she asked with a grin, like she was daring me to say it, as if that was what I wanted. I wondered if it was what she wanted too.

"You should do whatever you need to," I told her, and that must have been the wrong answer, because she didn't speak to me again for a year. I read about her wedding in the society page of the city newspaper. I read about her divorce there too. Milestones in a life, reduced to line items below the fold.

"Do you miss them?" Jack asks, taking the next exit, strip malls and Starbucks and Steak 'n Shake blipping past us like meager landmarks. "I mean, the three of you were close, right?"

"Sure," I say, and my gaze flits out the window, inspecting the pockmarked asphalt. We're headed into the heart of the country now, these rural backroads where the trees clot thick overhead and anyone could disappear in an instant. Next to me, Jack keeps on smiling, and I think how I don't know him at all. He could be anyone. He could want anything from me.

After we met for coffee, I went home and googled Foxwell Enterprises. It's a legit organization from the looks of it. Proper website, proper 501(c)3 status, even a proper annual report with a balance sheet and cash flow analysis and cheerful pictures from their annual gala. Last year's theme was masquerade ball, and everyone wore funny hats. I don't know what that has to do with their mission statement, which according to the site involves "seeking justice in the country's most unusual cold cases." It sounds like a passable line, but that could all be a masquerade too, couldn't it? After all, just because it's a registered charity doesn't mean it's got good intentions.

"Brett had a lot to say about you when I met her." His hands are steady on the wheel, everything about him so even, so cool. "She told me you might be interested in working with us."

Barbed wire tightens in my chest. He's picking at every wound I've got, but he seems to think this is normal chitchat, like it's just the two of us getting to know each other. *The cute one,* Brett said about him. Not that she probably thought he was cute. She just knew I would. She knows me well, knows all my secrets.

And I know hers.

"Let's not talk about it right now," I whisper.

Another smile, tighter this time. "That's fine," Jack says, and doesn't ask again.

It's early afternoon when we stop off at Jimmy's Burger Shack, and I'm sure we're almost there now, because I remember this place. My dad used to take me and Sophie here on the way home from road trips.

"Best cheeseburgers this side of the Mississippi," he used to say.

When the front door swings open, part of me is sure we'll hear him again. My dad's rich, booming laugh, ricocheting off the walls.

But all the faces inside are empty and unfamiliar, their gazes going right through us. It's been a long time since I've been here, and the world changes more than you expect. We might be getting closer to home, but home isn't getting closer to me.

Jack and I order at the counter and find a table in the back, the cleanest one in the place, though at a roadside stop like this one, that isn't saying much. While we're waiting for our food, Jack unfolds a weathered piece of paper and smooths it on the table. It's a hand-drawn map of Velkwood Street.

"Do you remember the layout of the neighborhood?" he asks.

"Sure," I say. "There were only eight houses. There's not much to remember."

Jack nods. "So, if you make it inside," he starts, and then gives me a quick shake of his head. "*When* you make it inside, start with the places you've got the most connection to. Your house. Grace's house. Brett's house."

His fingers slowly trace the curves on the map, and I lean in, watching him, wanting him a little, even though I don't know him.

But he's got other ideas. He glances up at me and asks a question that takes my breath away.

"Were you friends with anyone else in the neighborhood?"

Shame flushes through me. "No," I blurt out, and instantly, I feel caught like a bug under glass.

This was the one thing we all agreed on. Whenever we were asked, Grace, Brett, and I always said it was just the three of us. Nobody else, no other friends.

Across the table, Jack squints at me, looking ready to say something, ready to call me out, but a server sidles up to our booth, depositing a red tray of greasy food in front of each of us. I exhale, grateful for the reprieve.

"No," I say again, as I dip a french fry in a tiny cup of ketchup, my fingers shaking. "There wasn't anyone else."

The server shuffles away, but Jack doesn't move for his food. He keeps watching me, his face cold as stone. I brace for it, the accusation, the first rumble of an avalanche I'll never be able to stop. Only he doesn't say anything. He just unwraps the foil around his burger, his hands moving slowly, carefully.

"So," he says, "start with those houses. With the people you know."

"Makes sense," I murmur, as if anything about this does.

As we eat in silence, I gaze down at the map, still splayed out on the table. Each of the eight houses is clearly marked, five on one side of the street and three on the other. And there's something else, something I wouldn't expect anyone to include. The small valley at the end of our street. When we were kids, that's where we used to go and hide, as though we could simply wait there long enough to outlast the world.

"We'll be safe here," I used to whisper to Brett, and sometimes, she even pretended to believe me.

When we're finished, Jack picks up the tab, which is the least he could do. We don't speak the rest of the way in the car, an hour of strained silence. I scan the radio, but all the stations drop off, one by one, as if even they don't want to venture this far.

The *Welcome to Our Town* sign whizzes past the window, and my insides turn to porridge. We're here, back in the place I came from. The place that's been beckoning me home.

Through the passenger window, I watch a string of landmarks flash by.

The abandoned shopping mall, all the store signs blotted out with black paint.

The basketball court where Grace's twin brothers shoved her down when we were kids, cracking open her skull on concrete. Brett and I had to sit with her until the paramedics came.

The other state highway, the one that leads north out of town, far away from here.

For years, I've wanted to forget this place. But staring at it again, it feels like I never left.

Even after all this time, there are still a few businesses remaining on Main Street. A tattoo parlor with a *Help Wanted* sign in the window. A little diner on the corner with an attached gas station.

As we pass by, I can't help but shiver.

At last, Jack turns down a narrow street, the curbs crumbling, everything crumbling. Yet even through the decay, I recognize it. Carter Lane. This is the subdivision next to ours, the shells of abandoned split-levels dotting the street like empty dollhouses.

After our neighborhood went spectral, this whole town might as well have become a ghost right along with it. Property values plummeted, and soon the government was buying up the nearby allotments and turning them into lookout stations where they could monitor our neighborhood. Or what was left of it. That was back when they believed they'd solve this whole thing, like it was nothing more than a Sunday crossword puzzle.

Jack pulls into the last driveway on the left. "Our accommodations," he says, the Camry engine cutting out.

But I don't move. I hadn't considered this part, how we'd need to stay somewhere nearby. When it comes down to it, I hadn't really considered any of this. No logistics, no specifics of what happens next.

And now here I am, with a man I hardly know, in a place I wish I could forget.

"Is it only the two of us?" I ask, and that's when they emerge from the other houses. A dozen figures, maybe more, their faces wan in the afternoon sun.

"It's so good to meet you, Talitha," someone says, their voice muffled through the glass. In a flash, they've got the car surrounded, their hands groping at all the windows.

I don't know these people. I didn't ask to meet them. None of this was part of the plan, at least not my plan. I figured Jack and I would show up, and I'd walk down my street. Simple as that. No bells, no whistles. Just me taking a few steps, and it would be over.

But of course it's not that easy. We needed a permit just to get me this far. That means there's going to be more paperwork, more questions. And worst of all, more people.

I climb out of the car, slowly at first, as though they're wild animals, and I don't want to disturb them. They tell me their names, one after another, right down the line, but it's all a blur of fresh faces, their smiles sharp, their words sharper. My back pressed against the cool steel of the car, I stand perfectly still, searching for Jack, the closest thing to an ally, but he's vanished in the throng. Meanwhile, they pelt me with their cheerful commentary.

"We're so happy to have you here."

"We thought you'd never come."

"Are you glad to be back? Are you excited about your visit?"

They ask this last question as though I'm headed to Disneyland.

"I'll be excited when it's over," I say.

Jack emerges suddenly, clutching my bag from the trunk. "That's enough for now," he says, his hand on my shoulder, and the others recede like a restless tide, mumbling to themselves, their eyes still on me.

"We'll have more questions for her later," someone says, and Jack waves them off, as if they've already talked about this, as if there's a whole plan already in motion, with me at the unwitting center of it.

"Come on," he whispers and ushers me up a long walkway and through a red front door.

Inside, the house looks like a showroom, everything sterile and bleached and in its proper place. Cream-colored carpet, cream-colored walls, a cream-colored couch that's never been used, the cushions plump, the upholstery untouched.

"We can stay here as long as we need," Jack says, and it sounds more like a threat than a comfort.

I back away from him. "Who were those people?"

"Researchers," he says and drifts through the room, hollow as a cicada shell. "They're here to monitor our progress." Then he adds, almost under his breath, "It's a stipulation of the grant."

I nod, thinking how none of this should surprise me. Our little neighborhood inspired a whole slew of avid scholars. Back in the early days, everyone braced for it, an avalanche of ghost neighborhoods. The whole country—hell, maybe the whole world—worried it would become some kind of epidemic, all the broken-down streets eager to jump on the bandwagon and transform into specters.

Except that never happened. It was just our luck that it was just our neighborhood. One tiny street in the suburbs, lost to time, lost to the world.

I gaze out between the thin curtains. The street is empty now.

"You could have warned me about them," I say, and Jack lets out a thin laugh.

"You could have asked. I would have told you anything you wanted to know."

He hesitates before adding, "I'll still tell you anything."

This knocks me off-balance, the simplicity of it, the transparency. I turn toward him, grasping at what question I should ask.

"Why ghosts?" I say. "Why are you personally so interested in this? In us?"

He gives me that crooked smile again. “Why not?”

I roll my eyes. “You’re going to have to do better than that,” I say, and he holds up one hand as if to concede.

“I grew up with ghost stories,” he says. “My aunt used to tell them to me. She raised me on dowsing rods and Ouija boards and seances. All good fun, she’d say.”

For an instant, I imagine Jack as a bright-eyed kid, gripping a planchette, convinced he’d be the first one on his block to summon the dead. And in a way, that’s exactly what he’s done. Or maybe the dead have summoned him.

“So,” I say, “what does your aunt think about you spending your whole life with phantoms?”

“I don’t know,” he says, and all the joy vanishes from his face. “She’s been gone a long while now.”

A knot of pain twists inside me. It seems like everyone we love just ends up turning into ghosts. “I’m sorry.”

“Thank you,” he says. “I’m sorry too. For you. And for this place.”

“Thanks, I guess.”

I step back, leaning against the windowsill to steady myself. Everything stinks of bleach and stale Pine-Sol, the past scrubbed away like a nuisance. There’s no history here, no remembrance in these walls. Somebody used to live in this house, a family probably, but that was a long time ago. The ghosts chased them away. My ghosts.

“When will I be going in?” I ask.

“Tomorrow,” Jack says. “Or we could always wait another day. We’ve certainly got lots of questions for you if you’d prefer that.”

I shudder a little. “Tomorrow will be fine,” I say, and he smiles again, brighter this time. Men are always more charming when they’re about to get what they want.

And the truth is, I like him when he’s charming. We sit together on the living room floor, his maps and notes sprawled out in front of us, and he tells me everything he's learned about the street. Nearly twenty years of research, of minutia into how we lived our lives, an anthropological deep dive into the peculiarities of suburbia. It's nothing new to me, but I listen anyhow, because of the way Jack's eyes flash as he talks about it. Because of how fascinating he makes my tragedy sound.

"And you've always been at the center of this." He's breathless now, shuffling through a stack of old Polaroids, milky images of me and Brett and Grace all jumbled together. "I can't believe you're really here."

"I'm here," I say, and almost laugh aloud. I was a nobody in my old life, disposable as a leaky bag of garbage, but not in this place. I'm a guinea pig, but at least not an easily replaceable one.

It's almost midnight when Jack folds up his facts and figures, and we head upstairs. There are two bedrooms, side by side, and they've already been earmarked, one for him and one for me, as though this was all preordained.

"Let me know if you need anything," he says, and leaves his door open.

With the lights out, I curl up in my temporary bed. Everything about this place is cold and alien. I try to sleep, the blankets wadded around me, but when I close my eyes, all I can see is Sophie's face peering out of that photograph.

To distract myself, I thumb through my phone, pretending I'm just killing time, pretending I'm not looking for her. The one person who understands this. In my contacts, her name might as well be limned in neon, the letters pulsating accusingly in the dark.

Brett. I want to call her again. I want to tell her I'm here, that she should be here too, but I already know what she'd say.

"Leave it in the past, Talitha. Leave it where it belongs."

And she's probably right. Brett's always been right, even when it happened. That first day back after spring break. A Monday afternoon when we got the call.

"They're gone, they're all gone," someone on the other end of the line said, and I'm still not sure who it was. Brett's grandmother or maybe Grace's. We passed the phone around, each one of us getting the same message, trying our best to decipher it like we were reading tea leaves in the bottom of a cup.

I remember I didn't cry. I didn't scream. I didn't do anything except ask what had happened, bracing for a bearable response. A gas leak or a fire or an earthquake, something you could write on an insurance form or talk about in polite conversation. Still a tragedy, of course, but something banal. Something that didn't defy the laws of nature.

But that's not the answer we got, and all of us knew why. Wheezing, Grace collapsed in the corner, snotty tears running down her flushed cheeks, her fingers stuffed in her mouth, muffling her own scream. Brett, however, would have none of those hysterics.

"We've got to keep going," she said, and she's been able to do exactly that. I only wish I could keep up with her.

I tuck my phone in the nightstand, closing the drawer, closing off the possibility of calling Brett. Not tonight, not with what I'm about to do.

Through the wall, I hear Jack murmuring in his room, already half asleep. Part of me wants to go to him. Just to talk, I tell myself, even though that's the last thing I need from him. More of his book report questions about my life, about the woman he thinks I am, because he read a list of factoids about me in a declassified report or a tabloid headline, yellowed with age.

I crawl out of bed, wavering in the hall, loneliness aching in me. He's only a few steps away now. I could knock on his open door, I could pretend this is a normal night in a normal place. But the echo of my mother's voice still trembles through me.

You're not a very nice girl, are you?

So I turn away instead and head toward a narrow staircase in the corner, up to the attic. Up to the highest window where I peer outside.

You can see it from here, shimmering in the distance. Eight little houses and the street, thick as an artery, that connects them. It doesn't look like much in the dark. It doesn't look like much in the daytime, either. A dime-store illusion, a relic trapped in time.

All these years, I kept waiting, hoping the neighborhood would be like a nuclear exclusion zone, that maybe eventually the land would heal itself, and people could start venturing inside again. Only that never happened. Instead, it's become Area 51 for phantoms.

The government's done its best to fix the problem. They've tried hazmat suits and helicopters and a row of military-surplus tanks with little American flags painted on the side. Yet no matter which way they try to come in, they've never even gotten to the first mailbox. The street would always shove them back.

Except from this vantage point, I can see a whole row of mailboxes, glinting in the moonlight. I look for mine too, the plastic cracked with age, but it's obscured by a whisper of trees.

I never thought I'd come back, never thought I'd have a reason to. But here I am, and I can feel it, the way something's shifting in me. I feel so tired of running, so tired of keeping secrets I never asked for. Maybe tomorrow will fix that. Maybe I can finally rest.

In the morning, Jack finds me here, bleary-eyed and huddled in the window seat.

"Did you get any sleep at all?" he asks.

"I'll be fine," I murmur, and trudge down the narrow staircase after him.

He makes us both breakfast, and I fidget at the pristine table with its pressed linens and never-used silverware. It's as if they had this whole house vacuum-sealed and waiting, just in case I returned.

Jack sets a plate of eggs and bacon in front of me, and I nudge it with the tines of my fork, a gray wave of nausea rising within me.

"We don't know what's going to happen today," I say. "We don't even know if I'll survive in there."

"Grace survived," Jack says, and sips his orange juice.

I scoff. "Barely."

"She stayed overnight." Jack dips his dry toast into the runny yolk of an egg, splattering yellow gore across the plate. "We're only asking you to go in for a few minutes. An hour max."

This is so normal to him. He's been studying the neighborhood for years, like it's all a game, like it's all theoretical. But there's nothing theoretical about this to me.

I shove my plate away, uncertainty churning in me. This didn't seem like such a bad idea, even last night. But in the bare light of morning, everything feels different. Everything feels like an elegy.

Jack watches me from the other side of the table. "Do you want to go over the plan for today?"

I shrug, looking away from him. "There's not much to talk about, is there? I go in. I go home. I hopefully come back out again."

I don't say anything else. I don't move either, the house going sullen and quiet around us.

Jack puts his arms on the table, leaning in. "Last night," he says, "you asked me why I'm here. It's because I want to prove what really happened to your family. To finally get answers. To get closure. You could help us with that."

My eyes are on him. "And what if I don't want to prove anything?"

He sits back, taking a deep breath. "It's okay if you've changed your mind," he says, and I want to tell him yes. I want to ask him to take me home, even though I don't know where home is anymore.

But then I think again of that photograph, Sophie peering out at the world. Waiting for me to make good on my promise. Waiting for me to rescue her.

"No," I say, resolve hardening in me. "I'm ready."

It's only a few blocks away, a five-minute walk at most, but Jack offers to drive me. Before we leave, he puts something in his pocket, a good luck charm perhaps. I strain to see what it is, but he's too quick for me.

At the front door, I slip into my black bomber jacket, the one Brett loaned me years ago. I doubt she'd appreciate me taking her stuff back into the neighborhood. I always meant to return it to her. I always meant to do a lot of things.

"Let's go," I say.

The street is longer than I remember. This end of it was never developed, vacant lots looming all around us, but it's what's up ahead that really counts. There are orange pylons marking the spot where most people can't go. It's such a simple delineation. The living stay on this side, and the dead stay on the other, and only someone like me gets to cross between.

Jack parks the Camry in the middle of the road, blocking the traffic that isn't there, and as I climb out of the car, I realize we're not alone. The researchers from yesterday surge forward to greet us, an unwelcoming welcome committee. Three of them have their cell phones out, filming my every move, their hands shaking, their eyes wide and ravenous. Someone takes my pulse, their cold fingers pressed in my wrist, and I can't help but shudder at their touch.

"Anything you want to tell us before you go in?" they ask brightly.

Any last words, they mean.

"No," I say, and I expect they'll keep closing in on me, making more demands, making a circus attraction out of me, but Jack stands with me this time. He doesn't let them circle me. He stays at my side, the two of us in step until we get to the perimeter. Until the street won't let him any closer.

We seize up, staring at the emptiness where my life used to be. If I squint, I can see it there, even in the blaring daylight, the hazy outline of the neighborhood waiting for me. I wonder if Jack can see it too.

But when I peer up at him, he isn't looking at the street. He's looking at me.

"Remember not to stay too long." He reaches into his blazer and removes the item he pocketed back at the house. It's a small plastic timer, set for one hour. He places it in the palm of my hand, my flesh prickling at his touch.

"Thank you," I whisper, clutching it to my chest. Then I turn away and start walking.

This is the only way into the neighborhood. People have tried to sneak in elsewhere—even Grace tried every backyard and back door she could think of—but it never works. The neighborhood repels you like the wrong side of a magnet. You can only walk onto Velkwood Street the old-fashioned way: right down the middle of the road. So that's the route I'm taking.

I'm past the row of pylons now, the asphalt crumbling beneath my feet. Nobody's been this far in twenty years besides me and Grace, which means nobody can repair the road. It's falling apart in big clumps, potholed and forgotten with time, and everything past this point looks like a warning.

But I tip my head up and keep going. The boundary gleams up ahead, the mirage of my childhood flickering in and out of existence. As I step to the edge, I glance back once at the eager crowd congealing behind me, but even though they're no more than a hundred yards away, I recognize no one, not even Jack, their figures like tiny insects, like something make-believe.

There's only one thing that's real—the neighborhood unfurling before me. With my breath tight in my chest, I drift forward, just a few inches.

Just enough that I'm suddenly home.

CHAPTER 3

My head spins, everything in me going numb. It feels like I've been turned inside out, my skin flayed and tacked back on again, and maybe that's exactly what's happened. Maybe that's the only way to get into this place.

But what I know for sure: I'm here. Back on this street, back where I used to belong.

When I woke up this morning, it was the end of fall, but in this neighborhood, it's summertime, jubilant sprinklers cascading over lawns, the solstice sun baking the pale concrete. The street's bathed in jaundice yellow, the whole world like a desaturated photo. I try to remember if it ever really looked like this, or if this is merely a trick of the afterlife, this place becoming more a memory than a flesh-and-blood reality.

Either way, I'm looking into the past, and I'm not sure yet that I like what I see.

I inhale a ragged breath, and the thin air burns my lungs. I wonder how long I can survive here. I wonder how long anyone can survive.

At least I already know how long I'll stay. One hour and not a minute over. That's what Jack suggested, and after what happened to

Grace, I won't take any chances. At least not any more chances than I've already taken.

With my hands steady, I start the timer and then I start walking, right down the middle of Velkwood Street. It's only a few steps at first, my vision gauzy, as though I'm peering through a hundred layers of chiffon. The pavement is solid beneath my feet, but it barely feels real.

Our neighborhood was never built for subtlety, every house arrayed in candy-colored siding, the roofs with sharp, almost comical angles. We all lived in split-levels with the same floorplans, the mid-century equivalent to making it in suburbia, but that dream was a short-lived one. The street was dated, almost kitsch, by the time we started high school.

"We're stuck in the past," Brett once said, as she and I sat together on the curb, each of us devouring one half of a cherry twin pop we procured from the local ice cream truck. "We'll never escape it."

"You don't know that," I said, my fingers stained red. But maybe she did.

As I keep moving, I count the houses. All eight of them are here, right where they belong, three on the left side of the street, and five on the right. A lopsided arrangement, but it wasn't supposed to stay like this forever. We were supposed to get new houses, new neighbors, new possibilities. But that never happened. Instead, two of the houses had been vacant since we were in junior high, the *For Sale* signs still in the front yards, like a promise nobody could keep.

I don't look too long at them. I keep heading toward the place where I once belonged, the fourth house on the right, almost at the end of the street. Almost at the end of the world.

Nearby, there are empty cans of Coca-Cola abandoned on the curb, ants swarming around the sweetness, hundreds of them coming from every direction.

I'm passing Grace's house now, the second on the right, the slider windows gazing out at me, the pink trim glinting in the sun. Everything in Grace's life was always pink and bright and cheerful. Her mother would have it no other way.

"The problem with you girls is that you need to smile more," she used to tell us when we all stayed for sleepovers, and my stomach would always clench, because from the look on Brett's face, she wasn't ever thinking about smiling. She was always thinking of spitting right in Mrs. Spencer's eye.

The sun shifts in the sky, disappearing behind a patch of pale clouds, thick as marshmallow fluff. That's when I see them. Two people walking across the verdant yard. Grace's younger brothers maybe. It looks like them, arrayed in grimy Mötley Crüe T-shirts and hand-me-down Levi's, one of them holding a Spalding basketball. This is it, a chance to finally meet someone. To ask them what's happened. To ask them about Sophie.

They drift out of the yard and onto the street, their figures obscure and wavering. I squint at them, shielding my eyes from the blazing sun, but I still can't recognize them, and as they get closer, I realize why. My vision's clear now, but they're not. Their faces are blurred out, almost as if they're moving too fast, a hundred expressions flashing by at once, joy and dread and rage mingling together. Their skin's gray as a thunderstorm, but they don't seem to notice. They just keep moving forward.

Moving right toward me.

I seize up, my feet turned to lead, a scream lodged in my throat. I'm sure they've spotted me here, I'm sure this is it. But they pass me by, as though everything's normal, as though they don't see me at all. And that's probably for the best, because without a clear mouth to speak, I doubt they could help me much. I doubt they can help themselves much either.

I'm running now, away from them, away from everything, heading deeper into this neighborhood, even though I should retreat, back the way I came, back into reality. Except right now I'm not sure where reality is.

So I run toward the place where I grew up. Toward where my family should be.

Up ahead, at the house next to ours, there's another figure sitting out front. Only this one isn't the same as the other two. She has a face, and I recognize her in an instant.

Mrs. Owens, creaking back and forth on her half-rotted porch swing. A widow from way back, we used to think she was the only lonely person on Velkwood Street. That was a long time ago, back when we didn't know much about loneliness. Or much about ourselves.

"You don't belong here," she's saying, and hope threads through me, because I'm convinced she's talking to me. I sprint across the sidewalk, rushing onto her lawn, just glad to see a face, an actual face.

"How are you?" I blurt out, but she doesn't move, doesn't even flinch at the question. I watch her for a while before waving my hands in front of her. There's nothing, not a hint of recognition.

I'm right here, but I'm nowhere at the same time.

"Don't you listen?" she asks, her voice like rusted nails. "I told you already you don't belong here." She's scowling hard at something, and I follow her gaze until I spot it.

A frog sitting on her front step, staring off at nothing, its expression as impassive as the seasons.

"You should move along," Mrs. Owens says, still glaring at the frog. "You don't have much time."

And I don't have much time either. My house is only next door. I'm almost there. I'm almost home.

"Maybe we can talk later," I say to her, and I hope I'm right.

Grass crunches like brittle bone beneath my feet as I cross the yard. A sharp breeze shivers down the street, the air turning thick and fragrant with honeysuckle, like something out of a dream. I hold my breath and keep going, all the way up the narrow walkway that leads to my front door. Gladiolas creep along the perimeter of the house. The summer before I left for college, I planted the bulbs with Sophie, the two of us in old overalls, dirt caked beneath our fingernails.

"How long will it take them to grow?" she asked, her arms wrapped around my legs.

"A few weeks until we see the first sprouts." I pulled her close, and she hugged me a little tighter. "Three or four months before flowers."

She crinkled up her nose. "Why do they take so long to grow?"

"The same reason you do," I said with a laugh. "You've got to give things time."

Now the flowers have all the time in the world. And so does Sophie.

I'm on the front step now, everything I want and everything I fear wrapped up in this moment. My heart squeezed tight in my chest, I reach to knock on the front door, but I don't have a chance. The lock clicks on the other side, and my mother is suddenly standing right in front of me.

She doesn't look like those terrible figures from the sidewalk. Instead, everything about her is the same as I remember. Her wide eyes as blue as tidepools, a bolt of gray tucked behind one ear, the same furrowed lines between her brows.

"I'm home," I whisper, but the same as Mrs. Owens, she doesn't see me. Nobody can. In here, I'm the ghost, the trespasser, the spirit who can barely disturb the air.

She didn't even hear me at the front door. With her purse slung over her shoulder, she just happened to be heading out already. I fall back a step, huddling among the privet shrubs as she drifts down the cobblestone walkway. There's nowhere for her to go, but maybe she does this every day, pretending to pick up the groceries and run the errands and live the life that was pilfered from her, cycling through patterns of the past like they're a comfort rather than a curse.

Do they know they're ghosts? Do any of us ever know?

She slides into the driver's seat of our '92 Geo Metro, the one we bought brand-new with five thousand dollars in cash, like we were big spenders on the Riviera. I wait for her to start up the engine, but she only sits there, not moving, not doing anything at all. I want to reach out for her. But even if she were still alive, she probably wouldn't reach back.

"Is Dad around?" I say, but she doesn't answer. I can already guess what her response would be.

"Of course he's not here. Don't you know anything, Talitha?"

I know that Dad's gone for good, dead and buried a full five years before this neighborhood faded to nothing. Heart failure, they said, but I figured he just wanted to get out while he still could. My father was clever like that, always one step ahead of the rest of us.

"Don't let them get to you, Talitha," he would tell me. "People will try to grind you into dust if you let them."

I only wish I'd taken his advice.

The front door is still open, sunshine leaking into the foyer, so I slip past the welcome mat, an intruder in my own life.

Inside, the house is just like I left it, the scents of beef stroganoff and Windex mingling in the air. The shag carpet, the color of autumn leaves, bristles beneath my feet.

"Hello," I say to no one in particular, and as always, no one answers.

Up the stairs, the living room is empty. No trace of anybody besides the portrait slung on the wall, our faces frozen in that garish K-Mart studio with the mottled gray background. Sophie was only a baby then, her cheeks ruddy, her watery eyes gazing off into nothing. She didn't want to be there. None of us did, but Mom insisted. Sophie fussed the whole time, only brightening when I let her wrap her tiny fingers around my thumb. It didn't matter what went wrong. I could always make her smile.

I hated that picture, the way Mom forced it on us, all of us in our itchy Sunday best, but staring at it now, it's almost comforting. It's almost better than a memory, because it's real. It's something you can hold on to.

I pass an oak coffee table, Avon samples scattered across it, tiny tubes of mauve lipstick and pale packets of Skin So Soft. For years, my mom was the street's resident Avon lady, and that meant goodies galore. Brett and I used to lie in wait, watching every week for the big brown box to arrive in the mail. When we were sure no one was looking, we'd pillage what we could, spiriting a pocketful of loot off to Brett's bedroom where we'd take turns putting makeup on each other, giggling the entire time like petty bandits.

"You look perfect," Brett would whisper, and I'd just blush. That is, until I got home, and my mother saw me.

"Don't touch my stuff again," she'd say, gritting her teeth, her hands clenching into fists, but I'd always stare back at her, wide-eyed.

"I don't know what you're talking about," I'd say, even though I was wearing the evidence on my face.

The ancient appliances in the kitchen whir pleasantly in the background as I keep wandering, exploring my own life like it's an archeological dig. I'm in my old bedroom now, and I want to open my dresser drawers, raiding everything, yanking out the past. But I can't touch any of it, my fingers as insubstantial as mist. I try to steady myself against the wall, but my hands go right through the plaster. If the doors to the rooms weren't already open, I wouldn't even be able to walk in. Everything's closed off to me.

"Are you here?" I call out, moving slowly into the hall. "Can you hear me, Sophie?"

No answer. I glance down at the timer. Fifteen minutes gone already. That doesn't seem possible, but then again, I'm not sure what is possible here.

I'm ready to start back outside, to try again with my mother, to plead with her, anything to make her listen. But then I hear it. That sweet voice clear as a windchime.

"Do you know what you're doing? Do you know where you've been?"

Sophie. I rush toward the sound, my feet in a tangle. Downstairs in the rec room, I find her, surrounded by an army of knockoff My Little Ponys, their nylon hair in knots, half of them collapsed on their backs, their gnarled legs in the air, as though they've lost a most fearsome war.

And Sophie, grinning and gap-toothed in the middle of them.

"I'm here, baby, I'm finally here," I say, my words blurring together. I collapse on the floor, reaching out for her, desperate to take her hand, desperate to hold her, but it doesn't matter what I want. My fingers go right through her.

She doesn't even notice. She's like the rest of them now. I'm sitting next to my little sister, and I'm as invisible as air.

"Sophie," I say over and over, as though this is a fairy tale, and repeating her name enough times will break the spell. "I told you I wouldn't forget."

She keeps playing, lining up the ponies and knocking them back down again. It's such a simple thing, so normal, so Sophie. Her hair tucked behind her ears, she hums to herself, a lullaby I taught her, and though she can't hear me, I close my eyes and sing along too. It isn't much, but at least it's something we can do together.

The timer in my pocket ticks down, minute by aching minute,

but I pretend not to notice. I pretend nothing exists beyond this room with its tacky wood paneling and its old ceiling fan, dusty and creaking overhead. Everything here has been past its prime for years, but I don't care. All I want is to curl up on the tacky velour couch and never leave. Even if she doesn't see me, I'd rather be here than back out in a world that can't see me either.

"You have to go now," Sophie whispers, and though she's staring at her toys, I can't help but wonder if she's speaking to me.

"Baby?" I lean closer to her, my hand outstretched. "Can you hear me?"

But she never glances up, not even so much as a flutter of her eyes. I'm nothing to her now, a distant memory, a vestigial limb.

And she's right: I need to go. That's what I agreed to. That's the only way I won't end up like Grace, her sanity lost to time. Lost to this place.

I start across the room, hesitating in the doorway. "I love you," I say, but at the sound of my voice, Sophie never even flinches.

Outside, in the driveway, my mother's still sitting behind the wheel of the Geo Metro. She hasn't started the engine. She hasn't done anything, her body slumped over, as though everything in her surrendered long ago.

I kneel next to the driver's seat, the door hanging open. "What can I do?" I ask, but she doesn't look up, her eyes gone cold, the expression on her face never changing.

That face. The first one I ever saw, the one I couldn't forget, even though I've tried. She was nineteen when she had me, thirty-nine when she vanished. That makes her a year younger than I am now. I'm staring at my own mother, and somehow, I'm the elder.

Down the sidewalk, there are more ants swarming around the abandoned Coca-Cola cans, so many now that it looks like a shadow devouring the concrete.

Suburbia. We were supposed to be aspirational. We were supposed to be the American Dream incarnate. But that's the problem with dreams. They rarely come true the way you expect them to.

And besides, this wasn't even really the suburbs. This wasn't really anywhere. Our neighborhood was almost an hour away from the nearest city, too far to be anything but a nothing town.

The houses stand sentry around me, the ones that have been empty for years, and the ones occupied only by ghosts. Despite the decades, most of them are still dazzling, the gutters clear, the siding never fading.

All except for one. On the other side of the street, the last house sits there with lichens splotching the porch, the front steps sagging. I shouldn't look at it, I shouldn't remember, but it doesn't give me a choice. An upstairs curtain flutters, and I hold my breath, waiting for her.

Enid, the one we left behind.

I tell myself I won't walk up that driveway. I won't get one step closer. I never promised Jack that I'd visit every house, and I certainly never promised myself.

This was a simple plan: come back for Sophie. But nothing is turning out the way it was supposed to.

Next door, Mrs. Owens is still on her porch, still staring at that frog, which hasn't moved an inch, its dark eyes glassy and mournful.

"You don't have much time." Mrs. Owens swats at the frog with a broom, narrowly missing it. "Why won't you listen to me?"

My skin prickles, and I clutch the timer in my trembling hand. Ten minutes left. I should head back, but I already know I won't. Not yet. There's still one more stop I need to make.

The flimsy screen door is flapping open in the wind, and I sneak inside. Brett's house hasn't changed, the walls butter yellow, the floors gleaming with Glo-Coat. In the dining room, there are three cabinets packed to the brim with commemorative plates, the kind people used to buy for way too much money out of the backs of magazines. There must be a hundred of them, each design more garish than the last, Christmas trees and Princess Di and Elvis Presley and baseball players whose names I never did know. Brett's mother loved these things, loved wasting half a paycheck every month on them.

As if on cue, her voice carries in to greet me. "Brett? Is that you?"

I hesitate, wondering if at last someone can see me. She materializes in the doorway, dirty slippers on her feet, her greasy hair slung over her face. She's wearing that same thin nightgown that she's owned for thirty years, the one that was threadbare and see-through from the get-go.

"Hello, Mrs. Harrington," I whisper, but the empty expression on her face doesn't change.

"Brett," she says, her voice no more than a rasp. "Where are you, honey?"

She's getting closer now, and I reach out for her, to take her hand, to help her along, but she shuffles right past me.

I shouldn't be surprised. Brett's mom barely noticed me when she was alive. I can't imagine she'd bother with me now that she's dead.

The overhead light is sallow and dim, and she shambles on as though every step is agony. When I'm sure she's gone, I keep moving. It's not much farther now, just down a long hallway to the last room on the right.

Brett's bedroom.

Inside, the single lamp in the corner is flicked off, but the glow of permanent summer spills through the double-hung window, illuminating the walls. I'm expecting something to be waiting for me, sprawled out on the floor, the same thing we left here that night twenty years ago.

The same thing I've been trying to forget ever since.

But the room's empty, except for the remnants of Brett.

A poster of the Cranberries tacked up over the dresser, the tape yellowed, the corners sagging.

Shelves packed with dainty ceramic figurines in the shape of frilly little girls in frilly little dresses, their faces hand-painted, their tiny hands clutching a different number, one for each year of Brett's life, right up to the age of twenty. Right up to the time this place ceased to exist.

A cache of mini liquor bottles stuffed under the bed, Fireball whisky and Southern Comfort and DeKuyper Pucker Sour Apple Schnapps.

"Home sweet home," Brett used to say when we'd walk in, and then she'd flash a harsh grin like the whole world was a big joke to her. Brett was all sharp edges, broken glass in the shape of a girl. She knew what she wanted—to get off this street and out of this town.

And she had her reasons, the kind I couldn't quite fathom, at least not when we were kids. Reasons that came home every day at five thirty, grumbling under his breath, as he settled down on the couch with a Miller Lite and a grudge.

We all knew somebody like him, the sort of man that got mean young and stayed that way. The kind that left a constellation of bruises on Brett's arms that everyone in the neighborhood refused to see. Even Grace wouldn't listen when Brett tried to talk about it. I was the only one who ever heard her, for all the good it did.

"What can we do?" I'd ask, my hand entwined with hers.

"Grow up," Brett would say, her gaze dark as the grave. "We have to grow up. We have to get out."

So that's what we did, one aching day at a time. The two of us reclining on her daybed, our legs in a tangle, the tiny latch on the brass doorknob twisted, sealing out the world.

"Nobody will bother us now," Brett would whisper, her lips pressed to my ear, her long, dark hair cascading over us, the same color as mine. We rotated through cassettes, the sound of Dolores O'Riordan's ethereal vocals crooning out "Dreams" and "Zombie" and "Ode to My Family."

Brett hasn't been in this room for twenty years, but it doesn't matter. She's everywhere, lingering in the air, the scent of her strawberries-and-cream body lotion, the one she used to buy on sale at the mall.

I don't know what I'm hoping to find here. Maybe I'm just looking for Brett, even though I lost her a long time ago, lost her in a hundred different ways.

There's someone else who lost her too. Another shuffle of anxious feet in the hallway.

"Brett?" That rasping voice, hollow and lonely as heartache. "Can you hear me, honey?"

Brett's mother, a walking catastrophe. She must do this every day, all day, searching in vain for a reckless daughter who's long gone. A daughter with no desire to return. Not that anyone could blame her. Whenever Brett tried to talk about it, tried to tell the truth, her mother would always wave her off like a gadfly.

"We could have done worse, kid," she'd say to Brett, as though they'd won a raffle for deadbeat dads and had to take what they could get.

I look down at the timer again. Three minutes left. I need to get back outside. But that furtive basket of liquor glints up from beneath the bed. There's a bottle of peach schnapps on top, the label faded with time, half the syrupy liqueur already gone, an imprint of Brett's red lipstick around the rim. My hands tingling, I reach out for it. It's a nothing motion, but somehow, it's enough. I'm suddenly gripping the tiny bottle. It's solid in my hand, the first thing I've been able to touch.

I slip it into my pocket along with the timer, and then I'm gone, back into the hallway. I pass Brett's mother on the way out. She's making circles in the kitchen, her feet dragging on the linoleum.

"Brett," she keeps saying, and I can still hear her behind me even as I disappear onto the street.

Back out in the open, I drift down the middle of the road, this place sitting in my belly like a stone, like it wants to weigh me down. To keep me here.

Overhead, something starts to shift, the endless summer ebbing away. The sunlight leaks out of the sky, the color fading from a lemon yellow to a deep, irrevocable blue.

I turn back toward my house, searching for Sophie, even though she isn't there. Even though she wouldn't see me if she was. But there's someone else on the street now. In the driveway across the street from ours, the door to the decaying house has swung open, and a figure lingers on the front step.

A figure that's looking right at me.

"Talitha," she whispers, and though she's a hundred yards away, I can somehow hear her voice. I can see her face, too, those tragic eyes, that red hair the color of an October bonfire, everything about her looking like a calamity in the making.

"Hello, Enid," I say, and shame seeps through me.

We shouldn't have left her behind. None of this would have happened if we hadn't left her.

The world is shifting around me now. Ants are covering the sidewalk, up and down both sides of the street, the cement crawling with darkness. On Mrs. Owens's porch, the frog is still sitting on the step, but something's wrong. His eyes have gone filmy, his mouth gaping open. I edge closer to him, wanting to help, wanting to set him free, but it's far too late. A final, bottomless moment, and he deflates into nothing, his skin reduced to a leathery pile, like a balloon with all the air let out.

Grace's brothers are back, pacing the street, their arms flailing. They exhale shrill, muffled screams, their mouths blurry, their agony seeping out. Everything's seeping out now, this whole street in disarray.

I whirl around to face Enid. "What's happening?" I ask, my heart thrumming in my chest.

Her face blanches. "It's not my fault," she says, as though that's an explanation.

The timer screeches in my pocket, and part of me wants to ignore it. Part of me wants to stay, to protect Sophie, to protect everyone, but Enid only shakes her head, her eyes gone wild. She screams something at me, something I can't quite hear, but I know I should run, and that's exactly what I do.

The neighborhood bleeds past me, the air gone fetid and gray. At the end of the street, I look back once, hoping to see Enid again, hoping she'll say something else, but it's too late. She's vanished in plain sight, and I can't linger here another moment. I take that last step toward the shimmering threshold, just an inch, just enough that I vanish too.

When I open my eyes, the air is chilled, and a dozen pylons are scattered at my feet, half of them knocked over. I'm back on the other side of the perimeter, back in my own reality. Whatever that means.

It's dark now, and the street's empty. There's no one waiting for me. No sea of keen researchers. No Jack, either. I wasn't expecting a jubilant homecoming, but I figured they'd at least stick around.

But I also figured it would still be daylight. I was only inside for an hour. Night shouldn't have come so quickly.

I stand here, frozen, the midnight breeze biting at my flesh. I don't know what I should do. I don't know where I should go. Then something in the darkness crackles, sharp and sweet. It sounds like it's coming from behind me, from the place I just left. It sounds like it's beckoning me back.

I won't listen. With my guts churning, I rush past the row of pylons and the empty lots where the people never did come to build their dreams.

The night pushing closer, I turn the corner, and I'm back in the other subdivision. Carter Lane. The bland house where I stayed last night materializes at the end of the street, and in an instant, I'm up the walkway, pounding on the door, my fists clenched, my body aching.

Jack answers, his face going wan the moment he sees me. "Talitha," he says, like he barely remembers who I am.

"Where were you?" I glare at him. "I set the timer like you told me to. I went in for an hour. But then I come back out, and you've all gone home?"

Jack's lips move silently, as though lost in prayer. "You don't understand," he says at last.

"Understand what? That you're running a really crummy operation here? Because I understand that perfectly well."

My cheeks burning with rage, I realize I must be yelling, my voice carrying up and down the street, because the other researchers are pouring out of every house on Carter Lane, their complexions as pallid and strained as Jack's. All of them are drawing closer now, and I back away, because I don't like the looks on their faces. Watching me like they've seen a ghost.

"Talitha," Jack says finally, and my name sounds like an apology, "you've been gone for three months."

CHAPTER 4

They surround me in an instant, ushering me inside and sitting me down on the pristine couch in the living room, the plump cushions stiff beneath me. This whole house feels like a movie set, and I've suddenly become an extra in my own life.

The researchers swirl around me, one of them clutching a leather satchel.

"We promise it won't hurt," they say, as they dig into their bag of tricks. Stethoscopes and blood pressure cuffs and tongue depressors along with a tray of metal implements, all of them like torture devices in miniature. With smiles plastered on their faces, the researchers turn this bland room into their own private operating theater, a makeshift clinic in a makeshift place.

I want to tell them no. I want to run, but I'm too exhausted, my head spinning. They go for my heart first, listening in.

"Vital signs are normal," they say, and I'm not sure if I'm relieved or not. Maybe things shouldn't be normal. Maybe there should be some lingering sign of where I've been and what I've seen.

Jack kneels next to me, a clipboard in hand. "How are you feeling?" he asks, and unlike the others, he sounds like he genuinely means it.

"I'm not sure," I say, my limbs heavy, my gaze fogged. I still feel halfway between, wearing the past and the present at the same time.

The others elbow Jack out of the way as they prick my finger like a spindle in a fairy tale, the blood coming fast.

"She might be dehydrated," they say, as though I'm not sitting right here.

"I'm not thirsty," I say, but someone brings me a glass of water anyhow, and they all stand back and wait until I drink it, one careful sip at a time, their owl eyes fixed on me.

"What are your names again?" I ask, my guts roiling, and they repeat them to me, one after another, but by the time we get to the last of them, I can't remember the first or any of the names in between. My mind's a blur right now, and all I want is to close my eyes. All I want is to go back home.

Jack's still studying his clipboard. "Did you see anyone over there? Your family or any of your old neighbors?"

I nod. "But they didn't notice me."

Except for Enid. In spite of everything, she saw me.

A few other researchers breach the door, and they lean in close, their shadows draped over my face, their hands reeking of iodine. They've got needles now, the silvery tips glinting in the incandescent light.

"We're not asking for much," they say, as the metal plunges into my arm, as cold and impersonal as a stranger's handshake. Their lips pursed, they take half a dozen blood samples, filling vial after vial with fragments of me.

"What are you looking for?" I ask, but nobody answers. I squirm on the sofa, my nervous hands rifling through my pockets. That's when I feel it there.

The bottle of peach schnapps from Brett's room.

"Here," I say, passing it to Jack.

He takes it from me, the label uncurling at the edges, the neon-orange liqueur sloshing inside. "What is this?"

"A souvenir," I say.

His eyes are on me. "You brought this back with you?"

"It's the only thing I could touch."

He inspects it again, from every angle this time, like he's just uncovered a coelacanth. "What's the significance?"

I hesitate. "I don't know," I say, even though that's a lie.

Brett. She's the significance.

The others keep bustling around me. They're trying to feign order, like they've got a protocol for this, like they've done it a thousand times before, all of them pushing for a closer look at me, their bug beneath a magnifying glass.

"Stand up," somebody says, and they position me against a blank wall like a prisoner before a firing squad. One of them disappears outside and returns a minute later with a bright yellow device covered in knobs and needles. I stare at it for a long moment, trying to comprehend what it is. Then as they flip the switch and it crackles to life, a knot ties tight inside me.

A Geiger counter. They've got a Geiger counter.

"Is that really necessary?" I ask.

"Yes," they say, and I wonder if they know something I don't.

I hold my breath as they run the counter over the tiny bottle. And over me. But there's nothing, no sharp crackling. Whatever I brought back with me, at least it isn't radioactive.

I settle down on the couch again, breathing a little easier. "I imagine it'll be a hassle now that I'm back."

"What will be a hassle?" Jack asks as he scribbles a note on a clipboard. Jack is always scribbling something, his entire life a never-ending list of bureaucratic checkboxes.

"Proving I'm still alive," I say. "You must have declared me dead, right? Or at least reported me missing?"

No one will look at me now. They don't even move, and for an instant, it feels like I'm surrounded by plastic mannequins, each of them with a knit brow and sour face.

Jack breaks away from the others, pacing toward the other side of the room, his back to me. "We didn't know what to do."

I watch him, confusion trickling through me. "What does that mean?"

"It means we just kept monitoring the area to see if anything changed. To see if you came back."

"You didn't tell anyone?" I gape at him. "I vanished for three months, and you just pretended it didn't happen?"

"Like I said, we weren't sure what to do." His cheeks burn with shame. "We already knew you didn't have any living relatives."

The truth is I don't, but it still doesn't make me feel any better. I could have disappeared for good, and nobody in the whole world would have known. I'm sitting right here, but it's like I don't exist.

"I'm done now," I say, and shove them away, as I struggle to my feet. A few of the researchers try to come after me, but I rush toward the stairs and up to a room that's the closest thing to mine I've got left.

I'd rather run farther—away from this street, away from this town—but there's no way for me to get there. I didn't even drive myself here. I'm trapped in this place, a block away from home and nowhere at the same time.

I waver in the bedroom doorway, waiting to see if anyone follows, but they're all still downstairs, arguing about what to do next.

"We could put her in quarantine," someone says. "That would force her to cooperate."

"I don't think that will be necessary," says another. "Plus, we didn't quarantine Grace Spencer when she returned."

"But Talitha was in there longer. We don't know what she brought back."

"A tiny bottle of alcohol." Jack's voice now, calm and clear. "That's the only thing she brought back."

My head aching, I stumble across the room toward the nightstand. My cell phone's still inside, exactly where I left it. Both hands shaking, I try to turn it on, but it's gone dead. Of course it has. It's been three months, abandoned in a drawer. My charger's there too, so I plug it in, staring at the little battery icon like it's a lifeline.

"We should let her rest," someone's saying, their voice rising up from downstairs. "We can try again tomorrow."

A few more fervent murmurs, the last meager vestiges of a fight. Then all at once, a rush of movement, all of them drifting together as the door opens, the outside world leaking in for a moment before it slams shut again. They leave an emptiness in their wake, a hollow echo on a street filled with them.

But at least they're gone for now. I settle down in bed, my hands over my eyes. This is the first quiet I've had since slipping through the veil between here and there. That's when I notice it, so slight that it was impossible to detect downstairs. My skin is humming. Everything in me is humming. I feel more alive than I have in years. Maybe more alive than I've ever been.

I should feel robbed, three months of my life siphoned away in an hour. But then I've lost far more time than that. Twenty years of stasis, of empty questions, of telling myself I couldn't fix it, but always wondering if I really could.

There's a creak on the stairs, and I freeze, waiting to see if one of them stayed behind. If there's somebody with a handful of needles and ill intentions eager to get the last laugh.

And it turns out one of them did stay. Jack materializes in the hall outside my room.

"I'm sorry about that," he says. "I'm sorry about everything."

He doesn't come any closer, not even a step inside my makeshift bedroom, an invisible border suddenly between us.

I say nothing. I just glance back at my phone, silently willing it to charge faster.

Jack hesitates, grasping for something to say, a salve that can make this better somehow. "Are you hungry?" he asks finally.

It's nearly eleven o'clock, and we order a pizza from the only place in town.

I linger at the downstairs window, waiting for the delivery car to pull up. When it arrives, my body drifts forward, ready to run. I could rush outside, beg for help, for an escape. The driver might even accommodate me. He might give me a ride into what's left of town. To a bus stop or a rest stop or any place at all. But then what? I've got nowhere to be and nothing to go back to. Not my rented house, not even my La-Z-Boy couch. I imagine my sleazy landlord's gluttonous face as he collected a whole twenty bucks from the pawnshop when he hocked my entire life to them.

So when the doorbell rings, I simply stand back in the corner as Jack answers.

The driver peers in the house, his jaw gaping like he's sneaking a peek into the Amityville Horror. "I didn't know anybody still lived out here."

"We're just passing through," Jack says with a bright smile. He's always smiling, always cheerful. I wonder what that's like.

The driver shakes his head. "I wouldn't recommend staying very long." His eyes shift to me, still huddled in the corner, and a spark of recognition flashes on his face. "Do I know you?"

This catches me off guard. Right after it happened, Brett, Grace, and I were local celebrities, an infamous trio. But that was a long time ago, and I wouldn't expect anyone to remember now.

"No," I say finally. "I'm nobody."

After the driver leaves, taking my only chance of escape with him, Jack and I sit together at the table, the same place we had breakfast only this morning. Except it wasn't this morning for anyone but me. It was three months ago, all the way back in November. A different year, practically a different lifetime.

And now here I am, eating a slice of congealed pizza in a house as sanitized and barren as a hospital suite.

I glance around at the décor and down at our ceramic plates, everything the color of eggshells, the color of nothing. "Did this house come fully stocked?"

Jack nods. "Researchers have been moving in and out for years."

Of course they have. All of them convinced they'd be the ones to break this whole thing wide open. Yet nobody's been able to learn anything. Until now anyway.

When we're done, Jack clears the table, and I collapse on the couch, the cushions starting to give beneath my body. This place feels a little like mine now. My home a block away from home.

The clock on the wall ticks away slowly. It's almost midnight, almost time to turn in. But after everything, I'm not tired, and apparently Jack isn't either, because he edges into the living room, gripping his clipboard again.

"I was hoping you could help me," he says, something in his eyes as bashful as a child.

My brow arches. "Help with what?"

"You said you saw a few people over there." He holds up a list of names. "I'd like you to tell me who."

He settles on the floor, sitting cross-legged next to the couch. Like the two of us are old friends who've always reminisced about a neighborhood of ghosts.

"Let's start with your house," he says, a red pen in hand. "The Velkwoods. Caroline Velkwood."

"Yes," I say with a grimace. "I saw my mother."

He checks off her name. "Sophie Velkwood."

I nod, trying to ignore the ache in my chest.

"Now let's move on to the other houses," he says. "Kirsten Spencer. Grace's mother."

I shake my head.

"The Spencer twins. Grace's brothers. Bobby and Bert."

I shiver, their twisted faces still lingering in the margins of my mind. "Possibly," I whisper.

Jack's eyes flick up at me. "What does that mean?"

"It means possibly," I say and won't elaborate.

With a sigh, he moves down the list. "Marie Owens."

"She's still there," I say, "sitting on her front porch."

And what's left of her frog is there too.

"The Hawkins. Father, Oliver, and his daughter, Enid."

"No," I say, a knot in my throat. "I didn't see either of them."

That's a lie, of course, but Jack believes me. And why wouldn't he? He's got no way of knowing. Every word out of my mouth could be an invention, and he'd be none the wiser.

His red pen scans the next names on the list. "The Backmans. Parents Raymond and Lindsay, and one son. Del."

This one catches me by surprise. I passed their house, the first one on the right, but I barely thought about them. They were almost as bland as this room, a "filler family" my mom used to say. A homemaker mother and a handyman father and an insipid son who was my age. I probably wouldn't remember Del at all if he hadn't also been Grace's fiancé.

"A mistake in the making," Brett always said, and I would just toss my head back and laugh, because she wasn't wrong.

I fidget on the couch. "I didn't see them."

His head down, Jack studies his checklist like it's a most precious artifact. "And finally the house next door to yours. Brett's house."

"All right," I whisper.

"Nicole Harrington?"

Brett's mother. "Sure," I say, "she's still there."

Still wandering the house, searching for all the things she'll never find.

"And how about her husband Samuel Harrington? Brett's stepfather."

"He's not there," I say, the words slipping out before I can catch myself. I force a smile and add, "Or at least I didn't see him."

The clipboard sagging in his hands, Jack sits back, satisfied. "That's everyone," he says, and I count them up in my head, the same way I've counted them a thousand times before.

Thirteen. That's how many people we lost. Just one neighborhood, and a whole universe too.

I shiver again, wanting to escape this place, wanting to think about anything else. "I should get a chance to rattle off questions to you now."

Jack gives me that crooked smile. "Ask me whatever you want."

My head humming again, I lean toward him, debating where to start. "Why did the others have all those medical supplies today?"

He purses his lips, sucking in a heavy breath. "Like I told you, it's a stipulation of the grant."

I inspect him, my eyes narrowed. "To have a fully stocked bag of needles and vials?"

"We need to be ready to examine anyone who returns from the neighborhood."

That means me or Grace or Brett. I imagine our names were scattered throughout the grant application, promises that they'd bring one of us here and turn us into a most obedient specimen.

And that ended up being me. The one without a life. Without a home.

I wonder about Jack, what place he calls home. "Where do you live when you're not here?"

He chirps up a laugh. "When am I *not* here?"

"Don't you have someone waiting for you?" I seize up before saying it. The question I've been dying to ask since he bought me a cup of coffee. "Aren't you married or anything?"

His cheeks turn pink, as though he honestly didn't believe I'd ever thought about it. "No," he says. "Never."

Relief threads through me. "Me neither," I say.

At this, he smiles again. "I know."

Now it's my turn to blush. Of course he knows. Jack long ago memorized every detail about me, my whole life like a Trivial Pursuit game to him. Like something that can be unraveled, one meaningless inquiry at a time. But now I want to unravel him. "You told me about your aunt," I say. "What about your parents?"

His face goes gaunt, like this was the one thing he didn't want to talk about. "They're not dead, if that's what you're asking," he says. "They just don't care."

Shame sears through me, and I wish I hadn't said anything at all. "At least your aunt cared," I offer.

He nods, his gaze unfocused. "She used to say the dead care too. 'Probably more than the living,' she'd tell me. Because ghosts know everything. They know all our secrets."

At this, my throat closes up. "I hope that's not true," I whisper.

Unease settles into the room, an unwanted houseguest. Jack does his best to change the subject, telling me more about himself. How he earned a PhD in environmental engineering from a university in Cleveland. How his advisor pulled a few strings and got him an internship with a think tank in Cuyahoga County that studied the Velkwood Vicinity. How that internship turned into a grant, and the grant turned into this. An endless rigmarole that led him right where he wanted—into the company of ghosts.

"You didn't hope to do anything else?" I ask. "To be anyone else?"

He tosses up his hands. "Back when I started, this seemed like enough."

"Is it still enough?"

"If we find the answer to life after death? I think that'll be enough."

I lean back, the couch shifting beneath me. "So what happens when you figure this place out? What are you going to do then?"

"That depends on what we learn, doesn't it?" Another smile, the kind he knows he can use as a weapon. Or a good luck charm.

Not tonight though. After the day I've had, there will be no luck for him or luck for me.

"That's enough for now," I say, and start to stand, my skin humming again, louder than before. For a moment, I wonder if Jack can hear it too. Then I don't wonder anything, because my vision blurs out, and the room tilts around me.

Jack jolts forward, his arm looped around my waist, steadying me. "Do you want to go to the hospital? Just as a precaution?"

I shake my head, everything clearing again. "I just need to rest."

Except apparently rest doesn't need me, because even once the lights are out, I still can't sleep. I curl up alone in bed, the shadows shimmering around me. At least my phone's fully charged now. I prepaid the plan through the end of summer, which is the only reason it still works. Otherwise, it would have been turned off weeks ago.

My head heavy, I scroll through my new messages. There are only three of them, all from the same person.

Brett.

your holiday card came back did you move?

hey checking in again send me your new address when you get a chance

Talitha, are you all right? Call me.

This silly ritual of ours, the only remaining tether between us. Yet it was enough. The rest of the world had forgotten me, but not Brett. Even from hundreds of miles away, she knew something was wrong.

I read and reread her messages, my fingers aching. I want to text her back. I want to tell her where I've been. She's the only one who might understand. But that also makes her the only one who knows why I shouldn't have returned to begin with.

My head droops back, the world spinning a little around me. I should have known better. I've spent years telling myself there's nothing left, no reason to return.

But now that I've been inside again, I know that's not true. There's every reason. Sophie, for one. And Enid. I remember again how she saw me, how she spoke to me.

Enid. Always the strange one. If there was anything the whole neighborhood could agree on, it was that. And they didn't even know the things about her that Brett, Grace, and I knew.

Like the first time we realized she wasn't quite like the rest of us.

A bright rainstorm in the heyday of April, all of us in our hand-me-down slickers and rubber boots. We were only eight years old then, sharing the same second grade class, waiting together on the sidewalk, eager to climb on the yellow school bus.

Except Enid had other plans. She crouched in the center of the street, gawking at the cement. We joined her of course, just to see what the fuss was about. It took a moment to see them on the slick pavement, thin and pink and lifeless.

Earthworms. Enid was staring down at half a dozen earthworms, each one crushed by our parents' passing cars, their bodies sliced in two.

"It's all right," Enid cooed, as she ran her fingers along their sticky corpses. "I can fix you." Then she turned to us. "And you can help me."

With the raindrops thick as tears sliding down our hair, she made us put our hands atop hers, our tiny fingers tangled together. The storm suddenly stopped—in a way, it felt like time had stopped—and as we huddled in a circle, four lonely little girls, something happened. Like a sharp jolt of electricity passing through us.

Enid exhaled a small giggle, as though she was in on a joke the rest of us couldn't fathom. Then she went right down the line, peeling up the two halves of every worm from the wet concrete. I remember holding my breath while she put them back together again, their bodies fusing with no more than a flick of the wrist.

"There," she said brightly.

We helped her release each one in Mrs. Owens's garden, all of us watching in reverent silence as they wriggled back into the darkness. In the moment, it didn't seem so strange that our friend could do something like that. Everything in the world is new to you at that age, which means everything is possible. It wasn't until I told my mother that I realized my mistake.

"Don't you lie to me, Talitha." She sneered and snapped a dishrag at me. "What have I told you about girls who are liars?"

Panic clenched in my throat. "I'm sorry," I said, and I didn't mention it to her again. I didn't mention it to anyone except Brett.

"How do you think Enid did it?" I asked.

"It's just a magic trick," Brett told me, but from the quiet, scared look in her eyes, I could tell she didn't really believe that.

After that, I pretended I'd only imagined it, that we'd all imagined it. Because we were so young then, the memory soon turned misty, the way all memories do, and it became easier to believe it never happened at all.

Now I know it did happen, and that worse things were to follow. And that Enid would keep waiting in that neighborhood, that she's never stopped waiting there. After all these years, she still might be able to help.

I might be able to help.

It's almost sunrise when Jack turns over in bed and sees me standing in his doorway.

He squints up, his eyes bleary. "Talitha? What is it?"

"I want to go back," I say. "I want to try again."

Jack spends the next two days trying to talk me out of it.

"You don't have to do this," he keeps telling me. "We haven't even sent the bottle or your blood samples off to the lab yet."

"You can do that while I'm away," I say.

It doesn't help that I've had a dozen dizzy spells since then. It also doesn't help that Jack's witnessed every one of them.

"I'll only stay an hour," I insist, as though it's a compromise. That'll put my return right around May, the bright bloom of spring. That doesn't sound so bad. I'll get to skip the rest of winter, which is honestly a bonus.

In the evening, I sit up at the attic window, watching the neighborhood gleam in the distance. I wonder how I would have spent these last few months if Jack hadn't shown up at my door. Probably the same way I've spent the last two years—fading into the background of my own life, as anonymous as a Jane Doe. At least in this place, I can do something. At least in this place, I *am* something.

It's Thursday, the night before I'm headed back, and I'm scrolling through my messages again, staring at the last three from Brett. I tell myself not to call her. I call anyway. She picks up on the first ring.

"There you are," she says, as though this had all been a game of hide-and-seek, and at last she's won. "I was worried I'd never hear from you again. Are you mad at me?"

"No," I say, and I already regret this, because I know what her next question is going to be.

"Talitha, my god, where have you been?"

I close my eyes. "Home," I say. "I've been home."

A long, agonizing silence. The same sort of silence I've been expecting from her. That's why it took me two days to call.

"So," she says, "the cute boy convinced you to go back?"

I steel myself to her. "No," I say. "I convinced me."

"Did you get a nice homecoming?" Even through the phone, I can hear Brett smiling. That lovely, wicked smile. "Did they throw you a parade right down the middle of Velkwood Street? The prodigal daughter returns?"

"They couldn't see me."

"That must have been a mercy," she says with a sharp laugh. "None of them?"

"Except Enid." Everything in me goes cold. "She could see me."

At this, Brett seizes up. "How is Enid?" she asks, all the vitriol in her voice melting away.

"I don't know," I say. "Things were confusing over there."

"That's why you shouldn't have gone back."

"Maybe not," I whisper, "but I'm trying again tomorrow."

The years stretch thin between us.

"Well then," Brett says, "should I just use your mom's address for this year's Christmas card? Because it seems like that's where you'll be living now."

"That's not what I want," I say.

"What do you want?" she asks, her words like jagged ice.

The question hangs in the air, heavier than it has any right to be.

"I want your help," I say finally. "Brett, I can't do this alone."

"Don't do that to me, Talitha. Don't ask me to go back there."

Another bottomless silence, and I'm sure there's something else she wants to tell me. But all she does is laugh again.

"Have fun on your trip down memory lane."

And with that, the line goes dead.

"I'm sorry," I say, even though she can't hear me. Even though no one can.

CHAPTER 5

The next morning, I try again to call Brett, one more time to say a proper goodbye, but it goes straight to voice mail. I hang up without saying a word. I don't blame her for ignoring me. She told me she wanted no part of this. I'm the one who keeps trying to drag her into the past.

But then we've been dragging each other all over for the past twenty years. From home to college to the city and now back again, our lives an endless loop. An endless chase.

The last time I followed Brett somewhere was for the opening of her latest endeavor. It was held outside the city in a big blocky building that had been a former Macy's back before it was ceded to rats and decay during the recession. Now thanks to Brett, it was a community art museum complete with three galleries, a theater stage, and an art deco–style lobby that looked like Daisy Buchanan should be dancing the Charleston in it.

This was what Brett did for a living, what she'd done ever since we finished college. An independent contractor, they called it, a cross between a designer and historic preservationist, but it was a lot more than that. Brett was the human incarnation of Spirit Halloween, taking old, derelict buildings and transforming them into something new, something brimming with possibilities. She'd swap a department store into a museum, turn a faded strip mall into a block of affordable apartments.

Our neighborhood might be long gone, but she could spend the rest of her days repairing other ones.

That night, for the opening, I'd brought my boyfriend with me. A corporate accountant named Stefan. We dated for a year, though it felt like a decade. He milled about the artwork, sour-faced and stoic, for less than an hour before making an excuse to head home.

Brett watched him walk out the door, a smile blossoming on her lips. This meant she had me to herself for the evening.

I only rolled my eyes. "You could have just told me not to bring him."

"Why do you bother with boys like him?" she asked, and all I could do was shrug.

"He's good enough," I said, even though I knew damn well he wasn't. Even though I knew he left early so he and his bubbly blond co-worker could spend some quality time together investigating the satin sheets at his condo. I wouldn't call him until tomorrow, because I wanted him to think I didn't suspect. It was easier that way.

But there were reasons to stay, too. Everything about him—from his pressed khakis to his endless talk of Roth IRAs and 401Ks—was so achingly normal, so apple pie American, and that was oddly comforting. Back then, part of me honestly believed that if I tethered myself to somebody normal, then maybe I'd become normal myself. Or at least not the walking tragedy that I was. That I still am.

Brett, however, never cared a bit about being normal. For the opening, she'd designed one of the exhibitions. A wide-open partition filled with silver balloons and a light show of bright blue and lawn green and fresh-from-the-vein red, all splashed against the thin walls like a tie-dye tapestry.

"What's it supposed to be?" I asked, gazing up into the neon glow.

"Anything you want," she whispered, her hand suddenly entwined with mine, her touch softer than velvet. I remember staying that night at her apartment, a weird little warehouse loft in the Strip District, and how we drank too much rosé. I slept on the couch as always, one room and a million miles away from her. Even when Brett and I were in the same place, there was always an unbreachable chasm between us. She was right there, but she still felt like just another ghost.

"It doesn't have to be this way," she said the next morning, but I pretended not to hear her as I walked out the door.

I'm still thinking about her, as Jack and I climb into the car so he can drive me back to Velkwood Street. There's no welcoming committee joining us this time—it's just the two of us.

I hear Brett's voice again, echoing inside my head. *Why do you bother with boys like him?*

Except Jack's not quite like the other guys I've known. He's certainly not normal, that's for sure. Nobody ordinary has ever been this obsessed with ghosts.

As we turn out of the driveway, I notice something on him. A necklace dangling over his T-shirt, a charm at the end of it. A titanium compass. Only it's bent a little in the middle so that north doesn't quite point in the right direction anymore.

"From your aunt?" I ask, and it's a total guess, but Jack smiles, and I know instantly that I'm right.

"You asked me before what she would think about all this," he says. "And I think she'd love it. This neighborhood. Everything we're doing here." He hesitates before adding, almost sheepishly, "She always wanted to prove that ghosts were real."

"And you told her you would try, right?" I gaze at him. "At the end of her life, you told her you'd find her again?"

Another guess from me, another small smile from him.

"It might not seem like much," he says, "but I made a promise to her."

I can't help but laugh. "I know what that's like."

A promise to the dead. Sometimes it feels like the only promise that matters. Other times, it feels like nothing at all.

With another block to go, he tells me about her, his aunt Maggie. The way she raised him from age three, how the two of them would seek out the paranormal everywhere they went. Summer trips to the Queen Mary, spring breaks to the Winchester House, both of them standing in the back of every crowd, taunting the ghosts, begging them to come out and play.

"She called us occult tourists," he says with a chuckle, and he's blushing now, and I like it more than I expect to.

Part of me doesn't want to ask, but I do anyway. "What happened to her?"

"Cancer," he says, and a flash of pain twists on his face before he adds, "It's a lot different than what happened to you and your family."

"That doesn't make it hurt any less."

"Doesn't it?" he asks, and that's when I look up and see we're already here. At the end of Velkwood Street.

The Camry engine cuts out, and Jack starts to get out of the car until I hold up one hand.

"I'll go it alone," I say. There's no reason for him to risk it. Nobody but me should get any closer than this.

I open the passenger door, the timer in my pocket, the disintegrating concrete heavy beneath my feet. It's a long walk this time, even longer than before. That's because I know where I'm going now. And I know what's waiting for me.

"Be careful," Jack says, and he's standing outside the car, watching me.

"I'll do my best," I say, as if my best matters here.

I'm past the pylons when I realize they've all been set back up. I'm not sure if Jack's compatriots did this, or if it's the work of something else. I'd rather not ask.

Instead, I squeeze my eyes closed, and without glancing back, I take that final step. The only one that matters.

When I open my eyes, it's summer again, the sun bright and yellow and inviting in the sky.

"Hello," I say to no one. With my hands trembling, I start the timer, and then I start walking, making note in my mind of all the houses, trying to be more clinical, more focused this time. The first two on the left are abandoned. The first one on the right belongs to Del's family.

He was so easy for me to forget. Not for Grace, though—she was crazy about him. Her house sits right alongside his. The boy and girl next door, the two of them so perfectly wholesome, like something straight out of a Bible study class.

"Expand your horizons, honey," Brett always told her, but Grace never listened. She and Del had been off and on since junior high, and when this place vanished from the map, I can't remember if she was still wearing the engagement ring, the one he'd bought on sale at Sears for $99.99 plus tax. She must have taken it with her though, because she didn't leave it behind in our dorm. Brett itemized everything before we sold the stuff to an off-campus pawnshop. Afterward, we donated the money, all seventy dollars of it, to a local women's shelter.

"Grace would like that," Brett said, and I nodded eagerly, even though we both knew we had no idea what Grace would like anymore. We also had no idea if there was any Grace left or just someone occupying the body of the friend we used to have, a fractured mosaic of a girl.

At least Grace did the decent thing and fell apart all at once. I almost admire her for it, especially since I took the hard way out and fell apart a little at a time, crumbling bit by bit, year by year, until there was barely a husk of me.

Now here I am, back where I started.

The frog is back where he started too—on Mrs. Owens's porch. And she doesn't seem too happy about it.

"I don't know how many times I've got to warn you," she says. "It isn't safe for you out here. It isn't safe for any of us."

Shuddering, I turn away. At the end of the street there's the last split-level on the left, Enid's house, but she isn't outside anymore. I keep walking, down a steep slope, headed to a place I haven't visited yet. It's the small valley from Jack's map, the one past all the houses, past the dead end. The gray water lines all run off here, the detritus of our lives flowing this way. All the things we don't want, the parts of us we're desperate to leave behind.

And right in the middle of the hillside is a wide, empty culvert. It's made of thick, rusted metal, and when you peer inside, there are only shadows staring back at you.

The culvert isn't part of the gray water lines. According to the city plans, it isn't part of anything. It leads to nowhere, an inadvertent impasse, a bureaucratic oversight. But us kids, we knew better. You could follow it through the earth, crouching down, crawling on hands and knees, and if you could stomach the murk and the mud and the hungry darkness, then you'd come out the other side on a street they'd never developed. A vacant allotment, the place that was supposed to be built after ours.

But I was never brave enough to take that path out. Instead, I just stayed right here. This spot in the valley where we used to hide after school. Me and Brett mostly, the two of us sprawled out in the spindly grass near the culvert, our bare feet caked thick in mud. We lost a thousand hours here, our legs tangled together, Brett's scent of strawberries and cream always overwhelming me.

"Let's run away together," she whispered one long ago afternoon as she plucked a handful of dandelions from the dirt.

"All right," I said, staring up at the slate-gray sky. "We have to take Sophie, though."

"That's fine." Brett knotted the dandelion stems together. "Sophie's cool."

"What about Grace? And Enid?"

Brett shook her head. "You're not responsible for saving the world, Talitha."

"I'm not trying to save the world. I just want to save us."

"And how about you?" She finished tying the dandelions together in a loop, and with a grin, she placed the crown on my head. "Who's going to save you?"

I only laughed. "I've got you for that."

Above me, the sky fades out, the light in the neighborhood gone sour and blue. It's happening again, night coming all at once, and this time, I won't be on my own for it. There's something on the other side of the hill, a shadow edging nearer. Maybe Grace's faceless brothers again. Or maybe someone else, someone worse.

I don't want to find out. My breath shaky, I climb inside the culvert, grit beneath my feet, the darkness devouring me whole. I crouch down, out of sight, my legs pulled into my chest, rocking softly back and forth, anything to steady myself, anything to make this moment go away. And maybe it works, because no one comes down the hillside. Whoever it was, they've moved on now.

Except that doesn't mean I'm safe. And it doesn't mean I'm alone. Next to me, there's a flash of something, a figure hazy in the dark. A figure that was already hiding inside the culvert.

"Hello?" I whisper, my heart seizing in my chest, and it takes a moment for me to realize what's happening. To sense it in the shadows, the slightest of movements, the pressure against my palm.

Someone is holding my hand.

And they won't let go.

CHAPTER 6

I try to wrench away, I try to scream, but the figure in the shadows shushes me.

"Talitha, please don't."

That voice, soft as chiffon, ethereal as twilight. Enid. She's the one sitting next to me, her hand wrapped around mine. I hold completely still, thinking how this shouldn't even be possible. I couldn't touch anyone or almost anything the last time I was here. But then Enid isn't like the others. She never has been.

I turn toward the opening of the culvert, the world outside glimmering a somber shade of sapphire. "What are we hiding from?"

"I'm not sure," she whispers.

"You're not the one doing it?"

For an instant, her eyes flash in the dark. "Not this part."

A long moment passes before I ask it. The question that's haunted me for twenty years.

"How about the rest of it?" I gaze at her, the vague shape of her body wavering in the shadows, everything wavering. "Did you cause the rest of this?"

Enid seizes up, her hand gone colder than before. "It's what you wanted, isn't it?" she asks. "You told me to help you. So that's what I did."

Outside, there's thunder brewing in the distance, quiet and unmistakable, and I wonder suddenly if I'd be safer out there with the unknown than in here with her.

"I won't hurt you," she says. "I promise, Talitha."

"I know," I say, and reach into my pocket, feeling it there. The timer ticking against my body. No doubt I've lost ten minutes already, two weeks back in the real world. My hour will be up sooner than I expect, the moments dissolving around me. I can't stay here the entire time. I can't hide forever.

I squeeze her hand tighter. "What happens if I go back out there?"

"It depends," the voice in the shadows says.

"On what?"

"On you."

I peer into the place she must be, still trying to fathom her face, obscured in the dim. "What does that even mean?"

"It means you get to decide, Talitha."

I exhale a thin sigh. It's always riddles with Enid. She's been like this since we were kids, speaking in nonsense and nursery rhymes. You could holler at the sky and get a clearer answer.

"I'll take my chances." I untangle my hand from hers before crawling out, a slick of moss beneath my palms.

At the rusted mouth of the culvert, I stumble out, back into the valley. No one's waiting here, but that doesn't mean it's safe. With the pale blue light blaring down, the ants are returning now, clotting together in the mud, and they're not alone. Spiders and millipedes and iridescent beetles the color of springtime, their tiny legs and tinier antennas all gnarled together, slick carapaces stacked atop one another in endless piles. I can't even take a single step without crushing a hundred of them.

And there's something else, something that was never here before. A crevice in the earth, no wider than the tip of your thumb, no longer than a girl's body. My body perhaps. Or Enid's. I step to the edge and gaze into it. Darkness crawls within.

I should feel more surprised, more shocked at the spectacle this street is making of itself. But I'm not. Even before this neighborhood disappeared off the map, things were already falling apart. For a long time, I thought it was this spot, this dire strip of real estate. I told myself the ground was rotten beneath us, and that's why everything was going wrong. But when I shared my theory with Brett, she just let out a harsh laugh.

"It's not the land," she said. "It's us, Talitha."

Instantly, I knew what she meant. The way the people who populate a street can poison it. How the things they say and do seep into the soil, deeper than death, so deep that no one can ever excavate it. All our families believed we belonged on this block, nestled in our pretty little houses. But we didn't just break ground here. We broke everything.

The sky hums overhead, its dark melody trembling through my bones, as Enid emerges from the culvert, dainty as a teacup, her skin practically glowing. This is the first time I've seen her up close in twenty years. She hasn't changed a bit, not one speck of age on her. She's still wearing her favorite outfit from high school, a hand-me-down baby doll dress with tiny daisies on it, the hem unraveled, her sky-blue Hard Candy nail polish chipped away at the edges.

Enid. The pity invite, my mom used to call her. Whenever there was a birthday party or a summer sleepover in the neighborhood, you had to ask Enid too. That was the rule, even if you didn't want to.

"She's so fucking weird," Grace said with a sneer when we were thirteen. "Did you see her talking to that garter snake on the way to school the other day?"

"What's the big deal?" I shrugged as we sat together in my backyard. "Snakes aren't so bad."

But Grace wouldn't let it go, darkness clouding her eyes. "She's like a reverse Snow White. But instead of bluebirds and butterflies, she only attracts creepy things."

"Leave her alone," I'd say, but none of them would listen. Not even Brett.

"You're too quick to take in strays," she told me later, as she pleated an immaculate French braid in my hair, fine as cornsilk, the two of us perched in front of my bathroom mirror. "Stop trying to save everyone, Talitha."

I bristled at this, even though she was right. I was constantly trying to rescue all of us. From what, I didn't even know. Maybe everything.

"I just don't mind Enid," I said finally.

I could never understand why they did. She was just a little odd, those arcane eyes swirling with secrets. There's no crime against that. Of course, there probably should be a crime against what she did here, fracturing time and space, turning our whole world into a tomb. But she wasn't the only one responsible. The rest of us always try to forget that part.

The pale blue light fades above us, and Enid gives me that quiet smile that looks like heartbreak. "You were always so nice to me," she says. "Like you meant it."

This digs a knife deep in my chest. "You know I meant it. You were my friend."

She brightens a little. "You're my friend too. That's why I want to help you now. You came back for Sophie, right?"

"Yes," I say, and something tugs tight inside me, because I realize for the first time that maybe I should have come back for Enid, too. The invisible girl we all happily left behind.

Overhead, the sun emerges as if it's only fashionably late, everything turning a golden yellow again. In the dirt at our feet, the insects have receded now, disappearing into the darkness where nobody goes but them. I shiver, wondering when they'll come back, wondering if they'll bring more friends with them.

But Enid isn't worried about any of that. She's motioning me on. "Hurry now," she says, the two of us climbing the side of the hill.

I squint up at the sky. "How long does it usually stay daytime?"

"However long it wants." Enid quickens her steps. "And besides, it's never really night. It's never really afternoon either."

For once, I know exactly what she means. This is a place without time, the same day on repeat forever, like a record on a turntable that never stops skipping.

We return to the street, the sidewalk solid beneath us. Enid's house is the closest to the valley, to the runoff from our lives, which makes sense in a way. She always took the brunt of everything, the girl nobody bothered to care about. The girl whose very birth was a tragedy, her mother's uterus going septic overnight, her vitals crashing so quickly that she never got to hold her baby girl.

In spite of herself, Enid was born into death, and it was borne into her.

"Even her own mom didn't want to stick around," all the so-called adults on Velkwood Street would gossip, but even when I was young, I scoffed at that, because it wasn't Enid's fault. All us girls were delivered at the same cut-rate hospital with the same cutthroat doctors.

"More like terrible prenatal care," I said, but nobody wanted to talk about that. The truth can be so tedious to some people.

That meant Enid was left with her father, which was basically the same as being left with nobody at all. When he wasn't at work, he spent all day out in the front yard, baking his leathery flesh like he was roasting chicken skin.

He's there right now, snoring in a plastic lawn chair, a dented can of Bud Lite in one hand, the latest issue of *Playboy* in the other. Or what was the latest issue of *Playboy*, the airbrushed face of former teen idol Tiffany grinning back. *All Grown Up and Totally Nude*, the cover promises in bold cream-colored letters.

It's been twenty years since I've seen Enid's dad, and in all that time, I wonder if he's even woken up long enough to realize he's a ghost.

Enid barely seems to notice him. We're halfway across the street, nearly to my front door now, when we spot Grace's brothers. The two of them slouched on the curb, their blurry eyes staring out at the blank horizon, searching for something. And when we get closer, I can hear it too, the very thing they want, its tinkling melody rising up through the endless summer air.

An ice cream truck, so near that it could be on the very next street.

"They'll be waiting a long time," Enid says as we sneak past them. "That truck never comes this far."

Of course it doesn't. It's just another illusion like everything else here. The outside world keeps leaking in, but nothing ever quite makes it through. Nothing except me.

Together, Enid and I start up the familiar cobblestone path, past the driveway and the privet shrubs.

"Go on," she says, and opens the front door for me, as if I have to be invited into my own home.

Inside, the warm scents of cinnamon and cardamom waft through the house. Mom's been baking today. From the welcome mat, I can see her up the stairs, drifting back and forth in the kitchen, a frilly apron tied around her waist. It's so nostalgic, so painfully familiar, and for a moment, everything feels safe. Like I never left. Like I never had to leave.

Enid's looming right next to me, barely tethered to earth. "Would you rather talk to her?"

I shake my head. "Not yet," I say. Besides, I'm not sure my mother wants to talk to me.

"This way, then." Enid tugs my arm, and the two of us head downstairs. To the basement rec room where we find her. Sophie, still playing with her toys. I wonder if she's always playing with her toys now. If this is all eternity has to offer.

At least she looks happy, especially now that we're here. She glances toward the doorway, her face lighting up like it's Christmas morning.

"Hello," she says brightly, surging forward, and for the first time, it feels like I'm really home.

"Hi, baby," I whisper, but Sophie brushes right past me and wraps her arms around Enid's legs instead. The same way she used to wrap her arms around me.

"Hello, little one," Enid says, and a dagger twists in my chest.

Enid, her surrogate sister. A replacement for me.

I fall back a step, away from them, away from this place. I shouldn't have come here. I should have known better.

Enid must sense this in me, my wavering resolve, because she regards Sophie now. "I've got someone who wants to see you."

Sophie blinks up at her. "Who?" she asks, those blue eyes as strange and tempestuous as the sea.

"It's your sister. She's right there." Enid motions to me, as if that will be enough. As if she can will this to happen.

But when Sophie turns toward the doorway, her gaze locked on the spot where I'm standing, there's not even a flicker of recognition on her face. "Where?" she asks, waving her hands in front of her.

Enid purses her lips, pensive for a moment. "Try to talk to her," she says to me. "Try to make her hear your voice."

"I'm here, Sophie." I take a step closer. "I'm right here."

The air crackles around us, the scent of ozone rising up out of nowhere. Sophie reaches out slowly, and I hold my breath, wanting this to be it, the moment everything shifts. But her hand goes right through me.

"There's nothing there," she says, her nose crinkled as she retreats nonchalantly, settling down on the floor among her toys.

Nothing. That's a good description of it. I collapse cross-legged next to her, my head in my hands.

But Enid isn't so easily deterred. She crouches next to Sophie. "Talitha wants me to tell you she's here. That she came back just to see you."

Sophie tilts her head. "This is a funny game," she says. "We've never played this one before."

I look to Enid. "Tell her it's not a game."

"Your sister says it's not a game."

Sophie giggles. "She probably would say that too. You're good at pretending to be her." She leans in, giving Enid that gap-toothed grin. "What else would Talitha tell me?"

My head lolls back. "That I'm sorry," I whisper.

The minutes tick by. Sophie goes back to her army of toys, and Enid goes back to staring off, infinite secrets swirling in her. There are three of us in this room, but it feels like we all occupy different universes.

Sophie positions her red pony named Sam in the middle of the floor. Her favorite toy, the one she took everywhere with her. But after all these years, his plastic legs have gone gnarled, and he topples over. Smiling, Enid reaches out to set him back up again, and that's when I see it. The tips of her fingers are going gray. One after another, they're shriveling away, just a little, just enough that you can see it, the way death twists in her.

The death this neighborhood put inside her, long before the others were ghosts. Way back when she was the only ghost we knew.

It's a rule that nobody ever tells you, a rule I couldn't imagine, not until what happened here: when you have a haunting, there always has to be the first specter. That's her. She's what started all this.

Enid notices me staring. Her cheeks flushed, she hides both hands. "It's nothing," she says, and I already know if I ask her about it, she won't tell me. So I say something else instead.

"What does my sister think happened to me?"

"Sophie," Enid whispers, "what happened to Talitha?"

At this, Sophie stops playing, her hand frozen in midair, her pony's blank eyes staring up at me. "She went away," she says finally.

"Where does she think I've gone?" I ask.

"Where, Sophie? Where is Talitha?"

"Mom says she's with Daddy now." Sophie nods solemnly, as if to confirm it. "She says they're happier there."

My breath heaves in my chest. "She thinks I'm dead?" The question sits in my belly. "Tell her I'm still alive. Tell her that you're the ones that are dead."

"Are we though?" Enid asks, and she sounds genuinely curious.

I gape at her, dread churning through me. "What else would you be?"

Enid shrugs. "Perhaps we're all ghosts," she says, as if being a specter is no more than a point of view.

And maybe she's right. Maybe in this place, they're alive, and I'm the phantom. I certainly feel as unreal as a spirit, like I'm being plucked out of my own body. I'm everywhere and nowhere at once.

I remove the timer from my pocket. It's been fifty minutes already. Back on the other side, it must be almost May now, sap running from the trees, dandelions sprouting up between every crack in the sidewalk.

A strange notion ripples through me. I think how easy it would be, how I could forget the timer altogether. Toss it in Sophie's toybox and pretend it doesn't exist. If an hour in here is three months over there, then one week would do the trick. Seven days in this rec room would be enough to erase every other choice I've ever had, decades dissolving around me, my whole life dissolving. I could be a modern-day Rip Van Winkle, shipwrecked in suburbia.

All I have to do is close my eyes and wait.

Enid watches me, a shadow on her face. "Are you all right?"

"I'm fine," says Sophie, brushing the purple mane on a bright pink pony.

"I wasn't talking to you, honey. I was talking to your sister."

"What's wrong with her?" With a small frown, Sophie searches the room as though she might suddenly find me here. "Isn't she feeling well?"

"No," Enid says as she moves toward me, pressing one hand into my clammy forehead. "She's not."

Sophie snaps her tongue. "I didn't know ghosts could get sick."

I scowl. "I'm not a ghost. Tell her to stop saying that."

"Sophie, sweetheart, please stop accusing your sister of being dead. She doesn't like it."

Sophie makes her ponies dance in a haphazard circle. "Well, I don't like that she's dead."

Grief tightens in my chest, because this is pointless.

I clamber to my feet, and I'm nearly to the doorway before I turn back. "Come with me," I say to Enid. "Just to the end of the street. And bring Sophie."

She hesitates, as though this is all a trick. Then she looks to my sister. "Let's go for a walk, little one."

Sophie giggles. "Is that what 'Talitha' wants?" she asks, making air quotes around my name.

"That's right." Enid holds out her hand, steady as the seasons. Still giggling, Sophie takes it, and the three of us start up the stairs.

Outside, my mother is sitting in the Geo Metro again, her body slumped, her eyes glazed over.

"I wish she wouldn't do that," Sophie whispers as we creep by.

We head down the road together, Sophie matching me step for step, even though she can't see me. This feels so normal. This feels like nothing ever changed.

Home. I'm home. That's what I tell myself, and it's at once the truth and a lie.

Mrs. Owens eyes us up as we pass. "What are you girls doing?"

Sophie grins at her. "Just going for a walk, Mrs. Owens."

"You know what's coming, don't you?" Mrs. Owens shakes that familiar broom at us. "You know we can't stop it."

"What's she talking about?" I ask, but nobody answers me.

Overhead, a tangle of clouds cascades past us, as we cut through overgrown lawns, mud creeping over our shoes, the earth practically alive around us.

We're near Grace's house now, the front door hanging open, and I can't help but glance inside. It's the same as I remember it, the walls painted a garish robin's-egg blue, the love seat in the living room made of bright red velvet, a stack of old teen magazines in the corner. Grace's magazines, all the ones she couldn't bear to part with.

We used to hang out there, me and Grace and Brett and Enid. Del would join us sometimes too. He'd sit at the table and let Grace dye his hair neon green with a tub of Manic Panic she shoplifted from the mall, their saccharine laughter ricocheting off the walls.

I sprawled out on the floor, watching them. "He's not so bad," I said to Brett.

"Then why don't you date him?" she asked, thumbing through an issue of *Seventeen* she'd grabbed from the corner.

"I don't mean for me," I said. "I mean for Grace. She seems happy."

Brett grunted, still reading her magazine, pulling at the long, flowing sleeves on her blouse. It was the hothouse days of August then, but I could see it there, the thing she was trying to hide beneath the hem. A bruise on her arm in the shape of a gruff handprint. Another memento from her stepdad.

"Do you want to talk about it?" I asked.

"Nope," she said, not looking at me. Of course not. There were things he did to her out in the open, and things he did to her in the dark, and most days, Brett didn't want to discuss any of it. No one except me ever listened anyhow.

"You should run," a voice, quiet as a tomb, whispered. Enid. She was facing the wall next to us, her knees tucked into her chest, her body coiling up like she was in a cocoon.

Grace rolled her eyes. "Are you conversing with spiders again?"

Enid shook her head, as a row of insects marched past her. "Millipedes this time," she said, and they seemed to dance at her command.

There are millipedes skittering at our feet now, but Enid doesn't seem to notice them today. Instead, we keep going, all the houses behind us now, the perimeter wavering up ahead.

We're almost to the end of the street when Sophie's face goes waxen, and she starts to back away. "I don't like it here."

I look down at her, my stomach clenching. "What's wrong?" I ask, but instinctively, I already know. This spot is the way out. A way they can't go.

"What happens if I try to take you with me?" I ask.

Enid shakes her head. "Nothing good."

This aches inside me, the hopelessness of it. "Why did you do this?"

A wounded look blooms on Enid's face. "You know why," she whispers. "You wanted this. All three of you did. Or don't you remember?"

"You're wrong," I say. "I never asked for *this*."

Enid reaches out for me, her fingertips grayer now. "You told me to fix it," she says, taking my hand, "so I fixed it."

Sophie stares up at us, her pale eyes shifting between Enid and the empty air I occupy. "Fix what? What was broken, Enid?"

Silence settles between us, neither of us wanting to say it aloud. The timer bleats in my hand, and I pull away from both of them. My heart heavy, I drift forward a step, ready to return. But that scent of ozone rises up again, and my skin starts to hum, everything in me shifting.

And apparently, I'm not the only one who can feel it. I turn back, and Sophie's eyes are on me now, a strange look passing over her.

"Talitha?" She's suddenly reaching out for me. "Is it you?"

"It's me," I say, my voice splitting in two, but it's too late. The shimmering veil tugs at me, its icy fingers stronger than I am, and I don't even have time to scream before I slip through the darkness.

Away from home, away from Sophie.

When I emerge on the other side, I expect it to be night again, and I expect to be alone. I'm wrong on both accounts. Jack is still standing next to the Camry, the same place I left him.

"Didn't it work?" he asks, and I stare back at him.

"Didn't what work?"

He tilts his head, inspecting me. "You were gone less than a minute."

I hold up the timer, my hand trembling. "I was gone for an hour. The same as last time."

Except it wasn't the same. She saw me. Sophie finally saw me. I can't keep her waiting now.

I turn back, pylons splayed at my feet, but I don't even make it half a step before my whole body goes numb, the past and the present ringing at once in my bones.

"Talitha?" Jack's voice warbling a thousand miles away.

"It's all right," I murmur, but the words dissolve in the bitter morning air.

One final moment, and the world goes black.

Everything happens in flashes, like my whole life's become a missing reel.

Me wilting to the asphalt.

Jack pretending to be a gentleman again, carrying me back to the car.

The blur of Carter Lane outside the passenger window and the opening of the front door, everything sanitized within. Then the stairs, as Jack brings me up and puts me in bed. He's on the phone in an instant.

"It didn't work the same way this time," he's saying, but I don't want to hear the rest.

"I need to get back to Sophie." I try and fail to sit up, everything in me humming again.

"Your sister can wait." Jack looms in the doorway, his figure backlit, the shape of his body looking like something that isn't there. "After all, she's waited this long."

I want to argue, but the world spins around me, and I'm out again before I can say a word.

I awaken to a shadow over my face and a needle in my arm.

"Don't," I whisper, but no one hears me. There are three figures in the room, maybe four, but I can't get a clear look at any of them.

"It won't hurt much," they say and take another blood sample and another one after that.

"You've got no right," I murmur, my muscles thicker than sludge, my arms flailing uselessly, but it doesn't stop them. They label the vials with permanent marker, their hands stinking of antiseptic.

"That's it for now," they say, and they're out the door before I can even curse at them.

I drift in and out, the world falling away before rushing back up again, memories surging through me.

"It's all our fault," I said to Brett a few months after it happened, the new reality of our lives settling over me. "They're dead because of us."

"You don't know that." Brett was like steel through everything. Not a trace of emotion, not a single regret. "And you know what would have happened to us if we hadn't gotten out."

"Maybe that's what we deserved."

She looked at me for a moment like she honestly wished me dead. "I won't apologize for surviving, Talitha."

"I'm not asking you to."

In fact, I asked nothing of her. Brett and I didn't speak for weeks after that, existing tenuously together in the same dorm room, an echo where Grace should have been. I pretended I didn't know any of them, not Brett or Enid or even my own mother, that I'd never been to a place called Velkwood Street, even though it carried my own name. I told myself I was someone else.

It almost worked for a while.

The next time I open my eyes, it's night again, and I can't remember where I am. If I'm still at home curled up in the rec room or if I'm back in the real world. If there even is a real world anymore. I feel like I'm sliding between, here and not here, and if I'm not careful, I'll get lost in the dark, an ant disappearing into a crevice.

"How are you feeling?" Jack's in the doorway, watching me.

"Better," I say, though I wonder if that's true. I struggle to my feet, already sure of what I want to do next—charge back in and get Sophie. But with my head still numb, I'm afraid I won't make it ten minutes in there.

"Are you hungry?" Jack says, and I let out a defeated laugh. This is starting to become a habit: me returning from the great beyond, and him buying me dinner like a consolation prize.

Tonight, he takes me into town, these streets that used to be mine, used to be so familiar. At the far end of the thoroughfare, there's a Chevron gas station attached to a diner, the kind where the waitresses wear funny pink hats. I remember this place well. Brett and I would come here every Friday night in middle school, the two of us in matching camisoles, choosing the same back corner booth, away from the counter, away from everyone. Our freshman year, Brett even got a job as a server, saving every penny she made for college, and I'd grin and sit in our same booth, gulping down bottomless cups of coffee while she was working. Anything to be close to her.

Part of me hopes that's the spot where we'll sit tonight, as though I can relive the memory, like a crumbling flower pressed between the pages of an old book. But with a tight smile, the hostess seats us at a table by the window instead.

I slump back in my chair, wanting to shed the day like an ill-fitting suit, but Jack's all business. We've barely ordered before he leans in.

"I've been discussing it with the others," he says, and he even gives me a few of their names. The researchers, the ones that keep dissecting me. "We're still trying to put some of the pieces together."

"Like what?" I ask, glancing over my shoulder at that corner booth. It's empty now.

"What happened that last night?" Jack's hand brushes against mine on the table. "Before the three of you headed back to college?"

My head snaps toward him. "Why does it matter?"

"Because," he says, "I think that's key to this whole thing."

An old jukebox in the corner wheezes out a song by the Cranberries, and I suddenly can't breathe.

"Nothing," I say. "Nothing happened. We went back to school. That's it."

For what it's worth, he pretends to believe me. The two of us wait quietly for our food, pretending this is normal, pretending I didn't just return from an afternoon with ghosts.

I remember how Jack has ghosts of his own. The compass he's always wearing, tiny and misshapen, glints in the jaundiced yellow glow of the diner. I don't want to talk about me anymore, so maybe we can talk about him.

"What happened to your necklace?" I reach across the table and touch the charm dangling at his chest. "How did it end up bent like that?"

He blushes a little. "At a séance."

I snap my tongue. "No way," I say.

He puts up both hands, as if in protest. "I'm not kidding. My aunt took me to this séance at the Stanley Hotel when I was sixteen."

"You tried to summon the dead at the Stanley Hotel?"

"We didn't *try*. We succeeded. Shaking walls, cold spots, murmuring voices. The whole nine yards."

"And your necklace," I offer.

"We didn't even see that until the next day," he says, everything in him bright and wired, as though he's telling the story for the first time. "It shouldn't have been possible. The compass is made of titanium. Not one jeweler could figure out how it happened. Afterward, my aunt said it was my personal proof of ghosts."

I smile for a moment and then a wave of shame crests over me. I only got him started on this to distract from my ghosts. But he's on a roll now, and he doesn't seem to want to stop. Once you get lonely people talking, that tends to happen.

"She died my senior year in high school," he says, gnawing his bottom lip, his hands fiddling with the paper ring wrapped tight around his silverware. "On the day of her funeral, I picked up a newspaper just to get a copy of her obituary, just because it felt like the right thing to do. And wouldn't you know it, but there was a haunting in the headline?"

I hesitate. "Us," I say. "Velkwood Street."

"I took it as a sign. You were right there, like I was meant to find you. Like I was meant to come to this place. And I thought maybe—"

He trails off, his eyes unfocused.

"You thought you could see her again."

"Maybe," he says. "But if I couldn't have that, then I just really wanted to prove her right. To find the world's biggest piece of evidence for the existence of ghosts, something way more than a bent necklace."

"I think we will," I say. "The next time I go over there. I think we'll make your aunt proud."

"I hope you're right," he says, and he looks ready to tell me something else, but the waitress shuffles over first and brings us two blue-plate specials.

We're almost done with dinner when Jack's phone buzzes, and he excuses himself to take the call. I sit alone at the table, watching him through the window as he wanders out to the sidewalk, pacing back and forth, speaking so quietly I can't hear a thing.

The waitress shimmies back to the booth, a steaming coffee pot in her hand. "Those researchers out on Carter Lane are always busy, aren't they?"

I shrug, not looking at her. "I guess so."

She pours me another cup of coffee, even though I didn't ask. "I remember you," she says, grit and grief in her voice. "And your friend Brett. Always a troublemaker, that one. But then, you're a bit of a troublemaker too, aren't you?"

This hits me dead center. "I don't try to be," I say, shifting in my seat, wishing she'd go away, wishing all of this would go away.

"Then you should leave well enough alone." She leans in now, and her breath smells of curdled cream. "Don't go back there. Don't bother them."

My eyes are on her now. "Why not?"

"Because nobody finds what they want by running with ghosts."

I heave up a laugh. "I don't even know what I want anymore."

"Then do what we want," she says, "and leave it alone, Talitha."

My mouth goes dry. "We?"

She takes a step back, and there they are, scattered across the diner like wedding rice. A dozen other patrons, all of them watching me, their eyes sliding over me, a silent interrogation.

The bell over the door jingles, and Jack returns to the table. He looks at me, not noticing the others or the way they're still staring.

"Is everything all right?" he asks.

"Fine," I say and shove the coffee cup away. "Can we go now?"

I'm quiet all the way back to Carter Lane, my trembling hands folding and unfolding in my lap. The night's settling over us, thick as motor oil, ice crystals clinging to the edges of the windshield. It's still the dead of winter. I didn't escape it. That's because I never escape anything. I'm a fly in the ointment of my own life.

But Jack doesn't look at me that way. I'm nothing but possibilities to him. I'm the woman that can unravel the riddle of his entire career, a solution instead of a problem. The only other person who's ever looked at me like that is Brett, and she won't even take my calls now.

Back at the house, we head upstairs together. In my room, there's only emptiness waiting for me. A bed, a dresser, the single bag I packed, when I intended to stay for no more than a couple days. I'm already running out of clothes.

"You can borrow this for tonight," Jack says, and gives me an old college tee. I read the name on the front. Case Western Reserve. I've never heard of it.

"Thanks," I say and change into the shirt, not bothering to close the bedroom door behind me. I don't look to see if Jack watches, even though I hope he does.

When I reemerge, he's waiting in the hall. "So you were really gone for a whole hour today?"

"That's what the timer said."

He nods, not saying anything else, just leaning against the wall, looking so calm, like he rescues girls from the beyond every other day. I stand here watching him, loneliness metastasizing in me. It's been a long day, a longer year, and I'm remembering what I wanted when he and I first met.

Maybe he's thinking the same thing, because he gives me that smile again. "I'm getting a shower," he says, and it almost sounds like an invitation.

I linger in the hallway, pretending not to hear him, pretending I don't want to take him up on the offer. He doesn't say anything else, but the same way I did, he leaves the door open, just a sliver, just enough that I can see flashes of him moving back and forth, backlit in the warm incandescent glow.

I tell myself not to look. I look anyway. It's been a long time since anybody noticed me. Or since I noticed anyone. I start to drift forward, my hand pressed on the door, ready to nudge it open. Ready to do something that would make my mother ashamed of me all over again.

But there's someone else who wants to be let in. A knock downstairs, staccato as a nervous heartbeat, and I roll my eyes. More of those awful researchers, no doubt, all of them eager to vivisect me. I'm their biology class experiment, a frog dipped in formaldehyde, my chest split in two.

I shouldn't answer. I shouldn't bother with them at all, but then they'll only come back later. And I'd rather get this over with. My feet heavy beneath me, I start down the stairs. Another knock, louder this time, and I can't help but scowl.

"I'll be right there," I say as I flip the lock and brace for it. The stench of them, of antiseptic and bad intentions. But when I open the door, something else hits me instead, something familiar.

A scent like strawberries and cream.

Brett's standing on the other side, flashing that sweet smile that could cut you in two. "Can I come in?" she asks, and my whole life crashes over me in an instant.

CHAPTER 7

It's always startling to see her, the way she looks like a fever dream, like something not quite real. That valance of dark hair over her eyes, those lips always painted bright red as a pomegranate seed. I've just come face-to-face with a street full of ghosts, but nobody's ever haunted me like she does.

"I tried to call you earlier," I murmur, my cheeks burning, my words blurring together.

"My phone was off," she says. "I took the first flight out this morning."

Because I asked her to. Brett's here because it's what I wanted.

We stand together for a moment, each of us on opposite sides of the threshold, our breath fogging in the cold. She glances down at me, at what I'm wearing. An oversized T-shirt, one that's clearly not mine.

Smiling, she leans against the doorway. "You look like you've been busy," she says, and I've never met anyone in my life who can make an accusation sound so cordial.

My throat constricts, and I don't even try to answer. Instead, I wave her inside.

Brett follows close behind, tracking in ice and midnight. "Who did the decorating?" she asks, scowling at the bland walls. "A Stepford wife?"

I look around, pretending to notice the place for the first time. "The researchers, I guess."

She turns to me, her eyes bright as hellfire. "And who are *they*?"

I swallow hard. "I'm not really sure."

There are lots of things I'm not sure of, answers I should know from questions Brett would have already asked.

I'm in the middle of the room now, my nerves gone raw, and Brett's right next to me, less than a step away. She doesn't have a bag, doesn't have anything at all. Just herself. That's always been more than enough. For an instant, I'm half convinced she might reach out for me. To embrace me maybe, the way old friends are supposed to do.

But she doesn't get a chance. A shuffle of steps overhead, and Jack comes bounding down the stairs, his skin still glistening from the shower. Brett eyes him up, like she knows what that means, like she knows what we were doing.

When he sees her, he smiles, recognition flashing across his face. This whirls my head for a moment. I'd forgotten they'd met before, that he went to her before he came to me.

"Brett," he says brightly. "This is a surprise."

"Not as much of a surprise as it is for me." She peers at him and then back at me fidgeting in his T-shirt. "I hope I'm not interrupting anything."

"Not at all," I say, even though I can't help but think that's exactly what she's doing. Brett's got impeccable timing, I'll give her that. She knew the precise moment to keep me from a mistake I was eager to make.

My hands clasp in front of me to keep from shaking. "How did you find us?"

"I asked in town," she says. "They told me all the researchers were on Carter Lane. From there, I just looked for the beat-up Camry in the driveway."

Jack glances at Brett and me, the past hanging heavy and sullen in the air. "How long's it been since you two saw each other?"

The question knocks me off-balance. "I don't remember," I start to say, but Brett cuts me off.

"Two years. It's been two years."

She's right. That's when I left the city and moved half a state away into that pigsty rental with the greasy landlord. I ran because I thought it would make a difference. That I could forget Velkwood Street. That I could forget her.

But I'm back home, exactly where I started.

Jack looks ready to say something else, but there's a whisper on the other side of the door and then three knocks right in a row, like a secret code.

"Exciting night," Brett says, and I hold my breath because I already know who it is.

Jack opens the door, and the researchers pour in, all of them with their sights set on Brett. They must have seen her come in. They must be watching us all the time.

"You don't belong here," they say.

"You're telling me," Brett says with a grin, but they don't break character, not for a minute.

"Guests need to have a permit," they say.

Brett gives them her best fuck-you smile. "Just tell me where to apply."

She edges forward, her jaw set, but Jack, always the peacemaker, intercepts first.

"This is Brett Hadley," he says to them. "You remember. We asked her to be part of this project last year."

Last year. It was really that long ago.

There's a moment of back and forth, Jack leaning in, explaining things, and all the researchers nodding back at him. "We can fast-track a permit," they say before turning to Brett. "We'll bring you a release form to sign tomorrow morning."

Brett does her best not to burst out laughing. "I'll be waiting," she says, as Jack ushers them to the door. "What's with the funeral procession?"

"They're just doing their jobs," he says and locks up behind them.

"And what are their jobs exactly?" Brett asks.

"They're post-doc students. Here on a one-year contract."

"And you're not a student," Brett says, circling him slowly, figuring it out as she goes. "So you're the one in charge."

Jack gives her that crooked smile. "That's not exactly how I'd describe it."

"But I bet it's how they'd describe it," Brett says, and it's clear she's right.

The researchers, each of them eager to impress Jack. Eager to get a good recommendation. No wonder they're all dour faces and all business. In this job market, everyone has to be.

Jack's still looking at Brett. "Are you staying the night?"

She turns to me, one eyebrow raised. "Am I?"

"If you'd like," I say, and my cheeks are burning again. I'm a forty-year-old woman, acting bashful as a schoolgirl. This is how it always is with me and Brett. I never know how to feel around her.

Jack, on the other hand, is as blithe as ever. "We've got plenty of room," he says, and in a flash, he's in the hall, digging through a linen closet I didn't know existed, procuring a blanket and two pillows and even a spare towel.

"Thanks," Brett says with a wan smile. She reclines on the couch, the cushions hugging her body, and Jack watches her, like he wants to say something else. Like he's got a script on a clipboard somewhere that could help him catalog Brett's memories.

But then he glances at the two of us, sensing it again. The past lingering in the air, potent as cigarette smoke.

He forces a smile. "I'll see you both in the morning," he says, and vanishes upstairs.

I should head up too. Back to my own room where I can sleep off this day that never ends. Only I already know I won't do that, not with Brett right here in front of me, sprawled out on the couch, her shoes kicked off, her long legs stretched out.

"It's cute," she says. "The way you two are playing house."

I back against the wall. "We're not playing at anything."

"You know," she says, "if I'd said yes to him, it would be me wearing that ratty T-shirt instead of you." Then she adds, as if to twist the knife, "We're just interchangeable to him, Talitha."

Embarrassment flushes through me. "You don't know that for sure."

"And you don't know for sure I'm wrong. He's nothing but a fanboy for ghosts."

I want to argue with her, but something shifts in me, my head going gauzy, my knees weak.

Brett puts out her hand to steady me. "You all right?"

I pull away before she can touch me. "I'm just tired," I say, but she doesn't buy it for a second.

Brett's not like Jack. I can't lie to her.

"It's that street, isn't it?" She sucks air through her teeth. "What's it even look like now?"

I stare back at her, suddenly remembering she hasn't seen the neighborhood in twenty years. After it happened, Brett wasn't like me or Grace. She never bothered to come back. The past didn't concern her anymore—she was only looking toward the future. She made the most of her parents' life insurance policy, paying off her tuition, paying off everything. Our college even waited until the end of the semester to get their payment, long past its due date.

"To honor your period of mourning," they told Brett, but I always thought it was because we freaked them out. The girls whose families were phantoms.

The same phantoms that are still waiting for us. "Would you like to see it?" I ask. "The old neighborhood?"

Brett hesitates, as if the notion hadn't occurred to her. "From a safe distance."

I lead her up the stairs, the plush carpet soft beneath our bare feet, our steps hardly making a sound. Not that we need to be quiet, not that Jack cares where we go in this house, but Brett and I are so used to sneaking around that it comes naturally to us now.

In the attic, we edge through the dark until we reach the smudged picture window. Outside, the neighborhood is waiting for us.

Brett gazes down at the thin row of shimmering houses. "It never changes, does it?"

She's right next to me, even closer than before, her long hair brushing against my arm, the warmth of her body radiating out. She's more alive than anyone I've ever known, everything in her firing on all cylinders.

One last glance, and she settles down in the dusty window seat, no longer looking at the neighborhood. She's only looking at me. "I missed you."

I breathe deep, and there it is again, that strange ache in my chest. I want to tell her I've missed her too, that I always miss her, but everything jumbles up inside me, and when I part my lips to speak, no sound comes out.

Brett knows me well enough. She knows I won't say it back.

"It's all right," she whispers, her head lolling, the weight of the day wearing on her. She's been traveling since morning, and in a way, so have I.

I curl up in the other corner of the window seat, a gulf between us. Brett's already half asleep now, but that doesn't matter. She reaches out for me anyway, her hand grasping softly in the dark. My heart tightening, I start to reach back, but then I see it again through the glass, the street wavering in the distance. It never stops watching, never stops accusing.

With shame draping over me, I wrench away from her and close my eyes.

When I look again, the sun is creeping through the picture window, and I'm alone.

It's morning now, probably well past nine, and Brett's long gone. I wonder for a moment if I dreamt last night, if I dreamt everything. Maybe I haven't been back to the neighborhood at all, and this is only the first morning all those months ago.

Then the throbbing in my head hits me all over again, and I remember it. Where I've been, how it's still in me. How I might never escape it.

Downstairs, there's a hint of smoke in the kitchen. Jack is busying himself at the stove, the scents of burnt bacon and burnt coffee wafting through the air, a morning in the making.

Meanwhile, Brett's reclined on the couch like she never left. She doesn't see me at first, so I linger at the bottom of the steps, watching her, the way she moves like a daydream.

There it is again, that sweet scent of hers. I can't believe she still wears that same strawberries-and-cream lotion from high school, but maybe I shouldn't be so surprised. Nothing ever seems to change for us. My head swimming, I shift on the steps, the house creaking around me, still watching Brett. When she notices me here, she rises at once, like an actor caught off guard, like she's desperate to keep up the performance. She parades across the room, and with her hands steady, she opens the front window, letting out the smoke from the kitchen, the thin trails mingling with sunlight.

"I figured I should let you sleep," she says, giving me an answer for a question I had no intention of asking.

I clasp my hands in front of me. "Thanks, I guess."

"Good morning," Jack says, and deposits three identical breakfasts on the table. We sit together, eating off plates the color of bone. A pale clock on the wall ticks by, every second an agonizing eternity. Brett's gaze keeps shifting between me and Jack, as if she's testing us, trying to figure out how many times I've worn this faded T-shirt.

I stare into my eggs, hating everything about this. I could tell her nothing's happened. I could also tell her it's none of her business, even though I wonder if that's really true. Brett and I have always made each other our business. We can go years and barely speak, but the moment we're in the same room, it's like nothing's changed, ancient jealousy stirring in us like we're still sixteen.

"Are you planning on going back home today?" she asks me.

"If I can," I say.

Brett gives me a tight grin, and it always astounds me, the way she can seethe through a smile. "How many more times are you planning to visit?"

I take a sip of black coffee, wincing at the bitterness. "As many as it takes."

Jack glances between us, oblivious to the world. "Talitha's managed to make some real progress."

"Like what?" Brett turns to him. "They're all still ghosts, aren't they?"

Nobody says anything else after that. We finish our meal in silence, the clock counting down every miserable moment. Jack's clearing the table when there's a knock on the door, and the researchers invite themselves in.

"Your permit has been approved," they say, and thrust a stack of papers at Brett. "Just sign here."

She takes a red pen from them, a devilish look sparking in her eyes. "Are you planning to steal my first born, too?"

They don't answer. They just wait until she scribbles on the dotted line before tucking her form in a folder and looking at me.

"Your turn now," they say, tearing a fresh needle out of its paper coffin. Again, they're all business, their jobs a never-ending checklist of items. I bet this sounded like a plum assignment when they applied for it. Hanging out with ghosts, discovering life after death. But everything's a bigger bureaucracy than you ever expect. I almost feel sorry for them. I almost feel sorry for all of us.

A needle in my arm, and I hardly flinch at the pain. Brett, however, is doing more than enough flinching for me.

"What's going on?" She watches as they take another tube of my blood, draining me bit by bit. "What are you doing to her?"

I hold up one hand, as if to say it's okay. Then I regard the researchers. "I want to go back in today."

They only shake their heads. "We need to wait for the results of your blood tests first," they say. "In the meantime, Miss Hadley can visit next."

Brett recoils. "No, Miss Hadley will not visit, thank you very much."

They turn to her, all of them at once. "Then why are you here?"

Brett looks at me, and something passes between us. "You'll have to ask Talitha about that."

Another three vials, and I'm still pressing a piece of gauze into a seeping needle mark when Brett pulls me outside.

"What are you doing?" She gapes at me, her breath fogging thick and pale between us. "What kind of tests are they even running on you?"

I shrug, fidgeting on the front step. "It's just for the research."

"For what? So they can figure that place out?" A sneer blooms on her lips. "Why would you ever want to help them?"

"You know why," I say, "Because Sophie's still in there."

"That's one reason." Brett glowers at the house. "Is there another?"

"No," I say. "Jack's not why I'm here."

"So he's just a fun bonus?"

I scoff. "Are we really going to do this right now?"

"You called me, remember?" She looks away, the facade fading for a moment, and all I can see in her eyes is hurt.

I start to say something, maybe to make an apology, maybe to make another excuse, but a voice floats outside.

"We can't let her go back today."

The researchers. They don't know the window's open. They don't know we can hear them.

"That's fine," Jack says, his voice thin and strained. "That'll give us time to survey the perimeter again. To double-check the new measurements."

"What new measurements?" Brett whispers, moving closer to me, her breath soft and sweet as spun sugar.

"I'm not sure."

Jack never mentioned anything to me.

"That will have to do for now," someone else says, and all at once, the researchers file out onto the sidewalk, marching past us like we're air, returning to the other houses on Carter Lane, all the front doors slamming, one after another. They come and go so quickly that I sometimes wonder if they're ghosts too.

Brett waits until they've disappeared before she looks at me again. "Why would it be changing now?" she asks. "Especially after all these years?"

I hesitate, thinking again of Enid's fingertips, the way they're turning gray. The way that spot at the culvert is splitting open in the earth.

Everything is shifting, but there's still so much I don't know. I've only seen what the neighborhood looks like now. We need someone who's been inside already. Someone who knows what the place was like before.

"Grace," I whisper. "We should talk to Grace."

"Good luck with that," Brett says. "Are we even sure she's living in the same place?"

"Where else would she be?"

That little shotgun house practically swallowed her whole ten years ago. For better or worse, she's still inside.

"I don't know, Talitha." Brett runs her hands through her hair, the sun on her face, the winter wind whipping bitterly around us. "She might not talk to you."

"But she might talk to both of us." I bite my bottom lip, my eyes on her. "Come with me?"

Without a word, we both already know she'll say yes.

I don't tell Jack where I'm going. I just bundle up in my black jacket, pretending this is a nothing daytrip between old friends.

"Have fun," he says, lingering at the front door, watching us go, that smile of his dipping just a little, like he knows something.

From the driver seat, Brett waves to him. "See you later," she says, as though she's won this round.

On the way out of town, we stop at the Chevron gas station, attached to the diner where Jack and I had supper last night. There's a woman smoking outside, the same one who served my coffee, still wearing her funny hat, slumped to one side.

Brett climbs out of the car. "Hello again," she says as she starts to fill the tank.

"Hi, Brett." The woman peers through the passenger window at me. "I see you found your girl."

Brett gives me a quick smile. "I did," she says. This must have been where she asked about us. Jack and I couldn't have missed her by more than a few minutes.

I sink down in my seat, counting the seconds until we're away from here. In the window of the diner, there's a faded sign. *Upstairs Room for Rent.* That room has been vacant since we were kids. It's right above the kitchen, the walls reeking of frying oil and Sunday dinners long past. I know because I've been in there. On her break from work, Brett used to grab my hand, and we'd sneak up the back steps, the two of us playing house, discussing where to put our invisible furniture.

"The dresser should go in this corner," I'd say.

"And of course, our bed should be by the window," Brett would say, and we'd laugh, make-believing a future together that would never come.

This future came instead, the one where we barely know each other anymore. I watch Brett, pacing impatiently next to the car, the world always too slow for her taste.

Nearby, the woman sucks her Marlboro down to the filter. "You two leaving town?"

The gas pump jolts to a stop. "For now," Brett says. "We'll be back."

A sharp guffaw. "I'm sure you will."

With a full tank, the rental car surges down the street, past the carcass of our small town. Empty storefronts, empty houses, empty hearts. This little speck on the map was on its way out years ago, and our street was the final nail in a coffin the world built for us.

Heading south on the state highway, you can see the rest of what we left behind. The boarded-up hospital where we were all born. A husk of an abandoned shopping mall. We lost a thousand hours there, lounging around the food court with Grace, the three of us sharing endless baskets of curly fries. In the tacky department stores, Brett and I always changing in the same dressing room, giggling like fools, zipping and unzipping dresses we could never afford.

It's a five-hour drive to Grace's house, Brett doing her best to make small talk, me doing my best not to fall apart. My head's still throbbing, the specter of that place hanging over me. Afternoon leaks in, painting the car interior a sallow yellow, and I'm drifting off in the passenger seat when I feel Brett watching me.

"What is it?" I ask, not looking at her.

"Why did you go back?" Her voice chafes with accusation. "You told me on the phone you didn't want to."

A dull ache in my heart. "I thought it would be different."

I thought she and I would be different too. We had plenty of chances. Two years ago, when the lease was up on my last apartment, Brett invited me out to brunch, the kind of place with bleached linen tablecloths and nothing on the menu for less than the price of a utility bill. It was exactly the sort of locale Brett had come to fancy, a reminder of how she'd upgraded in life. And a reminder of how I hadn't. I ordered the cheapest thing à la carte, even though she offered to pay.

She offered something else, too.

"Let's buy a house together," she said over a pitcher of mimosas. "Lots of friends are doing it now."

She brought it up as if the idea had just occurred to her, as if she hadn't been trying to invent ways for us to be together for years. Not that Brett needed to buy a house with anyone, not with the amount of money she had squirreled away in savings and IRAs and probably even tucked under her mattress. But then she wasn't trying to buy it with just anyone. She was trying to buy it with me.

"I'll think about it," I said, but I never did. Instead, I left the city altogether. I couldn't keep looking at her and remembering everything that came before. Everything we'd lost.

"You always run." Brett's hands are tight on the wheel. "That's the one thing I can rely on."

"I'm not running now."

"Sure you are," she says. "Instead of running away from home, you're running straight towards it."

The highway stretches long, the world blurring by. This is how I see everything—through a passenger window, always riding shotgun in a car that doesn't belong to me.

"So," Brett says, as though making polite conversation, "is my stepdad still dead?"

A long moment, the road whirring beneath us, the question curdling in my belly.

"I think so," I say at last.

Her eyes shift over to me. "Did you check?"

"I did."

"There was no body?"

I shake my head. "No ghost, either. Not that I saw."

Her nose crinkles, a trace of disappointment on her face. "I was hoping he'd rotted to dust by now."

"Maybe he has," I whisper.

She and I have never talked about this before, not a word, not since we left that last night, his corpse still warm on Brett's bedroom floor. He's *why* we left, all three of us sneaking off at midnight like fugitives. Which, to be fair, was exactly what we were. What we still are if anybody finds out what we did.

But Enid made sure nobody ever would.

"I'll fix it," she told us, and that's what she did.

As it turns out, the best way to cover up a crime is to commit an even bigger one. She wiped away the scene of a murder by wiping the whole neighborhood off the map.

"They'll never find out," Brett says like she's peering right into me. "Not unless you tell them."

I bristle. "Why would I do that?"

"Why would you ever go back?"

My heart holds tight in my chest. I want to explain. I want to make her understand this, but then we take the last turn and there it is. Grace's house, sitting grimly on the corner, the baby-blue paint peeling off in thick clumps, the porch sagging on one side like it's doing its best to escape itself.

Brett slides the rental into park, the engine cutting out. "I love what she's done with the place."

I droop forward, regret clotting in my guts. "This is our fault," I whisper.

"No, it's not." Brett climbs out of the car. "This is Grace's choice."

I unbuckle my seat belt. "Since when was any of this our choice?"

We edge up the front porch, every step moaning worse than the last. This whole place looks liable to collapse at the slightest sneeze.

"Are you sure you want to do this?" Brett asks, but then we hear it. A shuffling on the other side of the threshold.

"Grace?" I press my hands into the door, splinters biting back at me. "Are you there?"

A strained moment before her voice seeps out from the darkness. "You aren't invited. Nobody's invited."

"Please," I say. "We need to talk."

"Come on, Grace." Brett pounds on the door. "It's just me and Talitha. You know us."

"That's why I don't want to let you in."

At this, Brett chirps out a laugh. "You can't argue with that," she says, and I can tell she's ready to turn back, to walk away from our friend, from our only chance at understanding this. But I won't give up so quickly.

"I've been home," I blurt out, and on the other side, I can hear it. The way she seizes up, her whole life holding still around her.

"You went back?"

"Twice," I say, and that's apparently the magic word, because the door creaks open, and together, Brett and I cross the perilous threshold.

Inside, the place looks nothing like I'm expecting. It's dilapidated, to be sure, but it's even worse than that. It's an imitation of her living room from Velkwood Street. The walls painted robin's-egg blue, the love seat made of red velvet. Except all of it is fading out now, the walls smudged and sallow, the upholstery grimy as a bar stool. There are stacks of once-glossy magazines turning to compost in a nearby corner, and I notice suddenly how there's thin plastic taped over all the soaped windows. Grace is trying to barricade herself from the world, desperate to keep something out.

Or to keep something in.

"I'd offer you tea," she says, shambling across the floor, "but I don't want you to stay that long."

"Neither do we," Brett murmurs, her hands sliding along the crown molding. It crumbles at her touch.

On the other side of the room, Grace sinks down on the love seat, her form turning gauzy and gray, resembling a shadow more than a girl. "So what do you want?"

Her voice is sharp as thorns, yet familiar. Everything about this feels familiar. After all, we're together again, three best friends. Only there's a strange emptiness in Grace's eyes, and she barely seems to recognize us. I barely recognize her, either. Her hair's gone a bright shade of silver, a cluster of sharp lines around her mouth. Brett's barely aged a day, but Grace has apparently absorbed the years for both of them.

"We just want to ask you a few questions," I say.

The rusted radiator against the wall rattles on, the brittle floorboards shaking. "About what?" she asks.

"About the street." I back up a step, the shadows everywhere now. I wish I knew where the light switch was.

Still lingering near the doorway, Brett senses it in me, my faltering resolve. "Something's wrong," she says, filling in the things I can't seem to speak. "The researchers think the neighborhood's changing."

Grace gives us a languid sigh. "Maybe it is. We don't get to decide."

I roll my eyes. More riddles. She's starting to sound like Enid. We need to ask clear-cut questions. Something that's easy to answer.

"How long were you there?" I say, and I'm expecting the same thing as me: either a few months or a few minutes.

Grace's eyes go dark, her dire gaze set on the wall. "A year," she says.

My throat constricts. "You were in there for a year?"

She nods. "Until something forced me out."

At this, Brett edges closer. "Like what?"

"I don't know," she says, "but it's starting to come back."

My breath catches in my chest. "How do you know?"

"Because you brought it out with you, Talitha." Grace turns to me, her face gone gaunt. "It's in the room with us right now."

CHAPTER 8

I barely move. I barely breathe.

"Where is it?" I wheeze, and Grace motions behind me.

"There in the corner."

I turn slowly, every muscle in my body aching, until I'm staring at the very spot where she pointed.

Except there's nothing there. At least nothing I can see.

Brett tilts her head, taking a step closer. "Is it watching us now?"

Grace curls up on the love seat, nearly disappearing into it. "It's hard to tell. Especially since I'm not sure it even has eyes." Then she adds, her lips pursed, "It certainly feels like it's watching us though."

I try to steady myself, to pretend the fear isn't coursing through my body like poison.

"What does it look like?" I say, my voice hardly disturbing the air. "Other than not having eyes?"

"It's just darkness," Grace says. "Not much more than that. Unless you count the whispering."

In an instant, everything in the house goes quiet except for the ticking of the radiator. Brett and I stare at each other, both of us straining to listen. But still, there's nothing.

"If it's so dangerous," Brett says, her arms crossed, "then why doesn't it come after us?"

Grace picks up the nearest magazine, gone yellow and ragged, and flips through it as though she might find the answer there. "There's not enough of it yet," she says. "But there will be if you keep going back, dragging the past out with you."

Shame pulses through me. "I'm not dragging out anything."

"Of course you are." Grace looks at me now, something shifting in her face. Something I almost recognize. "Leave it alone, Talitha. It's not safe."

At this, Brett gives me her patented told-you-so look. I pretend not to notice.

Grace tosses the magazine on the floor, already bored with it. "Did you see anyone over there?" A hopefulness brimming in her eyes. "Like maybe Del?"

I shake my head. "I'm sorry."

She hesitates. "How about my brothers?"

My stomach churns. "Sure," I say.

She perks up, her gaze brightening, and it's the first time I can see her in there, the girl we used to know. A string of questions tumbles from her lips. "How are they? Did they ask about me? Are they still playing basketball at the end of the street?"

I try not to grimace. "They're fine," I say, and the quiver in my voice must give me away, because Brett raises an eyebrow at me. She knows I'm lying. She always knows.

But it's enough to assuage Grace, who settles back on the love seat. "I'm glad they're doing okay."

Okay is not the word I'd use to describe her brothers, but since I don't think the world has invented a proper term for what they are, I won't argue.

I glance down at the magazine she just tossed on the floor. It's an old copy of *Seventeen*, back from when we were still in high school, Katie Holmes' sanguine face staring back at me. My hands quivering, I step toward the towering stack of issues pushed up against the wall, and I start to sift through them. All of them are from the era of scrunchies and Y2K, each copy stacked atop another, their pages curled back, their covers sallow. Like the rest of the décor, Grace must have scoured the internet, procuring every piece of memorabilia from our childhood that she could find. Even this house is no more than a ghost.

Something rattles in the floor beneath me, and with my chest constricting, I shove the magazines away, the entire stack cascading lazily to the floor.

With a scowl, Grace looks up from the love seat. "So," she says, "did you just come here to ransack my house?"

"No," I say, breathing deep. "We're here to get your help."

She waves one dismissive hand at me, and I see it there. Her engagement ring. The diamond's gone dull, the gold band turning her finger green, but she's still wearing it, even after all these years. "Who told you I could help anyone?" Her gaze flits about the room. "Look around, Talitha. I can't even help myself."

"But you were there for a year—"

"No," she says, her mouth a harsh line.

"Why not?" Brett asks.

"Because if I tell you anything," Grace says, "then you'll go back there again. And you'll make this so much worse."

"Please," I say, already sensing it, the way this is all slipping away from me. "We need your help. Sophie needs you."

"Don't you dare, Talitha." Sorrow falls over her face. "You're not the only one who lost somebody in there."

A long, empty moment, the house quiet around us.

"You need to leave now," Grace says, and points to the corner, to the darkness only she can see. "And take that with you."

The door slams shut behind us as Brett and I trudge back to the rental car, night settling around us like a curse.

"So that went well," Brett says, and lets out one of her throaty laughs.

I don't say anything as she starts the engine, the road unspooling before us. This isn't turning out how I'd hoped. Grace didn't turn out how I'd hoped, either. That shotgun house is disintegrating around her. Soon, there won't be anything left.

"She's gone stir crazy," Brett says as if that's an answer.

"And what if she hasn't?"

"You mean, what if there really was a figure in the room with us?" She leans back in the driver's seat. "Then it would be hard to say what it is."

"Do you think it's him?"

"My stepdad?" She won't look at me now. "I don't know."

I slump in my seat, thinking of him again. Her stepdad. I remember the first time we met him. Brett and her mother were already living on Velkwood Street for a year before he ever came into the picture. It was a week before third grade started when Brett and I burst through her back door, giggling, only to find a heap of a man sitting at the kitchen table, all thick callouses and faded tattoos, the stench of sweat and WD-40 filling the room.

"Brett, honey," her mother said with a forced smile. "I'd like you to meet Samuel. You know, the one I told you about."

"Hello," Brett whispered, but she didn't move closer to him. Instead, she took a step back toward me, and I felt her shrink a little. Like she was standing right next to me, but there was suddenly less of her.

Samuel didn't say a word back to her. He just took one look at us, at the way Brett and I huddled together, our hands entwined, our secrets whispered in each other's ears. And instantly he saw something he didn't like. Something he wanted to break.

"That girl of yours isn't right," he would tell Brett's mother again and again, and his ugly hands curled into fists, as though he'd be the one to fix Brett. As though she needed to be fixed at all.

She and I learned not to hold hands out in the open after that, not to let any of the adults see us get too close. It's a strange and terrible thing, the lessons our parents teach us.

Next to me, Brett keeps driving, her hair tossed out of her face, her gaze set only on the road ahead.

"I meant to tell you this morning," she says, lobbing the comment at me like an afterthought, "I'm sorry."

I glance at her, the highway lights glinting off her skin. "For what?"

"For how I acted last night. I've got no right to say a word about your love life."

"But that never stops you." I smile. "You never liked any of my boyfriends."

"That's because they were always ridiculous." She smiles too, just a little, until her face goes hard as stone again. "So, is that what he is? Your boyfriend?"

"No," I say.

"He wants to be though. That way, you'll tell him all your secrets."

"You know I'd never do that."

"I hope not."

We drive for a while, the radio crackling with static between us.

"By the way," Brett says, eyeing me up, "I like your jacket."

"Thanks. It's yours."

"I know," she says with a grin. "It looks better on you."

It's past midnight when the *Welcome to Our Town* sign rushes past us in the dark. Brett takes the turn at the corner, the one so familiar. The one that will lead us to Carter Lane, to everything that's waiting there.

"Let's not go back," I say suddenly.

Eagerness flashes in Brett's eyes. "Where do you want to go?"

"Home," I whisper, and all the optimism in her is gone in an instant.

She doesn't argue, though. Brett keeps driving, through the rabbit warren of narrow streets, until she coasts to the end of our road. But even once the rental is in park, she doesn't move, doesn't flick off the engine.

"Don't worry," I say. "So long as you stay behind the line, it's safe."

She scoffs. "Nowhere is safe, Talitha. You should know that by now."

I climb out of the car, taking one careful step at a time. Behind me, I hear the car door. Brett's coming, not because she plans to cross the line, but because she wants to make sure I don't.

The row of pylons are standing sentry in the dark, marking the threshold.

My head goes heavy again, a flash of white-hot pain deep in my skull, this place sinking into me. I double over, just for a moment, just long enough that Brett's suddenly next to me, as close to our neighborhood as she's been in years.

But she isn't worried about that. She's watching me.

"Are you all right?" Brett reaches out slowly, carefully, her hand on my arm. It's the first time she's touched me since she came back, and it's like a jolt of spring lightning running right through me.

"I'm fine," I say, and pull away from her.

"It's not safe for you to go in there alone," she whispers, and I know she's right. If I collapse once I'm inside, I might never find my way back out again.

The perimeter is glinting a dozen steps away. Still a safe distance.

That's what I tell myself anyhow. But as I inspect it in the dark, I see it there, how the street looks different tonight. Brighter somehow. More inviting.

"Something's wrong," I say.

"You're damn right something's wrong. Talitha, you don't belong in there with them. You belong out here with—"

She hesitates, leaving the sentence dangling in the darkness. But I don't even have to ask. I already know what she was going to say.

You belong out here with me.

Except she won't speak it aloud. We've been doing this for years, this strange back and forth, neither of us saying what we mean. We can discuss the dead body we left on her bedroom floor, but we can't talk about us.

She entwines her hand with mine. "Please don't go back."

"Please come with me."

Pain washes over her face. "You know what happened to me in there. How can you honestly expect me to walk into that all over again?"

She's right. I shouldn't expect that of her. No one should.

She retreats, her hand falling away from mine, and I'm losing her, losing everything that matters.

"I have to stay," I whisper.

She gives me a sad smile. "I know."

At this, she turns away, and it feels like the slamming of a door in my face. Like goodbye. I can't stand the thought that she's leaving, how it could be another two years before I see her again. How it could be even longer than that.

I start to call out to her, desperate to say the right words that will make her stay, but all at once, I look down, and my body goes numb.

The pylons are gone. The whole row of them, just vanished at my feet.

There's something else, too. I was sure I was standing at least a dozen steps from the perimeter, a safe distance away. But now I'm right up to the edge, the darkness shimmering before me.

And I'm not alone. A voice rises through the air, garbled and distant, like someone murmuring through a tin can telephone.

Talitha.

I seize up, straining to listen. It's Sophie, I'm sure of it.

But then dread sticks in the back of my throat, and I remember how I can't be certain of anything in this place.

The rental car's headlights flash yellow in the dark, and Brett's ready to pull away. I want to go to her, to ask her to stay, but I don't get the chance. That's because the perimeter comes to me instead, the ground shifting beneath my feet, the air gleaming around me.

I don't even have time to scream before it devours me whole.

My vision blurs out, and by the time my head stops spinning, I feel it beneath my feet. Velkwood Street.

It's another clear day, the sky sulking above me. I should slip back through to the other side, the real side. I certainly shouldn't let this neighborhood pull me in, not like this. Not against my will.

But then I hear her. Sophie, singing that old lullaby I taught her back when we were kids. And that's all it takes. I'm stumbling forward, down the street, tracking her voice. It's so crystalline, so perfect, like a rapture you've been waiting for all your life.

Mrs. Owens is out on her porch again, her dark eyes following me. "You don't belong here," she says, and I tell myself she doesn't see me, though I wonder if maybe she does.

But only Sophie matters now. I keep listening for her jubilant voice. She's behind all the houses, down the steep slope and into the valley with the rusted-out culvert. Enid's with her, the two of them giggling, racing in haphazard circles, playing a game only they know.

I stand back and watch them, as if this is a favorite old movie I've seen a hundred times before.

They turn toward me now, and everything in the world holds still. I'm sure this will be like before. I'm sure she won't see me. But then a grin blooms on Sophie's face, and she's running, right for me this time, quick as a jackrabbit, and with salt tears stinging my eyes, I scoop her up in my arms.

"There you are." She buries her face in my hair.

I'm holding my little sister. She's real, everything is real.

"What are you doing out here?" I whisper.

Sophie beams with pride. "We're playing," she says.

I smile back at her. "Are you?"

"We sure are," she says. "It's fun too. I run after Enid, over and over, until she falls down and plays dead."

A chill rushes through me, like a spider crawling up my spine. "That sounds like an awful game."

"That's because it's not a game at all." Enid's creeping closer now. "You remember, don't you? This is where I died."

Shame settles in my bones. "I remember," I say, even though I wish I didn't.

That was the start of all this. Or at least it was the moment we realized it: that something in this neighborhood had gone very, very wrong.

It was toward the end of our junior year, freedom so close we could practically taste it. Brett and I were tucked back in the culvert, hiding together in the dark after school. It was a few days before prom, our dates a pair of best friends from the other side of town. Two boys whose names have been lost to time, or at least lost to me.

"They keep talking about where they want to take us afterwards." Brett was sitting right next to me, her face barely visible in the dark. "One of their uncles has a cabin out in the woods."

I drew up my nose. "A cabin? For what?"

Brett laughed. "What do you think?"

My cheeks flushed, embarrassment fizzling in my guts. "I've never done that before," I said. "I've never even kissed anyone."

Brett shrugged, the shadows dancing around us. "It's no big deal," she said like she'd done it a hundred times, even though we both knew she hadn't. Most girls our age had made out with a boy in a back seat or a basement or beneath the bleachers, but not us. We pretended we didn't know why.

Only in that moment, I didn't want to pretend anymore. My heart in my throat, I leaned closer to her, knowing I shouldn't, knowing that wouldn't stop me.

"Just for practice," I whispered. "Just this once."

Brett hesitated, savoring it, how much I wanted her. Then her lips were on mine, the whole world going dizzy. She tasted of roses and midnight, of everything I'd hoped for, of everything I never wanted to stop.

Only it stopped even sooner than we expected. Figures flashed at the end of the culvert, their outlines sharp as daggers, and Brett and I wrenched away from each other, terrified we'd been caught, terrified of what would happen.

Except this had nothing to do with us.

"Give it back," we heard someone say. Grace's brothers, their voices like broken glass. "Right now, you fucking weirdo."

And then a glimpse of someone else. Enid, holding their basketball.

"It rolled down here on its own," she said, speaking in an odd singsong, like a nursery rhyme recited backward. "I was just looking at it."

"And now you're done." The boys were on either side of her now, and even though they were younger than us, they were always so much taller. "Hand it over."

"What are you doing?" Grace's voice. She must have followed them down the hill. Always lagging behind, always wanting to be included. "Mom needs both of you at home."

"It's practically a party out there," Brett scoffed, and even in the dark, I could hear the long drawl of annoyance in her voice, the way they were spoiling everything for us.

With a grin, I drifted toward her again, her scent sweet and heady, my fingertips sliding up her arm, her skin prickling at my touch. I wanted this to last forever, but it didn't even last a minute. The figures flashed again outside, closer now, Enid backing away, still gripping the basketball, and the boys right beside her.

"Now, bitch," they said, and their hands were suddenly on her.

The next moments happened in fragments, distant images we could barely comprehend.

The boys' harsh voices, mocking her, the shape of them nearly blocking out the sun.

A shove, quick and fluid, no more than a flick of a wrist.

Enid's body falling toward us, toward the culvert.

The crack of her skull against rusted metal.

And then the worst sound, which was no sound at all. No yelp of pain, no rush of movement. Just unending, unfathomable quiet.

And finally a small sob. Not from Enid, but from Grace.

"It was an accident," she kept repeating, as if saying it enough times would make it true.

The boys rushed back and forth, their shadows darting across our faces. "Let's just go home," one of them said. "We could forget all about it."

Grace hesitated, and I could tell even in the dark that she was debating it. She was honestly considering leaving Enid in the dirt, like a piece of old garbage.

"You can't do that," I said, surging forward, Brett close behind me, her hand on my arm, steadying me.

Grace watched as we climbed out of the culvert, her eyes shifting between us. "What were you two doing in there?" she asked, and then all at once, something in her face changed, the realization sinking in slowly because she knew exactly what we were doing.

I wouldn't look at her. Instead, I knelt next to Enid. She wasn't moving or breathing or doing anything at all. Sometimes, it only takes a glance to know, to see the way death settles in a body, so quickly, so irrevocably.

"It wasn't our fault," Grace's brothers were saying, like that was the only thing that mattered. Not the fact that there was a dead girl splayed out in front of us, but who was to blame for it. Rage, acrid as sewage, rose up the back of my throat, and I suddenly wanted to reach out and snap their reed-thin necks. Then maybe I could pretend that wasn't my fault too.

Grace must have seen it on my face, because she seized her brothers by their wrists. "Go home," she said to them, "and call an ambulance. You hear me?"

They scurried off, a pair of wayward children who seemed to think the worst thing that could happen to them was being grounded for a week.

That left us here in the empty valley behind our houses, three girls and what was left of the fourth. Our almost friend, the one we only knew how to pity.

"She didn't deserve this," I said, and all the anger in me washed away until the only thing I could feel was regret.

We were all quiet for what felt like a lifetime. There was nothing we could say that could fix this. Instead, we gathered around Enid, staring down at her slight form. That faded baby doll dress. That chipped nail polish. Her whole life was an apology that no one would accept.

Except we should have accepted her. We never should have cast her aside.

"I'm sorry," I whispered. Then I did something I never quite understood, not that day, not even now. I reached out for Enid. My hand on her hand, her body already gone cold. It was such a simple motion, one that should have meant nothing, that should have done nothing. But instantly, I could sense it, the electricity of me flowing into her, like a galvanized frog in a Victorian lab.

Huddled at my side, Brett watched me, silently understanding in the way we always understood each other. With a deep breath, she followed my lead, taking Enid's other hand, and I could tell at a glance that she felt it too. Grace joined in last, maybe because she knew what was happening, or maybe because she didn't want to be left out. Her hand on Enid's forehead, all of us locked together, as though we were witches at an ancient altar.

This street was always peculiar, always poisoned. That was what we would whisper at sleepovers, telling stories about our neighborhood like it was a ghost long before it ever was.

But in that moment, all the poison and all the peculiarity weren't a liability. They became something we could use.

The sky shifted above us, fading to blue, fading to what looked like night, even though it was three o'clock in the afternoon.

"What do we do?" Grace asked, her hand trembling against Enid, her nerves getting the best of her, but Brett and I looked at each other, never wavering.

A long, agonizing moment, before Enid stirred, slowly at first, her limbs twitching to life, one at a time, as though her body was doing its best to remember what it was like to be alive. It's strange how quickly bodies forget things like that.

At last, she sat up, her eyes foggy and ethereal. "Thank you," she said, and she sounded different now, as if there was more than one voice lodged in her throat.

None of this is real, I told myself, because that was the only way to make sense of it. But as we helped her up, Brett on one side and me on the other, I touched Enid's wrist, her pulse pressing against me, her heart barely beating, no more than a gentle thrum every ten seconds. Too slow to be real, too slow to be living. We'd brought her back, against nature, against God, but we'd only done it halfway, trapping her between alive and dead, at once more and less than the sum of her parts.

Enid had always been the strange one, the girl who never seemed to belong in this world. Now she didn't belong outside of it either.

Sophie doesn't know any of this. She doesn't know why they're playing the game, why they're repeating the past. Maybe even Enid doesn't know. They're caught in this endless loop, these memories they can't escape.

All the things I can't escape too.

The sun shifts overhead, and Sophie squirms from my arms, her feet landing in the mud without a sound. "Let's go home," she says and doesn't give me a choice. In a flash, she grabs my hand and starts pulling me along, so much stronger than I remember. I'm stumbling next to her, trying to keep up, the two of us scaling the hill and heading across the street. Enid calls out behind us, but I'm only focused on Sophie now.

"Are you sure this is a good idea?" I ask. "Does Mom even remember me?"

At this, Sophie nods, a little pensive. "Sometimes," she says.

"Other times, I'm not sure. But then there are days I don't think she remembers me either."

When we reach the house, my little sister shoots me a bright grin before opening the front door where our mother is waiting inside.

She's standing in the kitchen, perched at the black oven we bought on sale at Montgomery Ward, back when my father was still alive. Thick strips of bacon are sizzling and spurting in a frying pan, everything about this so normal I want to cry.

I walk toward her, hope swelling in my chest. "Hello," I say, and everything in me is shaking.

My mother gazes into my face for a long time, a Virginia Slim pursed between her lips, and for once, I'm sure she can see me. "Are you a ghost?" she asks, disgust edging into her voice, as though she always knew that's how her oldest daughter would end up.

I steady myself at the counter. "I'm still breathing," I say, though I only half believe it. In here, it never feels like I belong among the living. But it doesn't feel like I belong among the dead, either.

The bacon blackens in the pan, the grease hot and slick around the rim, but my mother doesn't move to flip it.

"What about you?" I ask. "Are you dead?"

She rolls her eyes and takes a long drag of her cigarette, the ash floating around us like dirty snow. "Does it matter?"

"To the people out there, it does." I exhale a ragged laugh. "They've got all kinds of questions about you."

My mother looks hard at me now, suspicion boiling in her eyes. "Have you been giving away all our secrets, Talitha?"

I back away, just a step, just far enough that I'm out of her reach. "Only the secrets not worth keeping."

She keeps watching me, her lips moving silently, trying to form words, but I can't hear her, as the room shifts suddenly around us. Maybe it's the light, or maybe it's something else. All I know is my vision blurs, and when I look again, the burner's not on anymore. The stovetop's gone cold, and the strips of bacon are all raw. No burnt edges, no hot grease. My mother hasn't moved, not an inch, but in spite of herself, she's starting all over again. A brand-new pan, a brand-new cigarette.

From her pocket, she pulls out a Zippo, the color of dried blood, and lights up her fresh Virginia Slim. "I'm fixing dinner," she says, as if I don't remember, as if I just walked into the room. "Why don't you rest a while until it's ready?"

I gape at her, trying to fathom what just happened. But my mother and sister don't seem to notice. This is just another afternoon to them.

"Let's go play." Sophie pulls me toward the stairs. I want to tell her no, I want to run, but here we are, together at last. I won't spoil this.

But someone else might. Enid has followed us inside, lingering on the landing. "Talitha," she whispers, like she's passing a secret message to me. Like she's trying to tell me not to go with my little sister.

I won't listen. My head tipped down, I pass by her, but Enid reaches out, desperate to hold me back. That's when I glance at her, noticing it before she can pull away. It's no longer just her fingertips that are gray. It's her whole hand now, the rot leaching into her.

"I'll be fine," she says, hiding the evidence behind her back, and I think how I'll be fine too. Just so long as I keep following Sophie.

In the rec room, everything is as I left it, the wood paneling bowing on the walls, the motor on the ceiling fan whining like a lost puppy.

"You rest now." Sophie pats my arm as I collapse on the floor next to the couch.

I didn't bring the timer with me today. I have no idea how many minutes have passed. On the other side, it might have been a moment, or it might have been years. This place won't stop changing, and all the rules keep shifting right along with it.

I'm becoming Rip Van Winkle after all. That's certainly what this street wants to do to me. It's a fairy ring of our own making.

Somewhere far off, I hear someone calling to me.

"Talitha? Where are you?"

It sounds like Brett, even though it can't be. She must be long gone by now, headed out of town in her rental car. Away from here, away from me.

"I miss you," I say to her, but my voice dissolves, the words plucked out of thin air, silencing me, silencing everything. This neighborhood wants to keep me here. It wants me for its own, a missing piece in its never-ending chess game.

Enid's right—I should run, I should escape this place. But my head throbs again, the pain more searing than before, and that's when I see it. A shadow on the other side of the room, as broad as the wall, as endless as time.

This is what Grace warned us about. This is what she could see back at her house. What I can see now.

"Don't worry." Sophie nestles among her toys, not looking at me. "It won't hurt you. It never hurts anyone."

But even as she's speaking, her grin never fading, the shape is moving toward me, deliberately at first and then in long, impossible strides. It's everywhere at once, its lithe arms wrapped around me, the coldest touch I've ever felt in my life.

"Please don't," I whisper, but nobody is listening. Nobody's listened in this neighborhood for a long time.

On the floor, Sophie's still smiling, all her ponies turned toward me, their bottomless gazes watching. "It'll be okay now," she says, and even though I know she's wrong, I want to believe her.

But all I can do is close my eyes as the shadow embraces me tighter, and the world falls away.

CHAPTER 9

I fade in and out, the darkness slipping through me, twining between my bones, at once weightless and crushing. I still want to run, but with my body limp on the plush carpet, it's too late for that.

But someone else wants me to escape. A voice, distant and strained, calls out to me again.

"Talitha, come back."

It sounds like Brett, like she's returned for me. Like she never left me at all.

Except wherever she is, it doesn't matter right now. Not with this shadow settling deeper inside me, its wicked embrace as cold as a Yule midnight. Sophie's there on the floor, no more than ten feet away, but she doesn't seem to care what it's doing to me. She barely notices.

"Don't worry," she says dreamily. "It will be over soon."

And maybe she's right, because the walls fade out around me. I turn away, covering my face with both hands, and when I look again, everything's resurfaced, shimmering and new. On the floor, Sophie's vanished, but I'm still here, still in this rec room, a memory rising up inside me.

I see it again, the past as if it's still happening, me and Brett and how we used to be, the two of us on the first day of summer break before our senior year. Other kids went to Myrtle Beach to celebrate, but not us. Our families never left this street. Another reminder that it wouldn't be easy to escape this place.

"We have to get out any way we can," Brett would whisper to me when we were alone. After what happened with Enid, after what never stopped happening with Brett's stepdad—the way he'd leave marks on her body, ones the world could see and ones only his eyes could see—we didn't have much choice. We needed to run and not look back.

But we couldn't run, not yet. It's such a strange thing to be seventeen. So close to freedom, yet a thousand miles away. The future was unfurling before us, but sometimes, it didn't feel like our future at all. It felt like it belonged to someone else, someone luckier. Someone who didn't live on Velkwood Street.

Only that day was different because for once, we weren't thinking about any of that. We were only thinking of each other. After my mother left for work, I rigged up an old sprinkler that my dad bought back in the eighties. It was such a silly diversion, me and Brett out in the sunshine, running back and forth like we were kids again. Afternoon crept in, and we retreated inside, our swimsuits gleaming wet, our dark hair soaked through. Downstairs in the rec room, we collapsed on the floor, both of us nestling down together, our bodies stretched long.

Brett closed her eyes, her hand wrapped around mine. "Please don't ever go away," she whispered.

I smiled and pulled her to me. "Never," I said, because back then, it honestly felt like a promise I could keep.

The day heavy in our bones, we started drifting off, the two of us in a tangle, her head rested on my chest, my hand on her thigh. This was a danger, and we both knew it. Us getting this close in plain sight. It was an unspoken rule not to get caught, to be up before my mom got home. We knew we couldn't do this, not in this house, not on this street. But it had been a long day, the sun baking our skin to a delicate pink, and I told myself I'd wake up, that I'd hear the key jingling in the front door.

Only I didn't. By the time I opened my eyes, my mother was already standing over us.

"Get out," she seethed at Brett. "*Now.*"

For a moment, everything in the world stopped. Her cheeks flushed, Brett scrambled to her feet, wrenching away from me like that would be enough, like my mother would somehow forget.

"I didn't mean to—" she started to say, but my mother wouldn't hear another word.

"I said *out.*" She glared at Brett, and the next words spilled from her lips with such ease, like she'd practiced saying it a hundred times. "Before I call your stepfather."

There it was, the cruelest threat my mother could conjure, the one she knew would get Brett to do whatever she wanted. All those years and all those bruises, nobody ever bothered to help her, but that didn't mean they weren't paying attention. This street was fully aware of exactly how to hurt her most.

And this did hurt her, the pain spreading slowly across her face, like she was breaking apart from the inside out. Her head down, Brett did as my mother told her to, marching like a condemned prisoner to the doorway. She turned back once, her eyes on me, wide and pleading, silently apologizing for something that wasn't her fault. I wanted to reach out for her, to pull her back or to let her take me away from this room, away from this moment. But nothing could change this now.

A final desperate look, and Brett was gone, her footsteps a hollow echo up the stairs. My mother waited, her face gone gray, until she heard the door slam. Then she turned back to me, and time ceased to exist.

Even now, I can't say how long it went on. It might have been an hour or it might have been longer. The only thing that mattered was that I was standing inside my home, in a place that should have been safe, with a person that should have kept me safe, and I'd never been more afraid. In that instant, there was nowhere on earth far enough away from her.

"Do you know what they'll say about you?" my mother asked, advancing on me.

I scrambled from the floor, desperate to make it to the doorway, already knowing that I couldn't reach it. "I don't care," I whispered.

"Well, *I* care." Her face scrunched up and red, everything in her quivering. "Hasn't this family been through enough? Why do you have to make it worse?"

I stared at her, pain clenching inside me. "I'm not trying to make anything worse."

My mother let out a coarse laugh that could cut you in two. "No, you don't have to try, Talitha. It comes so naturally for you."

"We just fell asleep." I backed toward the wall, my throat constricting. "That's all."

"It's not all," my mother said, "and you know it. Everybody knows it."

At this, I snapped my tongue. "Then it turns out they're already saying things about me."

Immediately, I knew these were the wrong words. With her eyes clouded over dark, my mother closed the distance between us, and I retreated into the corner, my body collapsing into itself. I didn't know what she would do. I didn't know what she was capable of.

"Don't," I wheezed, but it was too late. Her fingers wrapped around my arm, pressing hard into my flesh, my bones feeling liable to break in her embrace. I let out a quiet little yelp, but that only made her tighten her grip more.

She leaned in, everything about her stinking of cigarette tar and regret. "You're not a very nice girl, are you?"

I don't know how I got out of that room. I don't know when it ended. Maybe Sophie called out from the top of the steps, asking for chicken nuggets for dinner. Or perhaps I went quiet and numb for long enough that my mother was sure I'd learned my lesson. Or maybe she just got too tired to bother with me anymore, her disappointment of a daughter.

One thing I do remember: afterward, there were no bruises on me, not a single mark that anything had happened at all. There should have been something, a red wheal on my forearm, proof of what she'd done. But my mother would never have allowed that. She knew precisely how to put her hands on me and get away with it.

I've tried for years not to think about this, not to remember anything, and now here I am, sinking into it, so deep I'm not sure I'll return.

There's a hand on my arm again, and on instinct, I wrench away. Only this isn't the same as before. This isn't my mother, the touch warm and familiar. Instantly, I'm jolted out of the memory, the shadow receding, as I stare up at her face.

Brett, kneeling next to me.

"Are you real?" I ask.

She smiles. "I hope so."

I keep gazing at her, part of me certain this is just another trick of the neighborhood. But then she drifts closer, that scent like strawberries and cream filling the air, and I'm sure it's her.

"Why are you here?" I whisper.

"Because I knew you would be," she says.

Sophie's gone now, her ponies in a haphazard pile on the shag carpet. It's just me and Brett and the weight of the past.

"How long have I been away?" I ask.

"Only a few minutes," she says. "I came in right after you."

She must have seen me disappear, an unwitting witness as the street swallowed me whole. This place, inviting you in whether you like it or not.

I struggle to sit up, everything in me swirling with these memories, this echo of who we were. Brett hovers over me, and I'm sure she'll pull me to my feet and yank me out of this place as quick as she can.

But she does something else instead. She curls up next to me, just like before, just like that moment I can't escape.

"Don't," I whisper, panic searing through me. "My mother will find us here."

Brett shakes her head. "No, she won't. Upstairs, I walked right past her. She can't see me."

Of course she can't. She couldn't see me before either. Brett's invisible to her. But we can use that to our advantage now, the two of us wrapped up tight, her forehead rested against mine. Brett, always feeling like home. This is the only time we've ever been safe here together.

Not that anyone's ever really safe. I sense it across the room, the way it's watching us even though it has no eyes. The shadow's retreated, reclining sullenly in the corner, the shape of it more defined. It's no longer as broad as the wall. Right now, it doesn't look much bigger than me.

"I can see it," I whisper.

"See what?" Brett asks, her fingers entwined with mine.

"That thing Grace warned us about."

Brett holds me closer, something frantic rippling across her face. "Why can you suddenly see it?"

I part my lips to say something, past and present sloshing inside me at once, but I don't get a chance. Sophie is standing in the doorway now, clutching her red pony named Sam.

"Who are you talking to?" she asks, her brows knit.

She's looking right at me, right at Brett, but there's nothing, not even a flicker of recognition in her eyes.

"I'm invisible to her too," Brett says. "But they can all see you now, can't they?"

I don't answer her. I don't have to, both of us understanding it at the same time. I'm becoming part of this place again. And it's becoming part of me.

"We need to get you out of here," Brett says, her hands still on me, trying to help me up.

I loll back in her arms. "Just a few more minutes," I murmur, like a kid who doesn't want to go to school today.

Sophie stares at me. "A few minutes for what?" she asks, desperation creeping into her voice. "There *is* someone with you, isn't there? They're trying to take you away again. Why are you listening to them?"

"Because," I say, gripping tight to Brett, "I don't belong here."

"Yes, you do." Tears, thick as heartache, in Sophie's eyes. "You can't go, Talitha. You have to fix this."

She says it like it's a fact. Like there's really a way to repair all this.

"How?" I move away from Brett and toward my little sister. "How can I fix this, Sophie?"

"By staying." She wraps her fingers around mine, the same way she did as a baby. "You have to stay."

Brett huddles next to me, taking my other hand. "Talitha, please," she says, dread seeping in, because she knows she's losing me. She knows I'm torn, not sure what to do next.

Across the room, something else is watching me. And edging closer.

I turn to Sophie. "Let's just go for a walk, all right?"

Upstairs, the front door is hanging open, but I hesitate on the landing, peering toward the kitchen. My mother's in the same place I left her, looming over the oven, the bacon still raw in the pan.

"Dinner will be ready soon," she says, and lights a fresh cigarette.

Even after everything, I want to reach out to her, I want to rescue her, but Brett's hand is still on mine. "Come on," she whispers.

Outside, the sky is fading to a crystalline blue, the strange night on its way. We don't have much time now. I stumble down the cobblestone path, Brett on one side and Sophie on the other. I'm the only thing in the world they can both put their arms around, the only thing that fully exists both within and without.

I want to savor this moment, this chance to be with the two of them, but we're not alone. I can sense it drifting through the front door, so near that I can hear its footsteps. I can also hear it whispering my name.

I tug Sophie nearer to me. "Is the shadow right behind us?"

She glances back and giggles. "Of course. Where else would it be?"

Brett won't listen. Her jaw set, she just keeps going. "It's not too far," she says, as though I don't remember the way, as though I can't navigate a straight line.

The houses stand sentry around us, the grass verdant and glistening, but this street looks different now. It's the slightest shift, but you can see it. The siding on all the split-levels has gone dull, a veil of grime clinging to everything. And there's something else. My chest tightens, dread clogging my throat, because I feel it an instant before it happens.

All the doors on Velkwood Street creaking open at the same moment.

On the sidewalk, the three of us hold still, even though I don't want to. Not with that shadow still tracking us.

"What's happening?" Brett whispers, as everyone left on Velkwood Street is emerging from their homes now. I twist around, counting them. They're all here, all except for Enid, their eyes blank, their faces pallid as sour milk.

"They've been waiting for you," Sophie whispers.

My body goes numb. "But why?"

"Because they know you can fix this," she says.

There it is again, that accusation, the possibility that it isn't too late.

But Brett doesn't care. She just wants to get out. "We've got to keep going," she says, and I stick with her. She came back to this place for me. I won't make her go it alone.

Except we're not really alone at all. The whole neighborhood is with us, drifting down their walkways, headed toward the sidewalk. Toward us.

Next door, Mrs. Owens rises from her porch. "I told you already, Talitha," she says, moving toward her front steps, that frog still perched there like a lawn ornament. "You don't belong here."

We keep walking, past Grace's house, her mother beaming at us from the front stoop, her eyes blank as fresh paper, that phony grin plastered on her face.

"You just need to smile more," she says. Grace's brothers are with her, flanking her on either side, their Mötley Crüe T-shirts grubbier than before, their faces still blurred out like they can't quite decide who they are.

Brett gapes at the sight of them. "Jesus Christ," she murmurs, pulling me closer, as we pass the last house on our left. Del's house. With his dumbfounded parents at his side, he's standing there in the yard. It's been so long that I barely recognize him, arrayed in the same faded cargo shorts he's always worn, the tips of his hair bleached a brassy blond, everything about him a blast from a past I'd rather escape. He looks like he'd rather escape too. He's staring off at the sky, mumbling the same question over and over.

"Have you seen Grace? Have you seen Grace? Have you seen Grace?"

He doesn't seem to be asking us. It's like he's screaming at the clouds, at the gods, at anything that will hear him. But this time, I'm the one who's listening, and his words twist inside me, the tragedy of it, the way he and Grace have been torn apart. Brett wants to keep moving, but I seize up on the sidewalk.

"We were with her," I blurt out. "Just earlier today."

His eyes shift to me, seeing me as if for the first time. "How is she?"

Brett scoffs. "Not great," she says, but he can't hear her.

"She misses you," I say, and I want to tell him more, but Brett tugs me forward.

Up ahead, at the end of the street, there's someone waiting for us. Enid, her gaze swirling with universes I could never fathom.

She nods at Brett, giving her a small smile. "Hello again."

Brett rolls her eyes. "I should have guessed that you could see me."

Sophie glances between Enid and the air Brett occupies. "Who's the other ghost, Enid? Who's trying to take Talitha away?"

I wish I could explain this to her, why I need to leave, but we don't have time. The others are coming from every direction, abandoning their front porches and front yards, their footsteps rumbling through the earth, their voices drawing nearer. One voice in particular, letting out a hoarse, pathetic cry.

"Brett, where are you?" Her mother, still wearing that same threadbare robe, all the despair in the world hanging over her. "Honey, are you there?"

Brett flinches at the sound of her voice, but she doesn't look back. She's so good at this, at pretending like her old life doesn't exist, not even when it's calling out for her.

But there is one thing she hasn't forgotten. "Is my stepdad still here?" Brett asks. "Is he the one doing this?"

Enid stares back at her as the sky fades out. "He's not the one responsible for this," she says.

Brett leans into me, trying to steady herself. "But he might still be around?"

"I don't know," Enid whispers, and everything in Brett goes heavy and quiet.

This is the one thing that can scare her, the possibility that he's returning. That even after all these years, she'll never escape him.

"You need to go now," Enid says, her hands clasped in front of her, the rot creeping all the way up her arms in thin, gray tendrils.

"But Talitha can't leave." Sophie yanks me back a step, away from Brett. "You know she needs to stay."

Enid only shakes her head. "Not yet," she says, and this roils me.

"What does that mean?" I ask, but it's too late. The crowd is past all the houses now, their gait steady and unrelenting.

And something else has gotten here first. The figure from the rec room, its obscure outline enveloping us, its cold fingers reaching out for me.

Brett gazes up at it, seeing it for the first time. "Talitha," she whispers, terror boiling in her eyes.

With a quick hand, she pulls me forward, toward the wavering border, no more than a dozen steps away, and I know what I should do. I should let Sophie go, the same way I left her behind the last time. But as the shadow draws closer, the crowd right behind it, rage rises up inside me.

I won't let this place have her. I won't lose her again.

I hold tight to Sophie's hand, and together, we rush forward, the road crumbling beneath our feet. I'll take her as far as I can go. As far as *she* can go.

Except she doesn't want to come with us at all. She thrashes against me.

"Please, Talitha," she says, all our neighbors right behind us, their breath hot and eager on the back of my neck.

The boundary shimmers before us. We're almost there, but at the last moment, I can't go through with it. I can't risk what might happen to Sophie, this little ghost who belongs in this haunted place. With pain rippling through me, I close my eyes and let my sister go.

Still screaming my name, she falls away from me, her pony slipping from her grasp.

"Wait," Enid calls out, panic slicing through her voice, but Brett and I won't turn back, as the gleaming perimeter swallows us up.

The world returns, one fragment at a time, the air thinner than I remember it, so thin I can barely inhale a deep breath. It's afternoon now, the sun blaring above us, and I blink into the day, the pylons at my feet, my whole body aching and raw.

Next to me, Brett's still holding my hand, still holding me steady. "Are you all right?" she asks, her eyes bleary, and I want to tell her yes, but even now, we're not alone. The researchers are gathered in a line, gripping their clipboards, with Jack at the far end. He steps forward.

"What have you done?" he asks, gaping at something near the perimeter. Something near us.

My heart tight in my chest, I glance at Brett, but she's not looking at me either. I follow her gaze, my hand slipping away from hers, the whole world wobbling a little when I see it.

My sister is standing right next to me.

CHAPTER 10

"Sophie," I whisper, falling to my knees next to her, but she doesn't move. She doesn't even flinch. She just keeps staring off, past the researchers, past everything, her gaze squinted, the light overwhelming her. It's so much brighter on this side than I remember.

"I don't belong here," she whispers, fat tears forming in the corners of her eyes. "Take me home, Talitha."

But I won't listen. Instead, I scoop her up in my arms, clutching her so tight she probably can't breathe. Not that I'm sure she even needs to breathe anymore.

All that matters is that she's here, my baby sister's here. She's not a distant specter anymore. She's real, and she's free, and she's holding my hand, her fingers spiraled tight around mine.

The researchers are drifting nearer, Jack at the forefront. They want to get a closer look. They want to be the first ones to examine a ghost.

But not Brett. She stands back, peering at my little sister like she's an invader.

"It's only Sophie," I say, and start to reach out to Brett, but I don't get a chance. The others are already flanking us, pushing us back a step, nearly knocking us toward the perimeter.

"Let's take her back for tests," the researchers say, and I grit my teeth, ready to argue, to scream at them to stay away from her.

But I already know they're right. It's impossible to tell from looking at Sophie what effect that place has had on her. Plus, they can answer the question I've been wondering for decades.

If my little sister is dead or alive.

"Let's go for a ride," I whisper, and ruffle Sophie's hair.

We take Brett's rental car, the researchers following behind us in their own vehicle, as if they don't trust us, as if it isn't safe to let us out of their sight.

Sophie curls up in my lap, burying her face against my shoulder. "Home, Talitha," she keeps murmuring.

"It'll be all right," I say, even though I don't know how. Even though I don't know why she's here at all. I let her go. Back at the perimeter, I did the right thing and released Sophie's hand at the last moment. She made it through anyhow.

Scowling, she turns away from me, peering at Brett instead. "Will you take me back please?" she asks, her voice no more than a wisp.

Brett forces a smile. "Maybe later, all right?"

I realize for the first time that Sophie can see her now. On this side, she can see everyone. And everyone can see her.

We head back to Carter Lane, back to the house where I've been staying. We're barely out of the car, Sophie gripping my leg, when the researchers pull in behind us and hustle toward my sister, wrenching her away from me.

"Stop it," I say, swatting at them, for all the good it does. Together, they whisk her into the living room, setting her down on that pristine couch, as they surround her like pus filling a wound. I hate everything about this. The way they're prodding her like they own her. The way my little sister is no more than a specimen to them.

I want to get closer, I want to take her away from this terrible place, but all I can do is fall back in the doorway.

"They need to make sure you're okay," I say to her, but I already know she can't hear me. She's too busy thrashing against them, her tiny hands curled into fists aimed square at their faces.

"Leave me alone." She gnashes her teeth. "You're all ghosts, you're all awful ghosts."

But there are too many of them flocking around her, and pinned on the couch, she's still so small. Sophie should be twenty-eight now, only a few years from the malaise of middle age. She should have grown up. She should have gotten a chance to skip school her senior year and pick a college major and pick a lot of other things too, like where to live and who to love and who to be. Instead, she's only eight years old, an eternal child whether she likes it or not.

She cries out, the tragic tenor of her voice cracking my heart in half, but the researchers barely notice. They bring out their stainless steel tray of implements, syringes and stethoscopes and surgical swabs, lined up like they're showing off desserts at a fancy restaurant. Huddled together, they whisper back and forth, their brows knit, their lips pursed. Then they turn in tandem and start in on her, their hands everywhere at once.

"I hate you," she shrieks, and I'm not sure if she's talking to them or to me. She twists against their rigid bodies, a needle in her arm, a thermometer jabbed under her tongue.

At last, Jack breaks away from the others.

"Is she dead?" I blurt out the question before I can stop myself. It's such a ridiculous thing to ask, and I want him to tell me no. I want him to say I'm worrying for nothing, that she's just a little girl, nothing more and nothing less. But he can barely look at me.

"We're not sure," he whispers.

"What the hell does that mean?" Brett brushes past me, closing in on him in an instant. "Sophie's sitting right there. How do you not know if she's dead?"

"She's got some vital signs," Jack says, "but not others."

Everything in me goes cold. "Which vital signs?"

"Her heart's still working," he says, "but it only beats a few times per minute."

His words steal the breath out of my chest. This is the same as Enid, ever since that day she died at the culvert. Sophie's trapped between. My little sister, wavering in an ethereal no man's land, not quite alive but not quite dead, either.

For what it's worth, she certainly doesn't act dead. Across the room, she kicks one of the researchers, knocking him back a step. "I want to go home."

I push past Jack and the others, finding a place on the couch next to her. "It's all right," I say, my hand on hers. "This can be your home now."

"Why isn't Mom with us, then?" Her voice is thin and scared. "And why can't you just come back? That's what we want. That's what all of us want."

Except it's not what I want. Sophie doesn't understand that.

She pulls away from me, her body folding in on itself, nearly disappearing into the oversized couch cushions. "You have to fix this, Talitha," she says. "You're the one who broke it. You and Brett and Grace and Enid. This is *your* fault."

At this, all the researchers stop and stare at her.

Jack moves a little closer. "What do you mean it's *their* fault?"

"Why don't you ask Talitha?" A glower settles on Sophie's face. "She knows exactly what I'm talking about."

Panic clenches in my throat. "No, I don't," I say as I struggle to my feet. Sophie must know about what happened. Probably from Enid, the two of them colluding in the afterlife.

The researchers are still watching me, and part of me is sure they know what happened. Or they're about to figure it out.

I look to Brett, but there's not a trace of worry on her face. Instead, she's already drifting toward Sophie, taking the seat on the couch I just vacated. "Come on, kid," she says, everything about her as casual as a July afternoon. "It'll be okay."

Sophie crosses her arms and scowls again. "You don't know that."

"Have I ever lied to you before?" Brett asks, flashing that devious smile, and suddenly Sophie can't help but grin back.

Brett, always able to fix everything. So long as we can keep Sophie from talking about that place, about what happened there, then we'll be safe.

I turn to Jack, eager to keep him distracted. "How did you know Brett and I were inside the neighborhood?"

He grabs the nearest clipboard and makes a note in red pen. "Somebody went down this morning to take a few measurements. They found Brett's car, the door hanging open, keys still in the ignition."

Then he asks, almost as an afterthought, "What happened over there this time?"

I hesitate. "I'm not sure," I say. "But I think that place is getting stronger."

Jack watches me. "What do you mean?"

"I didn't cross the threshold willingly. And I don't think my sister did either."

Everything's shifting, the rules of the game tilted against us.

Another needle in Sophie's arm, a clear liquid filling up her veins. She lets out a pitiful welp before sulking back, her eyes going glassy.

"A tranquilizer," the researchers say. "We should let her rest."

"I didn't give you permission to do that," I say, but they're surrounding us now, pulling Brett to her feet, ushering both of us to the front door.

"She'll be awake again in a few hours," they say.

"I want to be with her," I screech, doing my best not to bare my teeth at them, not to become a feral animal. "You can't keep me from her."

"We need to monitor her for a while," they say, as though that's an answer.

Brett, however, doesn't buy it for a second. "Why should we let you monitor her at all? What jurisdiction do you even have here?"

They form a line in front of us, cutting us off from Sophie, their faces smearing together. Then they start in, one by one, spitting their rapid-fire commentary at us. Almost as if they've practiced this.

"You can take her to a hospital if you'd like," one of them says.

Another nods. "But after where she's been, they'll insist on quarantining her."

"You might not see her again for days."

"Weeks, even. Is that what you want?"

They stare at me, the threat fermenting between us. If I don't let them do this, then they won't let me have her at all. They'll take her from my arms, and I'll lose her all over again.

Jack slips between them, an apology all over his face. "It won't be for very long," he says to me. "I promise."

And with that, the researchers nudge us across the threshold and slam the door in our face.

"Well," Brett says, "so long as he promises."

We linger on the front step, the brittle air of February brimming around us. I can still hear Sophie inside, murmuring my name as she falls asleep.

I go for the doorknob, twisting it hard and fast, but it's already locked. Not that it matters. Even if I break down the door or toss a rock through the window, it won't change their threat. It won't change anything.

"We don't even know them." I lean against the door, my knees turned liquid. "They could be doing anything in there."

"It's all right," Brett says. "We'll come back for her tonight. They can't stay awake all the time."

"And then what?" Hopelessness settles in me. "Where will we go?"

"Anywhere we want," she says, and of course this is Brett's solution. To run and not look back.

But it's not my solution. "We can't just leave. What if we can still get the rest of them out?"

Brett shrugs. "So what if we can?"

"Because," I say, my voice shaking, my breath fogging between us, "you heard Sophie. She said I can fix this. Don't you want that? Don't you want to help your mom?"

A small, harsh laugh. "If I wanted to help my mother," Brett says, "don't you think I would have gone back before now?"

Her question cuts between us, the truth of it. The finality, too.

"Besides," she says, tossing her hair out of her eyes, "what if Grace is right? What if by dragging them out, we drag something else out too?"

"Like your stepdad?"

Neither of us says anything for a long time.

Brett grasps the key to the rental car, as though it's the solution to all our problems. "We've got everything now. We'll get Sophie and we'll go."

But all I can do is shake my head. "I can't do that."

She backs away from me, her gaze gone fire bright. "It'll never be enough for you," she seethes. "You'll always want to save someone else."

I stare at her, incredulous. "We're not talking about strangers, Brett. What happened is our fault. *We* did this."

"And what about them? What about what they did to us?" Her hands clench into fists. "They knew what was happening. To me. To you. And they didn't care, Talitha."

"Not Sophie." Grief churns through me. "She never asked for any of this."

"No," Brett says, something softening in her face, "she didn't."

"And Enid. What about her?"

Brett scoffs again. "This is what Enid wanted. It was her choice."

"Was dying her choice too?"

"That wasn't our fault."

"But bringing her back was."

"Do you regret that now too?" Brett sneers at me. "You're upset if we don't try to rescue the dead, and you're upset if we do."

This burns inside me. I hate the way she's looking at me like I'm the enemy. Like we haven't been in this together from the get-go.

"I'm not leaving town," I say. "Not until we try to help them."

Brett senses it in me, the invisible brick wall that's suddenly between us. "Talitha," she says, but I won't listen. I just turn away and start walking.

The street's a blur around me, as I cut through overgrown yards and abandoned lots where houses ought to be, the tread on my boots wearing thin. My head down, I come out on the other side of Carter Lane where there's nothing but an empty highway, the one that leads north out of town. I lived here for half my life, but I don't remember ever taking that road. It's strange how many directions you can travel in the world and how few of those paths you ever choose.

Finally, I emerge in downtown. Or what's left of it. It's the middle of the day when everything should be bustling. There used to be a business district here complete with a chamber of commerce and a two-screen movie theater and a barbershop with a striped pole that spun day and night, even when no one was around. But those places are long gone now. This town's almost as much of a ghost as Velkwood Street, death and decay leaking into every storefront, the facades crumbling, the faded signs promising services that haven't existed since dial-up.

The only place that's open is that dastardly diner connected to the gas station.

The waitress glances up when I walk in. "Take a seat anywhere, honey," she says, and I realize she's the same one from before, her hat still crooked, her expression still as inscrutable as ever. She pretends not to watch me as I scurry toward the back. All the old-timers at the counter pretend not to watch too, but I feel their gazes, slimy as pondwater, tracking my every step.

With a sigh, I choose a booth in the corner. My booth, the one where I used to sit while Brett was waitressing. She hated working here, hated the way the old men pinched her ass, hated how she had to practically beg for tips. But it was her way out. Our freshman year in high school, Brett and her mom opened a joint bank account, the two of them saving for her future. For her escape.

"This will all be okay," she'd tell me after her swing shift, the two of us walking home together in the dark. Back then, I wanted to believe it—that maybe this town wasn't a life sentence. Since then, I've learned better.

After a moment, the waitress shimmies up to me, coffee pot in hand. I glance at her name tag this time. Delores. I almost remember her, an echo of a younger face. She knew my mother, I think. If I remember right, they didn't like each other, something about a PTA meeting gone awry. Petty grudges are the most stubborn grudges. Then again, nobody liked my mother. I can't blame her for that.

She fills up a coffee cup even though I didn't ask. "So where's your friend Brett?"

I stare off through the window, a constellation of gray fingerprints smudging the glass. "I don't know," I say. "I don't even know if she's my friend anymore."

"Sure she is. You two have been attached at the hip since you were kids."

My eyes turn sharply toward her. "What's that supposed to mean?"

She blinks back at me. "Nothing," she says. "I wasn't trying to offend."

But that's all anyone does here, the old-timers still eyeing me up like I'm a prime piece of meat.

"Pretty soon Grace will be here," Delores says, "and then you'll have the band back together."

I flick at my fingernails. "I doubt that. Grace doesn't get out much these days."

"Maybe not," Delores says. "But she'll come back now. After all, it was the three of you who started this."

Instantly I bristle. "Who says we started anything?"

She rolls her eyes. "Please," she says. "You could lie to all those reporters and researchers, Talitha, but you sure as hell couldn't lie to us."

I sit back in the booth, my arms crossed. "So what is it you think we did?"

She exhales an uneasy laugh. "I don't know, kiddo. But you better do something to make it right. Or else this is all about to get so much worse."

This chills me. "Why do you say that?"

"Look out there," she says and motions through the window.

I follow her gaze until I see it, tucked back behind a solemn row of houses. Velkwood Street. Even in the daylight, it's shimmering bright, as if limned in a halo, the glow pulsating out above the trees, beyond everything.

Even beyond its own perimeter.

All at once it lodges in my belly, the hideous truth of it.

"It's getting bigger," I whisper.

"No," Delores says. "It's getting hungrier."

I gag up a sob, because it's true. That's how it sucked me through last night. It's like a living organism. And it knows what it wants.

Us.

Delores leans closer, a spark of fear in her eyes. "You have to stop it, Talitha."

I retreat farther into the booth, my legs pulled into my chest. "I don't know how."

"I bet you do." The coffee pot quivers in her white-knuckled grasp. "I bet you just don't want to."

I'm ready to argue with her, to tell her she's wrong, but the bell dings over the front door, and Delores looks up. "There's your best friend now."

Brett's suddenly standing next to me. "I thought you'd be here," she says.

I shrug. "There's nowhere else left to go."

Delores regards Brett, a tight grin on her face. "Would you like some coffee, sweetheart?"

"Sure," Brett says, and slides into the other side of the booth across from me.

Delores fills up a cup. Then she glances between us as though she already knows everything she needs to. "I'll give you two a minute," she says and wanders off.

The florescent lights flicker overhead, and Brett and I sit silently in the booth. Neither of us moves for our coffee cup. Neither of us moves at all. We simply sit here, staring at each other until the sun fades in the sky, the darkness sneaking in like a thief. That's when I finally amass the nerve to ask her a question that's been nagging at me all day.

"You said you never wanted to go back there." I look intently at her. "So why did you?"

She gives me a defeated smile. "Because I'd prefer to live in a world with you in it."

The overhead light flickers again, and I turn toward the window, toward Velkwood Street. Though it's almost a mile away, it's gleaming brighter than a beacon.

This is all we have to look forward to. The way this neighborhood looms over everything. How it'll never stop coming for us. Not unless we run and don't look back.

"You win," I whisper. "Let's leave."

Brett peers at me across the booth. "When?"

"Right now," I say, and that's all she needs to hear.

We're back on Carter Lane, the split-levels slumbering in the dark. Brett was right—the researchers have to rest sometime.

She parks the rental car at the end of the street, and we go the rest of the way on foot.

The window that Brett opened yesterday isn't entirely closed, and we sneak into the darkened living room. It's empty, the only light reflecting from the stairs.

They have Sophie on the second floor now, sequestered in the bedroom I'd claimed as mine. Most of the researchers have gone home for the night. There's only a pair of them milling about, but they're busy filling out paperwork, the bureaucratic bane of their existence.

Next to them, Sophie's awake in bed, her eyes still bleary, but she manages to spot me and Brett, lingering in the dim hallway. With a single look, she understands why we're here.

She climbs slowly off the mattress, her legs unsteady. "I need to use the bathroom."

The researchers motion her on. "Hurry up," they say absently, and she's out of their sight in an instant and running into my arms. She feels colder than before, but I pretend not to notice.

"Come on," I whisper, and without a sound, we escape down the stairs and out the front door, the three of us rushing to Brett's rental car.

This should be our victory lap, our triumphant escape. But as the car surges down Carter Lane, away from the houses, away from everything, Sophie doesn't seem to understand. She doesn't want to go. Instead, she just keeps weeping, her voice so soft, so pitiful.

"You need to take me home," she says, and she's crawling away from me now, into the back seat, as though she can escape.

I pull her back into my arms. "Please, Sophie," I whisper. "It isn't all bad. You get to grow up now."

At this, her eyes go frantic. "Why would I want to do that?" she asks, and I honestly can't give her a good reason.

Something else is changing in her eyes. Something I can't quite explain. She stares up at me, silently pleading for me to fix it, even though I don't know what's gone wrong.

Brett glances over at us. "It'll be all right," she says, but a dull wave of nausea washes over me, as the car makes the last turn out of the labyrinth of streets, the farthest we've taken Sophie away from here.

"Maybe we should—" I start to say, but it's too late.

Her skin fading to gray, Sophie tries to climb away from me again, and when I reach out to hold her, everything in me goes numb. Her fingers are wrapped around my hand, but she doesn't feel like herself anymore. She doesn't feel solid, her flesh gone soft and strange.

"I can't leave," she murmurs, and with dread choking me, I realize why.

Sophie's falling apart in my arms.

CHAPTER 11

"Stop the car, stop the fucking car."

The words are tumbling out of me as I hold Sophie close, her skin malleable as a fistful of clay.

She's still sobbing, still thrashing against me, her shrieks ricocheting off the slick leather interior. "Please," she says, her voice fading, everything in her fading.

Brett hits the brake hard, and we all jolt forward, our bodies tossed like ragdolls.

"Reverse it," I wheeze, because I don't know what else to do. "Reverse the car."

"What's wrong?" Brett stares at me, her voice splitting apart.

"Take us back," I say, and the tears are coming now, hard and fast, as Sophie goes limp in my arms. We're losing her. We're losing my little sister, and there's nothing I can do, her taffy limbs pulling apart in my grasp.

Brett can't see any of this in the dark, can't understand what's happening, but she does what I ask anyhow, the rental lurching backward, the world flashing past us like we're rewinding a VHS tape.

"Is she breathing?" Brett asks, but then we glance at each other, both of us realizing at the same moment that knowing that answer won't help us. Sophie might not have to breathe regardless.

"Hold on, baby," I whisper, holding her close, trying to keep her together, to keep her whole.

At the end of the street, Jack and the other researchers are already streaming out of the house, clipboards in their hands. They could probably be condemned to hell and still tow their notes and red pens with them.

But we need their help now—we need all of them. Brett's barely put the car in park when I stumble out, still clutching Sophie.

"Fix her," I say, and pass her lifeless form to Jack, as though he knows what to do.

And maybe he does, because he kneels in the grass, laying out Sophie's body, like a cadaver on a gurney. A flash of panic across his face, and he hovers over her like he might perform CPR. Like that would help. If he even attempts it, his hands might go right through her.

"What exactly happened?" he asks, and I breathe deep, desperate to explain it, to understand it myself. But before I can speak a word, we both look down at her, seeing it at the same time.

Sophie, blinking up at us, her cheeks flushed, her eyes wide and clear.

"It's okay now," she whispers, and I reach out slowly and squeeze her hand. She's solid again, everything in her reverted back to normal. Or as normal as she can be.

Past a thin row of trees I see it wavering there. The Velkwood Vicinity creeping a little closer, shrouded in a pale yellow glow, the color of a moon that never sets.

I stumble back, understanding it beyond reason. That neighborhood is why she can't leave. She's part of it now, and it's part of her. Take her too far away, and it will pull her back, even if that means pulling her apart.

And the worst of it is that she doesn't even mind. She just stands up, her legs wobbly as a colt's. "I'm tired," she says. "Can you take me home, Talitha?"

I don't answer. All I can do is stare at the shimmering houses where we used to live, the way they're watching her. The way they're watching all of us.

The researchers are staring too, their gazes set on Velkwood Street, on all the possibility teeming within. Brett's the only one who won't look. She pretends not to see the gleam in the dark that's nearly blinding, our past a dubious neon sign. Instead, she turns and smiles at Sophie.

"Come on, little one," she says and leads her by the hand, the two of them wandering up the sinuous walkway into the nearest house, the one where I've been staying. The researchers start after them, and Jack looks ready to follow, but I catch his arm first.

"Why are you here?" I pull him close. "What do you know about what's happening to our street?"

He recoils a little from me. "Who says anything's happening?"

"You did." I won't let him out of this. I won't make this easy. "Yesterday, Brett and I heard you talking to the other researchers about it. Just tell me. How fast is it growing?"

His cheeks redden. "That depends. When you were in there for three months, it didn't grow at all."

"And since I've been back?"

"A few feet," he says. "And from what we can tell, it's still expanding."

He doesn't say anything more. He just disappears inside the house, that penitent look still hanging over him. I follow behind him, through the red front door and up the carpeted stairs the color of porridge, until I reach her.

Sophie, sitting up in bed, her eyes wide and bright. I loiter in the doorway, and though the researchers scowl at me, they don't say anything. There's no point now. Even if I wanted to try again, we already know I can't rescue my little sister. Sophie can't leave, can't go to a hospital, can't even have a house call from a proper doctor. Because any decent physician would take one listen to that sluggish heartbeat of hers and demand to spirit her away from here. And that can't happen now. We're trapped—in this place, in this moment.

But maybe not everything about this moment is so bad. Across the room, Brett's tucking Sophie in, the two of them looking so sweet together, so comfortable. Like no time at all has passed. Like we're all still kids on Velkwood Street.

"How are you feeling?" Brett asks, ruffling her hair.

"Not good," Sophie says with a frown. "Can you take me home now?"

"Not yet," I say to her. "These nice people still have some tests they need to run on you."

Sophie glares at the researchers. "But you're wrong," she says. "They're not nice. Not at all."

Brett can't help but chuckle. "They don't seem very friendly, do they?"

Sophie puts her head on Brett's shoulder and closes her eyes. The two of them, always unlikely confidants.

"Are you going to marry her someday?" Sophie asked me once, and the question clenched in my heart.

"Girls can't do that," I said, and back then, it was true. There were things that seemed so impossible when we were young, things I gave up on long ago, even though they aren't impossible anymore. There's the world we lived in then and the world we live in now and an unbreachable gulf between.

After that day she caught us in the rec room, my mother forbid Brett and me from seeing each other. That didn't stop us, of course, but it didn't make it easy.

"We don't have to stay here much longer," Brett kept telling me every morning when we met at the culvert before school. "It'll be over soon."

But I always shook my head. Because I understood something that Brett wouldn't admit: that we were talking about family, and family is the ultimate trap. It's something you carry with you for life—the people you come from and the marks they leave on you.

Brett wouldn't listen to me. She was sure she knew the secret of how to run fast enough to escape this place. And I wanted to believe she was right.

Only nothing got any easier. Because she was paying for it, my mother chose which college I went to. "Don't argue," she said, and opted for a state university in the middle of nowhere. Far from home, far from Brett.

"I'm sorry," I said when I got the acceptance letter in the mail, but Brett only grinned.

"It's okay," she said like she had a plan. Of course she did. At the last minute, Brett managed to switch schools, not telling anyone but me, and by then, there was nothing my mother could do except sulk about it.

"That girl will ruin you," she said, and though I didn't let her see it, all I could do was smile.

But my mother wasn't done with me, not yet. Before I left, she had one more trick up her sleeve. "You don't have enough money to stay in school on your own," she said. "If I find out anything about you two, I'll bring you home."

Then she hesitated, suddenly recalibrating, thinking of something better, something crueler.

"Or maybe I'll tell Brett's mother." She sucked in a heavy breath, savoring what she was about to say next. "And I'll tell her stepfather too. Then they'll bring Brett home instead. Is that what you want?"

My whole body went numb, the prospect of what she could do to us settling in my bones. "No," I whispered.

"Then be a good girl, Talitha." She gave me a smug smile, the threats falling from her lips like withered rose petals. "Don't get yourself into trouble."

My mother and I didn't speak all the way to school or when she helped me unpack my luggage in a dorm room I was sharing with a stranger. She didn't have to say anything. Her voice was already on repeat in my head, droning over and over until the words barely made sense anymore.

"What's wrong?" Brett would ask me when I'd make up an excuse why we couldn't spend more time together after class, why I'd pull away when she'd touch my hand.

"It's fine," I'd say, and she'd pretend to believe me. Only a few more years, I promised myself, but it felt like I was always saying that, as though my own future was perpetually out of reach.

Because she always followed behind me and Brett, Grace joined us sophomore year, and she pulled some strings with administration to get all three of us in the same dorm room.

"Don't tell my mom about this," I said to them, and they listened, for all the good it did. Because even then, I was careful. I kept Brett at arm's length, never signing up for the same electives with her, never studying together in the dusty stacks of the library, never really speaking to her at all, the two of us passing each other in the dorm like we were already specters.

"Did I do something?" Brett asked me one night after she stumbled home from a party down the hall, her breath soaked in cheap whiskey. "Is that why you hardly look at me anymore?"

But I only shook my head. "You didn't do anything," I said, and it was true. This was never her fault. Not that it mattered, not when it was her heart breaking.

"It's fine," she said, and by the end of the month, we were both dating other people, nothing boys we liked well enough. The boys weren't the problem. The problem was we already knew we'd never find anyone we wanted more than each other. Even though we wouldn't admit it aloud. Even though the timing was never right.

Now here we are, in the same place, and the timing's all wrong again. Brett squeezes Sophie's hand, but she doesn't get to stay. The researchers nudge her out of the way as they take my little sister's vitals. What's left of them anyhow.

Her arms folded, Brett wanders into the hallway. She glares at Jack and me, still doing her best to gauge her suspicions, to figure out exactly what's going on between us.

"I'll be downstairs," she says to me, as if it's a challenge. As if she's already sure I'll choose him over her.

In the bedroom, the researchers finish, and not a moment too soon. Sophie's swatting at them with both hands.

"Go away, ugly ghosts," she says, a sneer on her lips, the weight of the world in that tiny, pink-cheeked face.

"We need to call in some results," the researchers say, and they file out into the hallway, one by one, their medical bag zipped up. "We'll be next door if you need us."

Jack nods and says something else to them, but I don't listen. I just brush past them and head into the bedroom.

Sophie glances up at me, her gaze shining and pale and unreal. "What did you do to make Brett mad?"

"Who says she's mad?" I ask.

Sophie's eyebrows arch up. "Did you see that look she gave you and Jack?"

I did see it. I can't believe my little sister saw it too.

"Brett just gets like that sometimes," I say.

Only it doesn't convince Sophie. She keeps watching me, sadness dancing in her eyes. "You never did get married, did you?"

A long moment passes. "No," I say. "Not to anyone."

"What did you do with yourself then?" she asks, and her question hits me like a grenade. Because I have no answer for her. No list of accomplishments. Nothing at all.

"I survived," I say, and it feels like everything and nothing at the same time.

"That's more than some people did," Sophie says. "Better than Dad."

"It wasn't his fault he went away."

"I don't remember him anymore," she says, and she won't look at me.

"You used to remember," I say, perching on the edge of the mattress.

Sophie nods, a sadness clouding her face. "I used to remember a lot of things."

This chills me. My little sister, drifting out of reach. I've managed to rescue her from that place, but in a way, it hasn't changed a thing. She's still fading away right in front of me.

"That's okay." I cup my hands over hers. "I'll remember him for the both of us."

Sophie yawns and rubs her eyes. "Why isn't he with us?" she asks, pulling the thin comforter beneath her chin. "When the neighborhood vanished, why didn't he come back home?"

A knot tightens in my chest. "I don't think that's how this works."

I stay with her until she falls asleep. Then with my heart in my shoes, I turn off the light and close the door behind me.

Jack's waiting for me in the hall. He's alone now, the other researchers retreated home for the evening.

Home. What an odd word for this place.

Nearby, the door to his bedroom is open, the curtain pushed back from the window, the glow of Velkwood Street leaking in.

"I'm sorry about taking her from you today," Jack says. "That was one of the agreements in the grant. If we were able to bring anyone through, we needed to run certain tests on them right away. Before any evidence started to deteriorate."

That makes Sophie sound like no more than a crime scene.

"Is this what you expected?" I ask. "When you decided to chase after ghosts?"

Jack blanches at the question. "No," he says finally. "I figured it would be like the trips my aunt and I used to take. Shaking tables, white noise recorders. I didn't think it would be like this."

"You thought it would be fun," I say, resentment boiling in me. Our tragedy as his entertainment. As a good time.

I grit my teeth, wanting to throw him out of this house, even though his grant is funding it, but then I remember how he got here. He's the same as me, in a way. He has nobody, not his parents, not even his aunt. Chasing ghosts isn't his amusement at all. It's his salvation. Both of us lost ourselves when we lost our families. I can't hate him for that. Not unless I want to hate myself for it too.

An anguished moment passes before Jack says, "You know this isn't personal, Talitha."

I exhale a laugh. "You're wrong."

After all, what's more personal than your home?

He looks ready to say something else, maybe to ask me to stay with him and answer more of his useless questions, or maybe just to ask me to stay. I don't give him the chance. Without a word, I turn away and start down the stairs.

Outside, Brett's sitting in the backyard, slouched in an old lawn chair, the perimeter of the neighborhood glinting back at her. She doesn't look up when I slide open the glass door and take the seat next to hers. The seat I suspect she was saving for me.

Brett keeps watching the sky. "I'm so tired."

I nod. "It's been a long day."

"I don't mean like that." Her eyes are on me now. "I'm tired of running, Talitha."

These words tighten in my chest, nearly choking me. It's the same thing I thought before going back into the neighborhood.

"That's why this place is changing," I whisper. "Because we're too exhausted to keep our own secrets anymore."

Brett turns toward the gleam of Velkwood Street. "You mean, because Enid's too tired now to keep those secrets for us."

She's right. We left Enid to fix our mistakes. But you can only escape the past for so long before it comes looking for you.

"How did Sophie make it through today?" Brett asks.

My head tips up, the stars pulsing back at us. "What do you mean?"

"When we were in there, I saw you. You let her go at the last moment." Brett glances at me. "So why is she here?"

"Because everything's falling apart," I say.

The neighborhood is shifting, the boundary becoming permeable, the past and the present sliding together. We can't control it. Neither can Jack and the researchers. We're all at the whim of Velkwood Street.

"We need to take Sophie home, Talitha."

I grimace. "I'm not putting her back in that place."

Brett's face softens, her lips forming a silent apology. "But what else can we do?"

"We'll live here." I gaze down the street at all the identical lawns on Carter Lane. "We'll buy one of these houses, and we'll stay right here until someone can fix her."

"Fix her?" Brett gapes at me. "You want them to fix a ghost?"

"She's not a ghost." Sorrow aches inside me. "She's my little sister."

"Not anymore," Brett says. "She's already gone, Talitha. She's no more than an echo."

"That's not true," I wheeze, but I can't help but wonder if she's right. If that's why Sophie can't remember our father anymore. If that's why she seems like she's less of herself. Less of my little sister.

Brett leans closer in the dark. "You're thinking of going back soon?"

"I am," I say, but that's not all I want now. Not if Sophie can't be out here with us.

Brett keeps watching me, until something in her shifts. "You're thinking about staying," she says. "You're thinking about going back there and staying with her."

I don't answer. I don't have to.

"Why?" she asks, her whole face looking liable to crumble. "Why would you ever want that?"

"I can't leave her alone there."

"You already have," she says. "For twenty years."

"That was different." I slump back in my chair, regret hanging over me.

My head goes heavy again, and I feel it, the weight of that street, of everything we were. Of everything we can't escape.

The glow of the neighborhood drifts closer, lingering at the margin of the yard. Then all at once, it isn't at the edge of the yard anymore. It's in the yard, becoming part of it, the gleam suddenly sentient, its tendrils, gray as mist, stretching long and thin and ethereal.

And headed right for us.

We're on our feet now, backing away, toward the house, toward anyplace but here, the neighborhood swirling and bulging and alive. The houses themselves aren't moving—all eight of them never budge from the same spots where they've stood for decades. It's the glow around them that's shifting.

"We need to get Sophie and Jack," I whisper. "*Now.*"

Brett grabs my hand, and together, we run, the neighborhood pushing closer behind us.

Inside the house, the walls are starting to glisten, the past illuminating the plaster.

Upstairs, Jack's already in bed. "What's wrong?" he asks, his eyes bleary until he sees it. The neighborhood seeping into the house.

"Get up." Brett tosses him his boots, as I hurry into Sophie's room, scooping her into my arms. Only she isn't eager to go anywhere.

"Let's stay." She tries to wrench away from me. "It's where we belong."

I clutch her close. "You're wrong," I say, and rush with her into the hallway.

We're running again, down the steps and across the living room, Jack next to me, Sophie on my hip, Brett lagging behind us. My hands quivering, I fumble with the lock on the door, my little sister still trying to squirm away, trying to convince us to stay.

"Keep going." Brett's voice at my back, fear coursing through her. I take her advice, not hesitating, not until we're out the front door, the cold air rushing up to greet us.

We spill onto the street, the glow fading out, the gloom of the night returning like an old friend. The neighborhood isn't following anymore. We've outrun it for now. For however long that will last.

"What are we supposed to do?" I ask, but when I look back, my heart seizes in my chest.

The house is completely gone.

And so is Brett.

CHAPTER 12

Sophie whimpers in my arms. "Where did Brett go?" she asks.

"I think you know," I whisper.

Brett, who never wanted to come back at all. Who only returned to this town because I asked her to. Begged her to.

Now I've condemned her to this.

I hold my breath, my heavy heartbeat tracking every passing second. By now, a minute might have gone by on that street. Or it could have been longer. It could have been a lifetime. Time isn't the same for Brett, not anymore.

I can't leave her over there for another instant. After all, she didn't leave me.

I set Sophie down on the sidewalk, and I'm running, my feet carrying me toward the perimeter.

"Talitha, wait." Jack's right behind me, but he doesn't have to pull me back. The moment I reach the boundary, the neighborhood shoves me away, as if by an invisible hand.

I should have expected this. Of course, the border's impenetrable here. It can devour whatever it wants, but that doesn't mean you can waltz right in. If I want to return, there's only one way inside—I need to go back to the end of Velkwood Street where the pylons are waiting.

Jack drives me there in his beat-up Camry, Sophie restless in my lap. If I were a good big sister, I would put her in the back seat in a proper seat belt, but what's the point? She's barely alive either way.

"Take me with you," Sophie pleads, burying her face in my hair. "Don't leave me."

I pretend not to hear her. The car lurches to a stop, and I peel her off me.

"Keep her safe," I say to Jack, and he holds her back, kicking and screaming, as I climb out of the car.

This is the inverse of what I came here to do. I returned to this neighborhood three months ago to reach her, to rescue my little sister. Now I've gotten her back, and all I can do is walk away from her.

I move toward the perimeter, past the crumbling cement and overturned pylons. At first, it feels different, like maybe it won't let me in this time.

Behind me, Sophie's still screaming out, her tiny hands pummeling the windshield inside the Camry. But she's not the one I'm listening to.

There's another voice, whispering to me.

Talitha, where are you? Where have you gone?

It's the same voice that spoke to me the last time I stood here. Only the cadence is clearer now, sharp and calm and welcoming. And it doesn't sound like a stranger.

It sounds like me. Like my own voice calling out, beckoning me home.

And it's about to get what it wants.

Without hesitating, I take that last step, and the whole world dissolves around me.

On the other side, it's still night, the firmament painted a deep sapphire blue. This spins my head for a moment. It's been daylight each time I've arrived before.

There's something else different too. I'm not at the end of the street this time. My boots sinking in mud, I'm standing in the valley behind the houses, perched in front of the culvert. And when I turn around, there's no entrance behind me, no proof of how I got here. It's as if this street picked me up and dropped me like the hand of a god.

In the earth, the crevice has opened wider, the darkness writhing and alive. Enid would like this. She's been waiting for something to happen here for years. Sometimes, at night, back when we were still seniors in high school, I'd sneak off with a pack of my mom's Virginia Slims and meet Grace and Brett at the culvert at midnight. We'd always find Enid alone, scrounging in the dirt, her fingernails limned with black.

"It's got to be here," she'd say, a family of arachnids crawling up her back, as she kept digging deeper.

"What are you doing?" Grace glared at her.

"Looking for a way out," Enid said with a shrug.

At this, Grace and Brett just walked away, their pilfered cigarettes hanging from their lips. But I stood with her.

"A way out?" I asked. "There's a way out in the earth?"

"Of course," she said. "We opened it when I died."

Panic washed over me. "Enid," I whispered, "we're not even sure you really died."

"You might not be sure," she said, her eyes rising to meet mine, "but I am."

All around me, the millipedes have returned, skittering across the mud, and like I expected, they've brought friends. Cicadas climbing out of crackling shells. Spiders that never stop hungering, and ants and houseflies and beetles that never stop being the bait.

Shuddering, I turn away and peer into the culvert. I'm hoping Brett's hiding there, waiting for me to rescue her, but inside, it's empty.

So I keep going, climbing up the hill and onto the street. There's no sign of anyone—not Grace's brothers or Mrs. Owens or even Enid.

There's no sign of the house from Carter Lane, either, not a single piece of splintered wood or broken glass. It's simply gone, disintegrated into the neighborhood like a spoonful of sugar in hot tea. As I trudge forward, I remember what Delores at the diner told me.

It's getting hungrier.

This street will consume everything if we let it.

My heart tugs tight in my chest, and I wonder about what was inside the house. Brett. What if it devoured her too and didn't even spit out the bones? There's nothing to say this place won't consume us the same way it consumes everything else.

"Can you hear me?" The words nearly evaporate in the night air. "Brett, are you here?"

I listen for her, that sweet, devilish voice, but there's no reply. I feel like some superstitious kid huddled over a spirit board, begging for a long-lost ghost to hear me.

Besides, I already know where she might be. Back home. She'll want to see if her stepdad's still there. If he's still dead.

The front door to her house is hanging open. I find her mother sitting at the table, still wearing that threadbare robe.

"Talitha," she says, and it's the first time she's spoken my name since Brett and I were in grade school. "Are you all back for a class reunion?"

I nearly laugh aloud until I realize she's serious. She has no idea what's happening.

"Something like that," I say. "Is Brett around?"

"In her room," she says, and motions down the hall, like I forgot which way. Like I could ever forget.

When I walk into the bedroom, Brett's sitting cross-legged on the floor. In the same spot where we left her stepdad all those years ago. I remember standing here in the doorway afterward. We didn't bother to get close to him, didn't bother to check his pulse. There wasn't much point, not with that much blood seeping into the carpet. Instead, we just ran, the three of us piling into Grace's used Volvo, screeching out of her driveway an hour before midnight. Leaving Enid to clean up the mess we'd made.

Brett glances up at me, her eyes glazed over. "There you are," she says, like she hasn't seen me in years. "Have I been gone for long?"

I shake my head, kneeling at her side. "Only a few minutes."

"It feels like an eternity."

The shadow's lingering over everything, slipping through her the same way it slipped through me. I try to swat it away, but my hand goes right through it.

"My mother can see me now," Brett says. "I'm becoming part of this place. The same way you are." A quiet moment before she adds, "You shouldn't have come back."

I put my hand on her arm, her skin chilled. "You came back for me."

A scoff. "Stop trying to save everyone, Talitha."

"I'm not trying to save everyone," I say. "I'm only trying to save you."

She wheezes out a thin laugh. "You should have realized that was hopeless years ago," she says, and her words ache in my chest. The way she was always tossed aside when we were kids. The way she escaped, only to end up back here all over again.

There's another shadow now, the pair of them swirling and mingling on the ceiling, the darkness pooling over us. I look up at the shelves of porcelain figurines. Brett hated those things. Her mom used to buy them for her, even though she never asked. Now they're lined up on the wall, their blank eyes staring out, seeing everything and nothing.

"He's still here," Brett whispers. "I can feel it. My stepfather's still here."

My breath shudders. "How do you know?"

She blinks back tears. "Because I can smell him."

I inhale, and there it is. That stench like afternoon sweat and WD-40.

"Let's go," I whisper.

Her mother is still shuffling back and forth in the hall. "Brett?" she murmurs, even though her daughter is standing right here. She's been looking for her for so long that it's the only thing she remembers how to do now.

Outside, Brett and I move toward the end of the street, my arm looped around her waist, guiding her, all the houses smearing past us, a sea of eyes watching from behind smudged windows.

I pretend not to notice them. "We're almost there," I say, but when we reach the spot where we've come and gone before, it won't open up to us now. The perimeter's become a mirror, reflecting our faces back at us.

We're trapped in the belly of this place.

"There has to be a different way out," Brett says, gripping tighter to me. We start back down the road toward the culvert, but we need to pass by my house first, and that's enemy territory, especially since my mother's waiting for me. She comes bursting through the front door, a dishrag gripped in her hand like a weapon.

"Where is she?" Her face is turning red. "What did you do with Sophie?"

On instinct, I recoil from her, that built-in childhood reflex. Then I breathe deep and remember I'm not a kid anymore. I'm an adult now, or at least a close approximation, and my mother's nothing more than a specter.

"She's fine," I say. "Sophie's fine, Mom."

"How could you?" My mother glares at me. "You kidnapped your own sister."

I let out a harsh laugh. "And what are you going to do about it? Call the ghost police on me?"

"I should." She crosses her arms, her body broadening. "Is she asking for me?"

I seize up for a moment. "No," I say.

She sneers at me. "Liar," she says, but then she's suddenly not looking at me anymore.

Instead, she's got her eyes on Brett.

"You," she says, disgust simmering in her voice. "I should have figured you two were still hanging around together. Nothing ever changes out there, does it?"

Brett flashes her that sweetheart smile. "No, it doesn't, Mrs. Velkwood."

"Please stop, you two," I say, edging away a step, and that's when I feel them beneath me, writhing and restless. The earth is crawling with strange creatures again, some that I recognize, some that I don't, their shiny carapaces glinting up at us.

Brett and I gape down at them, trying to fathom what we're seeing, what this place is becoming.

My mother just rolls her eyes. "Vile things," she says, and stomps on a few of them before starting back toward the house.

When I don't follow, she whirls around and shoots me one of her familiar glares.

"Do you want to know more about what's happening here, or don't you?" she asks.

Brett and I each take a dubious step toward her, but my mother holds up one hand. "Not her," she says about Brett, and then points at me. "Just you."

I sneer, ready to argue, but Brett squeezes my arm.

"You go on," she says. "I'll keep looking for another way out."

And with that, she's gone, headed to the backyard. I part my lips to say something, but she's out of my reach before I can say a word.

"Are you coming or what?" my mother asks before disappearing inside. With a sigh, I trudge through the door behind her.

When I walk in, she's already standing in the kitchen. The shadow's returned, swirling between the drapes. Through the back window, I see Brett, moving in the yard, inspecting every spot, trying to figure out if there's another way to escape. That's all she's ever done: test this place for weaknesses, for emergency exits.

And once upon a time, it actually worked—we found our way out. If only we could have stayed gone.

"Sit down," my mother says, and with my head heavy, I do as she tells me, the shadow drawing nearer now. My mother doesn't seem to notice. She busies herself at the stove before depositing a plate right in front of me, two raw strips of bacon, the striations of fat as pale white as a maggot. I draw up my nose, withering away from the table.

"Do you think I'll poison you?" my mother asks, taking the seat next to mine, the acrid scent of her knockoff Chanel perfume nearly gagging me.

"Not on purpose," I say, and nudge the plate away.

I shouldn't sit here with her. After everything, I shouldn't even speak to her. But somehow, I can't help myself. I keep coming back here, waiting for her to say the right thing. Waiting for her to fix it.

Why are we like this? Why do we chase after the very people who chase us away?

"You were never grateful for anything I did," my mother says, her lips pursed as she fiddles with something, turning it over and over in her palm. I recognize it in an instant.

A gold pocket watch. It belonged to my father. She used to say everything in this house belonged to him.

"It's your world, and we're just living in it," she would say to him. And she's wasn't completely wrong. He was the one who chose Velkwood Street before it was even a real street. My mom never wanted to move here, never liked the look of the neighborhood, never liked the look of the whole town.

"There's something wrong," I remember her telling him the first time we visited, the three of us standing in front of an empty lot filled with even emptier promises.

But with his wide eyes and ornery smile, my father convinced her. "Small-town paradise," he used to say, and I could never tell if he was reveling in it or mocking it. Either way, he didn't stick around for long, that heart of his big enough for two daughters but not nearly enough to endure the world. On a cold December afternoon, he fell asleep in front of a football game and never bothered to wake up again, abandoning Sophie and me with our mother. At first, she honestly seemed like she wanted to try to make it work, the three of us together, survivors of a war we never asked to fight. Then she stopped trying, little by little, until resentment was boiling in her like hot oil, and I couldn't pretend anymore. She hated us—not every day, not all the time, but enough that we couldn't deny it.

"Why does she do this?" Sophie whispered to me one Saturday morning when our mother was on the rampage again, screaming and cursing and tossing all my little sister's toys into a Hefty garbage bag just because she'd forgotten to pick them up the night before.

"I don't know," I said, and pulled Sophie closer, as if that would be enough. As if I could protect her from the world.

But then there were days when I didn't need to protect my little sister. You could blink your eyes, and our mother would be almost normal again, a tight smile on her face, pretending like none of it ever happened, like we were a real family, healthy and happy and whole. She'd bake us sugar cookies at Christmas and foil-wrap our birthday gifts, and when we'd hear the tinkling of the ice cream truck down the street, she would grin and reach into her black leather purse.

"Here," she'd say, and hand me a five. "Hurry now."

And I'd smile back and do exactly as she said. Those were always good memories, the three of us sitting on the front stoop, eating our silver-wrapped Klondike bars, huddled so close together you would swear nothing could ever go wrong here. Sometimes, I'd see Brett in the next yard, holding a twin pop she'd bought for the two of us to share, and I'd give her a small shrug, as if to say I was sorry. I couldn't go to her on days like that, days when my mother felt like someone I could trust. On those afternoons, Sophie and I learned to soak up every moment, because what else could we do? This was the best we could ever hope for.

Now here we are, in the remnants of a kitchen in the remnants of our lives, the world a thousand miles away from the best we'd hoped for.

"So you and Brett," my mother says, her voice trailing off, and we both know she just asked a question without bothering to speak it aloud.

"It's nothing," I say, and the words sear through me, because it's true. She and I are nothing these days. Barely friends. Barely anything.

My mother exhales a strident laugh. "Sophie always thought

you'd get married," she says, and I can't tell if she's mocking me or pitying me.

I just shake my head. "Brett and I hardly even see each other anymore."

At this, my mother sits back, clutching the gold watch tighter, everything about her looking so smugly satisfied, like she got what she wanted after all.

"You said you would tell me what's happening here."

My mother doesn't answer, the silence coagulating between us.

This is pointless. She probably doesn't know anything anyhow. I roll my eyes, ready to leave, but before I can turn away, her hand is on my wrist, gripping me so tight I nearly scream out.

"Why don't you tell me? You were there, weren't you, Talitha?" My mother's gaze, hard as granite. "You know what happened that night."

I recoil from her. "You're wrong," I say, cradling my arm, the pain from her touch still echoing in me.

"Liar," she says, and there are murmurs all around us now, and the elegant skittering of insects at the windows.

"Talitha?" Brett's frantic voice from outside, and that's all it takes. I'm on my feet and out the door.

"You're running out of time," my mother calls after me, but I pretend not to hear her.

When I reach the backyard, I see them at once, coming at us from every direction. The others in the neighborhood, a shadow twining between them.

"What do they want?" I ask, and my mother appears at the screen door behind me, her eyes as dead as theirs.

"You," she says lazily. "Everyone wants you to set this right."

"They keep saying that." Brett grits her teeth. "But nobody ever bothers to tell us what it means."

The others are drawing nearer, and I don't know what they'll do if they get hold of us. Our hands wrapped together, Brett and I rush through them, past Mrs. Owens still holding her broom and Grace's brothers, their faces still not making up their minds.

They call out our names, but we just keep going, across the yard, easing down the side of the hill, Brett's hand on my arm, the two of us steadying each other.

They don't follow us any farther. Maybe because of what's waiting for us. We slide together in the dirt, the earth alive beneath us, spiders crawling up our arms, the crevice in the mud opening up wider.

I turn to Brett, but she isn't looking at the crevice. She's staring at the opening of the culvert, a wistfulness in her eyes.

"You were my first kiss," she whispers.

I smile. "You were mine, too."

"You always said it didn't count."

"We both knew it did."

"That's why your mother always hated me. Because she knew."

I shake my head. "My mother hated a lot of people for a lot of reasons."

"But I was the only one she hated for that reason."

I look behind us. The others still haven't followed, but that doesn't mean we're alone.

A slight movement at the bottom of the hill, and I suddenly see her.

Enid, a bundle of a girl, crouched in the mud. She must have been here the whole time. I wonder if she was here before, when I first arrived looking for Brett. Is it always so easy to glance right past her?

"Don't worry." Enid struggles to her feet. "The others never notice me either."

As she steps closer to us, my breath falters in my chest. It's not just her hands and limbs that have gone gray now. It's her whole body, her skin pale and cracking. The only color that remains on her is that wild hair, still red as a bygone autumn. Otherwise, she's fading to nothing, the death leaching into her, hungry and eager.

Death has always found Enid. She never asked for it—it was merely her birthright. Death found her from the first breath she ever took, back when her mother faded away in the city hospital right in front of the slack-jawed doctors and nurses. Death found her in our neighborhood where the ground was poison and the people could only keep secrets, not promises. And death found her when she called to it in the darkness—called to it because we asked her to—and brought it down on this place like a holy punishment of her own invention.

A week before I left for college, I sat with her on the sidewalk, just the two of us in the August afternoon, and asked her how it worked. How she could do the things she did.

"It's hard to explain," she said, as the earthworms crawled out of their dirt prisons to greet us.

I edged closer to her, thinking of the times we'd wrapped our hands together and made the world shift at our will. "Do you need us, or don't you?"

She only shrugged. "I can make it happen all by myself," she said, "but it doesn't work as well."

"Why not?" I asked, half-breathless.

She gave me that sad smile of hers. "Because we're stronger when we're together."

That's how we ended up here. Enid was able to do most of it on her own—ghost the neighborhood, ghost the people—but it didn't work as well as she'd hoped. She needed us to finish it.

She still needs us. We were raised in the decay of this neighborhood too. It belongs to us, the same way it belongs to her. "What can we do?" I ask, my heart aching, everything in me aching.

"We need all four of us to be here," Enid says. "We did this together. And now we're the ones who have to undo it."

Hope surges through me. "So it can be undone?"

Enid hesitates. "In a way," she says. "But we don't have much time."

Her shaking hands are clasped in front of her, her fingers crumbling away. The neighborhood is slowly disintegrating around us, but it's even worse for Enid. She's bearing the brunt of everything. The same way she always has. Our sacrificial lamb.

A millipede skitters across the toe of my boot, and above us, voices are coming nearer, figures at the top of the hill darting back and forth.

"We need a way out," I say, shivering.

"I know," Enid whispers, "but everything is closing up."

There's more murmuring now from over the hill. It takes a long moment for me to decipher it, the words they're speaking, and when I finally do, my whole body goes numb.

"Help us," they whisper. "Please help us."

Brett's eyes go wild. "How do we get out?"

Enid exhales a quiet sigh. "Come on," she says, and we climb the hill, the insects tracking our every step, their antennae brushing against our ankles, their skittering ringing in my ears. On the sidewalk, we dodge around Grace's brothers, as they scream silently, their mouths wide and gnarled. The frog is waiting on the curb, his body sinking into the concrete, a mountain of ants circling him from every direction. I shudder and try not to look back, as we make it to the end of the street.

"But it won't open for us," I say. "We already tried."

"It won't open again." Enid swallows hard. "But it'll open one more time."

The sky shifts above us, the air turning thin, and I feel something tremble through me.

"There," she whispers, and points behind us to a spot where the perimeter is shimmering.

Brett moves toward it, but I'm still watching Enid, the way the tips of her hair are turning a dull silver. She's holding this place open for us. She's the one letting us escape. And it's unraveling her.

"Thank you," I say before Brett reaches back for me, and we both tumble through.

Nobody's waiting for us when we return. No Jack, no researchers, no Sophie either. Just a yawning emptiness at the end of Velkwood Street.

At least we returned to the same place. At least we know where we are.

Back on Carter Lane, the researchers have set up shop in a different house, the Camry parked out front. The neighborhood didn't gobble it up. It didn't devour Brett's rental, either. Small mercies.

When we knock on the door, Jack answers in an instant. "I'm glad to see you again," he says, and regards Brett. "Both of you."

He leads us upstairs, this house cursed with the same plain layout as the one that vanished. They even have my little sister in the same bedroom, or at least a room that looks identical. A bed, a nightstand, a clock on the wall. Everything repeats here, the same way it repeats on Velkwood Street. Sometimes, it's like the whole world is a rerun.

But then I see my little sister, and it all feels new again. With sleepy eyes, Sophie rushes over to greet me in the doorway, her arms wrapped around my legs. "I was afraid you wouldn't come back," she whispers.

"I'm here," I say, though I wonder if that's really true.

The researchers usher Sophie back to bed, taking her vitals. Meanwhile, Brett and I stand with Jack in the hallway.

"How long were we gone?" I ask.

He won't look at us. "I'm not sure. Maybe an hour?"

Brett stares at him. "You don't know?"

"While you were in there," Jack says, "all the clocks stopped. Even our phones and computers aren't working."

Instantly, I understand why. Time is bleeding over, this side and the other side all mixed up into one.

"We'll keep monitoring Sophie overnight." Jack glances between me and Brett. "There's plenty of room at the house next door. You can stay there for the night."

"What about the other researchers?" I ask. "Aren't they living there?"

"Not anymore." Jack heaves up a ragged breath. "A few of them left town."

"Are they coming back?"

"No," he says sharply, and I can already guess why not. It's one thing to study a ghost of a neighborhood. It's another thing entirely when that neighborhood wants to study you.

I tuck Sophie into bed, and then together, Brett and I sneak next door like two kids out past curfew. Inside, the place is identical to the other houses, the walls and floors and furniture bleached white, blander than Sunday morning.

Brett looks around at the same couch and the same frozen clock on the wall. "Did they get everything in a bulk sale?"

The layout of the second floor is the same too, and I choose the room I had before. Brett picks the bedroom next to mine, the one where Jack stayed.

After surviving the day, I know what I should do. I should turn in. But instead, I linger in her doorway, watching Brett perched on the edge of the bed.

"I can still feel that neighborhood inside me." She runs her fingertips over her arms, as if wiping away the grit. "It's like I'm here and there at the same time."

I nod. "I know."

The blinds are open, and the glow of the Velkwood Vicinity fills up the room. It's getting nearer again. Maybe it will swallow us up in our sleep. Give it long enough, and maybe it will swallow up the whole world.

I tell myself it's not too late. We can fix this.

We can figure out how to get Sophie away from this neighborhood.

We can figure out how to help the others still trapped inside.

We can figure out everything.

That's what I pretend, even though I know the truth. Those moments are always out of reach.

But Brett's not out of reach. She never has been. My entire life, she's been standing right in front of me.

"You were the only one who ever believed me," she says. "Who bothered to listen at all."

"Of course I did." Brett was the only one I believed, the only one who mattered.

My mother never understood this. She always acted like one day, it would all work itself out, like I would forget Brett.

"It's just a phase," she said, and I cringed at those words, at the callousness of them. Because what do you ever really know about someone else's heart? Hell, most of us can barely decipher ourselves. Who are you to tell anyone that it isn't real? That they don't know who they are or who they love?

But that's just it, the real trick of it all: I let my mother tell me. I let her unravel everything. Back then, I pretended it was for the best, but that was never true, and I knew it.

And even once she was gone, it almost didn't matter. Because after everything, I couldn't look at Brett without remembering what we'd done. Without seeing her stepfather curled up like roadkill on her bedroom floor. Without feeling the ache in my heart where Sophie belonged. It kept Brett and me apart, turned us into strangers, as my guilt soured in me. The guilt I thought I could outrun. I told myself it would be easier this way, but there's never been anything easy about losing Brett.

My mother was dead, and she still won.

No, that's not entirely right. She's won so far. But it's not over, not yet.

Brett's watching me now. "Are you okay?"

I don't say anything. I just walk toward her. She keeps looking at me, like she doesn't believe I'm real. Like she doesn't believe this is happening.

I sit next to her on the bed, our thighs touching. "I've missed you," I say. "I always miss you."

It's the first time I've ever said this back to her. The first time I've ever tried to be honest about this. With her. With myself.

I drift closer to her, inhaling that sweet scent of strawberries, but she turns away, her head down, the weight of the world in her gaze.

"Just for practice, right?" she asks with a sad, defeated laugh.

"No," I whisper. "Just for us."

At this, her eyes flick up at me. I want to say something else. I want to say I'm sorry. For how much time I've wasted, that we've both wasted. But she's suddenly kissing me, her hands on my body, sliding up my waist, pulling me into her, and I'm kissing her fingertips, her neck, her back, my vision blurring, my skin electric and alive.

The halo of Velkwood Street leaks into the room, brighter than before, but together, we reach up and wrench down the blind, everything in the world falling away except each other.

CHAPTER 13

I awaken in the morning, Brett's long legs tangled with mine, the curve of her body pressed into me. I want this to last forever. I always want everything with Brett to last forever.

But I never get that wish.

A shadow in the hall, and I bolt up in bed, part of me convinced it's all the ghosts of Velkwood Street sent back to claim us.

Fortunately, it's far more mundane than that. It's only Jack, standing in the doorway.

"I don't mean to interrupt," he says, his eyes on the floor, his cheeks blooming red, "but your sister's asking for you."

He waits downstairs while I dress in the dim bedroom, my hands quivering. Brett sits on the edge of the mattress, her dark hair over her face, the sheets wadded up around.

"Are you coming with me?" I ask, but she shakes her head.

"I'll leave you two alone," she says, and I'm not sure if she means me and Sophie or me and Jack. Then I notice it there, sparking in her gaze. The sharp, unmistakable irritation, the way she feels like Jack's come between us again.

But she doesn't say that. She doesn't say anything. She just watches me go, as if it's the last time she'll see me.

I turn back in the doorway. "I won't be long."

At this, she perks up, giving me that devilish grin of hers. "Promise?"

I smile. "I promise."

Downstairs, Jack's waiting at the front door, and I walk to him, the two of us starting outside together, the glow of the neighborhood nearly blinding, even in the daylight. I stare back at it, silently measuring the perimeter, curious if it got closer overnight. Curious how much longer until it gets even closer. It could devour us all in a heartbeat. I wonder what it's waiting for.

Meanwhile, Jack's wondering about something else. I can see it on his face, even before he speaks it aloud. "How long have you and Brett been—"

He doesn't finish the sentence. He doesn't have to.

I give him a quick shrug. "That's hard to say."

Either Brett and I have been together since last night, or since we were kids. I'm not really sure which it is.

We're on the front step of the house next door, and Jack hesitates, giving me a sheepish look. "I don't think Brett likes me very much."

I let out a thin laugh. "What could possibly make you think that?"

Upstairs, Sophie is sitting on the bedroom floor, fiddling with two glass test tubes and a spare clipboard. "This is the only thing they had for me to play with," she says with a scowl.

I kneel next to her. "How are you feeling, little one?"

She crinkles her nose. "Not good," she says, and glares up at the researchers. "Those awful ghosts don't think I'm doing very well either."

I twist toward Jack. "Is that true?"

He motions me back to the hallway. "We're losing her vitals."

Alarm tightens in my throat. "Which ones?"

"All of them," he says. "Talitha, we can't find a heartbeat. She's not going to last out here."

I won't listen to this. I start to turn away, desperate to get back to Sophie, but Jack catches my arm.

"There's something else," he murmurs, his eyes clouding over. "The test results came back. *Your* results."

Dread coils up inside me. "And?"

"You won't last much longer either." He speaks the words as plainly as he can, the staccato rhythm of each syllable sounding so normal, so nothing. Like he's only giving me the time rather than giving me a death sentence. "That place is killing you, Talitha. It's slow, it's hard to detect, but it's there. Your heart rate, your metabolism. It's heading in the same direction as hers."

He glances at Sophie, who's watching us across the room as though she can hear every word. As though she already knew.

I stand here, trying to make sense of this new version of the world, one where I won't be in it much longer. "Is it too late?"

"I don't think so." A grimace tightens on his face. "But you can't go back there. It's not safe."

A painful sigh. "But what other choice do I have?"

We linger in silence, the two of us watching Sophie as she pretends to have a tea party with the test tubes.

"How about the bottle from Brett's room?" I ask. "What did they find out about it?"

"Nothing," Jack says. "It never made it to the lab. It turned to ash on the trip there."

The same way Sophie started to crumble in my arms. Nothing from the past can venture too far from this place.

Nearby, the researchers are observing Sophie, how she moves, the way her eyes are going gray around the rims, the way she's dying in plain sight. And I'm observing them, how there's only four of them left now, no more than a skeleton crew.

"A couple more left last night," Jack says. "I think more will be gone by nightfall."

I only laugh. "Who can blame them?"

This whole neighborhood is liable to vanish before dawn.

I return to Sophie, and the two of us sit on the floor together until she's too tired to play anymore. "When are you taking me home?" she asks, as I tuck her back into bed for a nap that never seems to end.

"Soon," I whisper and kiss her forehead. Then I return to the house next door. To Brett.

When I walk in, she's already dressed and scrounging around the kitchen, her bare feet padding back and forth on the pale floor. She brightens when she sees me standing here. "You want breakfast? I think I could whip up something."

"I'm not hungry," I say, and it strikes me that I haven't been hungry in a while, everything in me fading away.

Brett is rifling through the cupboards, yanking out boxes of stale cereal, but I keep my distance from her. It feels like it isn't safe to be close to her, like I shouldn't have been close to her last night either.

She glances up at me, her eyebrow arching. "You all right?"

"I'm fine," I say, but we both feel it. The sudden gulf between us.

She leans against the counter, the brightness in her dimming a little. "Now what?"

"We go back in," I say. "We figure out how to fix this."

"And then what?" She stares at me, incredulous. "Does everything go back to normal? Back to the way it was when we were kids?"

"I don't know," I say. I haven't planned that far. Not that I get a choice in any of this.

And there's someone else who didn't get a choice either. Someone we need to help us finish this.

"Come with me," I say. "Back to Grace's."

A heavy laugh. "What makes you think she'll agree this time?"

"Because she has to."

I ask Jack to keep an eye on Sophie while we're away. "Call me if anything happens," I tell him, and I kiss her forehead again. She doesn't even stir this time.

Brett drives us again, getting more than her money's worth on the rental car. We reach the edge of Carter Lane, and I hold my breath, half convinced it's already too late, that I'm the same as Sophie. One more turn, and I'll dissolve like seafoam into the pale leather passenger seat.

But Brett keeps going, past the corner where Sophie fell apart in my arms, and everything's normal. I'm still here, I'm still whole. At least for now.

The highway is narrow and endless before us, and as we take a sharp corner, Brett sneaks a glance at me.

"What's wrong?" she asks.

"Nothing," I say, and turn toward the window. "I'm fine."

"Please don't do this to me," she whispers. "Jack told you something this morning, didn't he?"

Her eyes are on me, just for a moment, just long enough that I feel caught.

She already knows. Or at least she knows enough. I need to tell her the rest.

"They got the blood tests back." I fiddle with the radio, anything to keep my nervous hands occupied. "*My* blood tests."

A chill settles into the car.

"And?"

"I'm changing," I say, and I try not to let her hear it, the panic seizing me, curdling in my blood. "The same way that Sophie's changing."

"And what does that mean exactly?"

"I'm not sure," I say. "Nobody is sure about anything."

Brett shakes her head, a flash of anger in her eyes. "I don't need their test results to figure out what's happening. I can *feel* it." Her hands tighten on the wheel. "That neighborhood is killing us, right? Slowly but surely?"

The whole world holds still. "Yes," I say. "If we're not careful, it will."

Back at the house, Jack said it isn't too late. Except he can't be sure of that. There might not be any way to stop what's happening inside me, my decay as inexorable as the pull of the moon.

And Brett's right—I can see it on her too. Just the start of it, only a whisper behind her eyes. She hasn't visited as many times as I have, but if I keep dragging her back, she'll end up the same way, the light in her slowly fading out.

We pass through a one-stoplight town on the state highway, and I gaze out at all the little houses as we pass by. Houses that don't look so different from the ones we left behind.

"What are they doing to us?" I whisper.

"Exactly the same thing that neighborhood's always done," Brett says.

The neighborhood that could have stopped all of this. They had so many chances, so many days that could have turned out differently. I remember the last time I hoped for something better. It was a week before we left for college, and my mother and I were sitting on our front step with Sophie. One of the final days when we acted like we were a family, like we hadn't already broken into more pieces than a person could ever repair. Everyone was outside that afternoon, sprinklers cascading over lawns, the scent of burnt charcoal rising up from Weber grills, the whole world as picture perfect as a promise.

Until Brett's voice shattered the day.

"Tell him to stay the fuck away from me."

Everyone on the street stopped to watch as she came bursting out of the house next door, her face streaked with shame.

The shadow of her stepfather lingered in the doorway as her mother rushed out after her. "Sweetie, please," she cooed, her hands cupped over Brett's, like she was comforting an errant child.

But Brett didn't move. "Don't make me go back in."

My stomach corkscrewed, and I searched the street, up and down, desperate for an ally, for someone who would admit they knew what was happening. That they knew it could be stopped right then and there.

But there was nobody on Velkwood Street who would do that. Instead, one by one, they all turned away. Grace's mother went first, glancing at a nothing spot in her garden, tugging a wayward weed from the dirt. Then the twins, passing the basketball back and forth like they were hypnotized by it. Even Grace twisted toward the other end of Velkwood Street, the same place that Mrs. Owens was looking, her gaze blank and hopeless. Del's family went back to their barbeque, and Enid's father went back to his nap. So far as they were concerned, it was the safest thing to do.

It was also the easiest, the one thing that took no effort at all.

Tears dripping down her chin, Brett looked at me, and I looked back, wanting to scream, to run to her, to do *anything*, but my mother's hand was suddenly on my arm, tightening around my wrist, and I knew there was no way out. And Brett knew it too, something in her face cracking just a little, just enough that I alone could see it. Then she turned away and followed her mother back into the house. Even now, more than twenty years later, I remember it so clearly, the sharp crack of the door closing behind them. Like a coffin lid slamming shut.

Afterward, Grace's mother wandered down the sidewalk, loitering in the front yard with my mother. "There's always some kind of scene with Brett, isn't there?" she said with a girlish giggle, like this was all such a delicious piece of neighborhood gossip instead of what it really was: a cry for help in plain sight. A cry nobody would answer.

My mother just stood back, her lips puckered in a sneer. "That girl's a troublemaker," she said, her eyes shifting to me.

Bristling, I twisted away, and that was when I saw her, no more than a shadow. Enid, sitting cross-legged in the shadow of her own house. She must have been there the whole time. We watched each other for a moment, and a silent understanding sparked between us, a realization that things didn't have to be this way. That we could change this if we wanted it enough. If we were willing to give up more than the world should ever expect a girl to surrender.

That night, after my mother took a Seconal and I put Sophie to bed by myself, I called Brett, my hands shaking, my heart in my throat. She picked up on the first ring.

"Are you all right?" I wheezed.

A wisp of a laugh. "What do you think, Talitha?"

Everything in me held tight. "I'm sorry," I whispered.

She wouldn't say any more about it. Instead, we talked about where we could buy our college textbooks for half price and if we were going to the mall on Friday night and how Grace had a new theory about how Enid had never really died at the culvert and was only playing possum. I sat on the other end of the phone, pretending everything was normal, but I kept silently promising myself this would never happen again. I would never stand by and say nothing like the others. I would stand with her, no matter what.

Because it didn't have to be this way.

By the time we pull down Grace's street, it's already past noon, and, in the naked daylight, her house on the corner looks even worse than before. The porch is sagging more on one side, a pale blue shutter drooping from its hinges, slate shingles knocked loose like missing teeth.

"You sure you want to do this?" Brett asks, but it's not Grace she's talking about. It's everything else.

"I'm sure," I say, and together, we start across the yard and up onto the rotted front stairs. I'm ready to knock when Grace's thin voice leaks through from the other side.

"It's open."

Without a word, Brett and I shuffle inside. We find what's left of our friend sitting cross-legged on her stained love seat, the cushions spewing yellow foam and heartache.

Brett latches the door behind us. "Grace, darling, you shouldn't leave the house unlocked."

"Please," she says with a grunt, fluttering one hand at us. "As if anything could get inside that's worse than what's already here."

A heavy silence lingers in the room, and for an instant, all we can hear is the mournful melody of this tired house. A tick of the radiator, a whisper in the faded walls. Grace doesn't ask us what we want. She doesn't seem to care, not about us, not about anything. A husk of a girl, a husk of our friend.

But we need her to be more than that. We need Grace to remember, to come back to us.

"Sophie's out," I say, the words tumbling from my lips. "We're able to get people out of the neighborhood."

I wait for it to hit her, the possibility of it. The way she could rescue her mother or her brothers or even her fiancé. But Grace only rolls her eyes.

"You're just making it worse," she says before glancing at Brett. "So you've been back home too, I see."

Brett recoils a step, the uneven floor lurching beneath her. "How did you know?"

Grace points to the wall behind us. "Because you've got one now too."

I don't want to listen to her. I don't want to believe anything she says. But I can't help myself. With Brett at my side, we turn toward the corner and stare into the darkness. There they are, two shapes shimmering right in front of us. The shadows that followed us out of Velkwood Street.

"You know what they are, don't you?" I ask, fear rasping in my chest.

"Of course I do," Grace says. "You know too. Keep looking, Talitha. You'll see it."

I swallow hard and keep watching the shadow nearest to me. The way we're the same height. The way it moves when I move, every shudder, every nervous tic.

And the one near Brett. It mirrors her as well. The same long legs. The same curve of the waist.

"They're us," I whisper, the realization settling like cancer in my bones.

We're following ourselves. These shadows are the remnants of who we were.

"Do you understand now?" Grace gathers herself from the love seat and wanders to a soaped window. "It's already too late."

But I won't give up that easily. "We've seen Del," I say. "He's still there. He's still waiting for you."

Grace tries to silence her face, tries not to react, but even though she's half-turned toward the window, she can't hide it, that faint hope in her eyes. "How is he?"

"He misses you," I say, and it's true. "You can help us now. You can help him. We need you, Grace. We've got to go back together."

"I know." Her weary gaze rises to meet mine. "That's why the street evicted me. It wanted me to find the two of you."

Her words, heavier than grief, take a long moment to sink in. "You knew?" I gape at her. "You knew we could reach Sophie, and you didn't say anything?"

Even Brett is caught off guard, her face gone ashen. "Grace, why didn't you tell us?"

"Because," she says, "if we fix this, what happens to them? They're already dead." Grace stares off at the opposite wall, at the vague shadow of herself splayed across the faded wallpaper. "You've noticed it, haven't you? The way they've changed. The way they aren't really there anymore. It's like they're fading away right in front of you."

"Like they're an echo," Brett whispers.

Grace exhales a defeated sigh. "Exactly," she says, and relief flushes across her face, as if she's grateful someone else finally understands. "They're only an echo."

"We have to try," I say, like I'm doing my best to convince myself, but Grace won't listen.

"You can't hold on to the past, Talitha," she says.

"But what if the past is holding on to us?"

The sallow yellow light in the room shifts, the overhead bulb flickering on and off, and I notice something that I hadn't before. The scent of this place, musty and heady. It's oddly familiar, like ozone and moldering heirlooms and too much barbeque.

It smells like home. Like everything we left behind.

"So what are you going to do now?" I ask Grace. "Spend the rest of your life rotting away here?"

She scoffs. "And what have you done with your life, Talitha?"

"Better than this," I say. "At least I'm still willing to try. Are you?"

Hurt flashes in her eyes, and she looks suddenly like the same scared girl who fled Velkwood Street twenty years ago. "Please leave me alone," she says, and the shadows are dancing nearer now, everything in the room alive and restless.

Brett puts a soft hand on my arm. "Let's go," she whispers, and with the light fading around us, we head toward the door.

I turn back once, peering past the shadows. Peering at Grace.

"We were always in this together," I say. "That was what got us into this. And it could get us out of it too."

Brett and I retreat to the car in silence. There's nothing just the two of us can do. We need to be together, all three of us. That's the only way.

The engine turns over, and Brett wrenches the wheel, ready to pull back onto the street.

"Maybe we could try—" I start to say, when the car lurches to a stop, both of us seeing her at the same time.

Grace. The shape of her, lingering in the pale glow of the headlights.

"I'll come with you," she says, resolve hardened in her eyes. "One last time."

CHAPTER 14

We drive home together, Brett behind the wheel, me next to her, Grace's slight frame sprawled out in the back. There should be so many things for us to say—where we've been, how we ended up here. But maybe none of those things are important anymore, the silence stretching thin between us.

I fumble with the radio, twisting the dials until a song comes through. It's staticky at first, but it's unmistakable. "Ode to My Family" by the Cranberries. This used to be one of Brett's favorites.

Her jaw set, she switches it off. "No oldies tonight," she says.

Behind us, Grace presses her hands over her face. "It's been a while since I've taken a trip like this."

"You mean away from home," Brett says, "or back home?"

"Either one." Grace turns away from us. "Whatever happens tonight, we'll probably regret it. We always do."

I want to argue with her, but I know she's right. After all, this isn't the first time we've driven this way together. On our last trip on this highway, we were heading home for spring break.

Brett didn't want to come back with us. She planned to stay at the dorm the whole week, but she never got the choice. The night before Grace and I were set to leave, we awoke after midnight to shrieks on every floor. Bleary-eyed, the three of us stumbled out into the hall, arrayed in our flannel pajamas, a parade of scared girls flailing back and forth, trying to flee the things that were hanging on all the walls and ceilings.

Millipedes. There were millipedes swarming everywhere. The same kind we always saw at the culvert. A little souvenir from home.

"It's like that place is following us," I said, huddling with Brett, the two of us closer than we'd been in months.

And we stayed close, even as the exterminators showed up the next day, tacking up their *Fumigation in progress* signs. They cordoned off the whole building with yellow caution tape, hurrying us out the door before we had time to argue.

Grace drove us home in her mom's used Volvo, the radio cranked up, blaring Third Eye Blind until my ears were ready to bleed. Grace chattered on, but Brett didn't speak almost the whole way back to Velkwood Street.

We were passing the county line when I finally asked her what was wrong.

"I got a letter from the registrar's office," she said. "My tuition isn't paid. My mother told me she'd take care of it."

Grace waved one hand at us. "It's probably just a mistake," she said blithely, as though all of life's problems were no more than a petty misunderstanding.

"I don't think so," Brett said, and I could hear the jagged edge in her voice, the fear roiling there. Brett never sounded afraid, not like this.

I asked her how much she owed.

"A thousand dollars."

It was nothing and everything at the same time.

"We'll figure it out," I told her, and in the pale light of the waning afternoon, she reached out and took my hand, everything in her cold and faraway.

At last, we pulled down Velkwood Street and into Grace's driveway. Her brothers were playing basketball, scowling at us that we were interrupting the game. Grace didn't even bother to say hello to them. A big silly grin on her face, she rushed next door to see Del, as though they'd been separated for eons.

But I didn't move. Instead, I lingered on the sidewalk with Brett. I wanted to stay with her, for that night and forever, but I couldn't even let my mother see that we'd driven home together. We both knew what that meant—soon Brett would have to walk through her front door and into her own private nightmare.

"Don't worry," she said, flashing me a tragic smile. "I'll keep my bedroom door locked."

It's nearly sundown when we coast into Jimmy's Burger Shack. This is the same place Jack and I stopped on the way to town all those months ago. The same place my dad used to take me and Sophie.

Brett and Grace head inside, but I fall back in the parking lot, my cell phone shaking in my hand as I call to check on Sophie.

"How is she?" I blurt out as soon as Jack picks up the phone.

"The same," he says, and I almost laugh aloud because of course she is. Except for nearly falling apart in my arms, Sophie hasn't changed much in twenty years. Why would I expect anything else?

"And the neighborhood?" I ask. "How is it?"

A long moment passes. "I'm not sure," Jack says finally. "Just hurry back, all right?"

The line goes dead, and I just stand here, staring at the phone. Across the parking lot, Brett's watching me from inside.

"You okay?" she mouths through the window, the glass muffling her voice, and I give her a small nod. Then I retreat to the car, sinking down in the passenger's seat, wishing I was someone else.

Back on the state highway, the streetlights flicker on, one by one. I sit back, my head humming. Brett got me a burger and fries for the road, the brown paper bag neatly folded over, but I leave it on the floor at my feet, untouched.

Brett glances over at me, worry creasing her brow. "You all right?"

I want to tell her I'm fine. It's the same lie I always give her, the lie she never believes. But for once, I just tell the truth.

"No," I say. "I'm not."

She exhales a broken breath, her gaze set on the road ahead. "What if we go back this time, and that place won't let us leave?"

"That won't happen," I say, but we both know that's only wishful thinking. It's impossible to be sure what that neighborhood will do next.

Brett doesn't ask about it again, but her hand finds mine in the dark, and she clings to me like I might slip away in plain sight. In the back seat, Grace curls up, her eyes closed. For a moment, I'm sure a shadow passes over each of us, but when we take the next curve, the shapes vanish like mist.

The *Welcome to Our Town* sign flashes up ahead, and this is it. We're almost home, no more than a mile away. That's when the red gas light comes on.

"We should fill up now," Brett says, "in case we need to leave in a hurry."

In case we even get a chance to leave again.

It's after dark now, which means there's only one place that's still open. The only place that's ever open these days. The Chevron station on the corner, the neon light in the diner window always glowing in the gloom.

Delores meanders outside, her hat still crooked. She glances into the car where Grace is sleeping in the back.

"Look at the three of you," Delores says, turning to me, a glint in her eye. "I told you that you'd get the band back together, Talitha."

Grace murmurs under her breath, shifting against the thick leather upholstery, as Brett pumps the gas. I shove open my door and wander closer to the diner, the emptiness yawning within. The regulars at the counter have thinned out, and all the tables are empty, even the booth where Brett and I used to sit.

"Where's everyone gone?" I whisper.

Delores is suddenly right next to me. "I'm not sure," she says. "Maybe they're at home. Or maybe they're far away from home by now."

Dread tightens inside me. "They're leaving?"

"They're afraid," she says. "We all are."

I peer at her in the darkness, a question brimming inside me. "You told me not to do this," I say. "You told me to stop running with ghosts. But what if running to those ghosts is the only way to fix it?"

She hesitates before shaking her head. "Then I pity you even more than I realized."

The gas pump jolts to a stop, and Brett forks over a fifty. She and I pile back into the car, and we drive through the rest of the town, past the boarded-up storefronts, their facades like bruised faces.

At last, we turn down Carter Lane, and my breath twists inside me.

There are only two houses left now. The rest of them have vanished since this morning, the neighborhood moving in.

Brett pulls into the nearest driveway, and Sophie comes rushing out one of the front doors to greet us. She leaps right into my arms, and I hold her close.

"How are you feeling?" I whisper.

She clutches me tighter. "Jack says I don't have much longer. But he's just an ugly ghost like the rest of them, so I don't believe him."

I start to smile, but then she pulls away from me, and all at once,

I see it. The way her whole face has gone more pallid. I grasp her hands, her tiny hands, the ones that haven't changed in twenty years. Except now they are changing. Her fingertips are fading to gray, the same as Enid's. The same way mine probably will if we don't fix this.

The rental car door creaks open, and Sophie brightens. "Hi, Grace," she says.

"Hello, little one." Grace ruffles Sophie's hair. "How have you been?"

"Better than you." My little sister curls up her nose. "You look like you're almost a ghost too."

Grace chokes out a laugh. "You're not wrong."

The night is growing grimmer around us, and the only light remaining is from Velkwood Street. It's blotted out everything else in the world. Even the moon has vanished in its wake.

We walk up the front path to the last house, Sophie scurrying past us. Inside, it looks the same as all the others on Carter Lane. Plain walls, plain carpet, plain everything. Besides Jack, there are only two researchers left now, their eyes limned red, their gait as shambling and uneasy as the dead.

Jack glances up when we come in. "Hello, Grace," he says, and again, it spins my head to remember they've already met. All those months ago, I was the last resort.

Nausea roils in me again, that place sinking deeper into my bones, and my knees nearly give out beneath me. The closer I am to home, the worse I feel. I move for the back door, out into what's left of the yard, not wanting anyone to see me like this.

But Brett doesn't let me get far. "Talitha?" she calls from the doorway.

I wave her off. "I just need some air."

"You need more than that," she says, and takes a step closer. "You haven't eaten in days."

I grin at her. "You know that's not true."

"Don't," she says, and there's not a trace of playfulness in her eyes.

We stand together in the harsh chill of the evening, neither of us saying anything, the gleam of the neighborhood saying more than enough in its silence.

"What if I say no?" Brett asks at last. "What if I won't go back again?"

"That's up to you," I say, and mean it. "But I'll go without you."

Brett scoffs, trying to play it off, but I can see it there, the pain dancing behind her eyes.

"This is how it'll always be, isn't it?" she asks. "I don't get any choice in anything. Either I fall in line with you, or I don't have you at all."

"It's not like that," I say, even though I know that's exactly what it's like. "I just want to help Sophie. I want to help all of them."

She shakes her head. "You know they did nothing to help us. They knew what was happening. They just didn't want to get involved. Now we should do the same thing to them."

There's nothing I can say to this. She's not wrong, but it won't change my mind. I slink back inside, and Brett comes with me, her head down.

In the living room, the last two researchers are gathered around Grace.

"This isn't what we expected," they're murmuring to Jack, their stethoscopes limp in their hands, and I remember what he told me before. How they never took Grace's vitals when she wandered out of the neighborhood all those years ago. She wouldn't let anyone near her.

But now it's clear what happened. The same thing that happens to everyone who lingers too long over there. Her pulse is the same as Sophie's, the same as Enid's. Slow and sluggish and barely there. Grace is at once alive and dead, a living ghost.

The researchers withdraw, still colluding with each other, trying to understand this place. Trying to understand us.

Across the room, Brett won't look at me. Her hands folded in her lap, she settles back on the couch, the cushions molding around her, everything about this the same as the first night she came here. We're trapped in this loop, our whole lives on repeat.

Only maybe we won't be trapped much longer.

"We'll head back first thing tomorrow," I say, even though I'm not sure who's listening.

Even though I'm not sure we'll make it until then.

It's after midnight when the house next door vanishes.

By then, the last two researchers have already hit the road, leaving everything behind. Empty vials and blood pressure cuffs and needles still waiting patiently in their paper wrappers.

Only Jack remains now. He and I stand on the front step together, watching the neighborhood edge closer.

"I'm sorry about this," he says, not looking at me.

I just shake my head. "You're not the one who did this to us."

Another moment, the neighborhood swirling at the edge of the lawn, so close you practically smell it. The scents of barbeque and ozone and something else, something as acrid as regret.

"You need to get out of here," I whisper.

That street devours everything that isn't part of it. If he's still here when it comes for us, he won't survive. Hell, I'm not even sure we'll survive it this time.

Jack loads his beat-up Camry with a stack of clipboards and papers, the remnants of a research project gone awry. But even once he's got everything he needs, he still lingers in the driveway. All the things he's worked for—his grants, his hopes, his promises to the dead—are unraveling in an evening.

And he's thinking of that promise, the one he made to his aunt. The one that brought him here. His fingers trembling, he unclasps his necklace and passes it to me.

"A good luck charm," he says.

I cradle it in the palm of my hand like it's a precious talisman. In a way, that's exactly what it is. "I'll bring it back to you."

He gives me that crooked grin. "I'm holding you to that," he says, and climbs inside the Camry, the door still hanging open. "Whatever happens, we'll return as soon as we can. We won't leave you out there." He hesitates before adding, "*I* won't leave you there."

I let out a small, sad laugh. "You might not have a choice."

As the Camry vanishes down Carter Lane, I slip the necklace into my jacket pocket and turn back. Brett's waiting for me in the doorway, the neighborhood illuminating her face like a silver screen starlet. She's outlasted Jack yet again.

"Are you sure about this?" she asks, her gaze set on the looming horizon.

I don't say anything. I just watch as the neighborhood drifts a little closer.

We sneak back inside and lock the door behind us, as if it will make a difference. Grace and Sophie are already waiting on the living room floor, the two of them wilted against the wall.

"We get to go home soon," Sophie says, all the brightness gone from her eyes. She's fading right in front of me.

An echo. That's how Brett described her. And she's right. There's not enough left of my little sister to take her away from here. There's barely enough left to call her my sister at all. I'm not even sure if returning home with her will be enough now.

But I have to try. Brett and I join them, all of us sitting cross-legged, the shadows dancing on the walls, the whole house alive and ravenous.

We don't run this time. We don't even move. The four of us in a circle, like pagans around a bonfire, our hands clasped together, as if that will be enough to tether us to earth.

The walls convulse, the plaster curling away in the corners, and I count silently to ten as everything starts to dissolve around us.

At the last moment, Brett looks at me, her fingers tightening around mine.

"I love you," she whispers, and the words ache inside me. I want to say it back, I want to say all the things we should have said years ago when we were kids, but by the time I part my lips to speak, it's already too late.

A final surge, and the glow of the neighborhood swallows us whole.

CHAPTER 15

When I open my eyes, the sky's gone dark, and I'm standing alone on the other side.

"Brett?" Her name on my lips sounds like an arcane language. "Can you hear me?"

There's no reply, not from her or from anyone else. I'm back home, maybe for the last time, and I'm on my own.

I edge forward, ready to run, but my boot catches on something. It's small, no bigger than the size of your hand. I lean down and pick it up, turning it over and over. A bright red pony, knots in its hair, its blank eyes staring off into nothing. This is Sam, Sophie's favorite. It's the toy she dropped when I inadvertently pulled her through with us.

Clutching it close, I start moving forward. The street is crumbling beneath my feet, even worse than the pavement back in the real world. The neighborhood is turning to dust, which means we don't have much longer.

And all the ghosts know it. They're watching me now, from behind the slider windows in their quiet houses and from the corners of their shadowy front porches. The houses are falling apart, one after another, their facades wilting, the vinyl siding peeling off like rotted fingernails.

I try not to stare back at them. There's only one thing that matters now: I need to find the others. And I already know where to start.

The second one on the right. Grace's house.

I creep across the manicured yard, sweet-scented like summer, and with my hands shaking, I knock on the front door, the only thing about the place that's still gleaming and new. Mrs. Spencer answers in a flash, as if she's been expecting me. As if everyone on this street has always been expecting me.

"Is Grace here?" I ask, and I feel suddenly like some silly kid, hoping my friend can come out and play.

Mrs. Spencer shakes her head. "I haven't seen her," she says.

Behind her, Bobby and Bert flit back and forth in the living room, their faces still strange and blurred, everything about them like a nightmare. I want to look away, I want to pretend I don't see them, but I just keep staring instead.

Mrs. Spencer notices me watching. "She did it, you know."

My gaze shifts to her now. "Who did?" I ask, my voice breaking apart.

"That weird little girl." She grimaces. "The one that lives at the end of the lane."

Enid. She's talking about Enid.

I steady myself against the doorway, but splinters bite at my skin, and I wrench away. The frame wasn't splintered only a second ago. It was brand-new. This place is falling apart faster by the minute.

"Why do you think it's Enid's fault?" I ask.

"Because she didn't like them," Mrs. Spencer says, and gives the twins a mournful look. "She didn't like my boys for some reason."

I nearly spit out a laugh in her face. *Nobody liked your boys*, I want to say. And Enid had more reason than most to hate them. I don't blame her that she silenced them for good. It's the one thing about this neighborhood I understand.

But I don't have time to argue right now. "If you see Grace," I say, "tell her I'm here and I'm looking for her."

"I will," Mrs. Spencer says, "if it's not already too late."

And with that, she slams the door in my face. That doesn't mean she disappears completely, though. A moment later, she's at the window, peering out at me through the torn curtain, the twins looming at her side, all of them watching and waiting.

With a shudder, I turn around, and the grass is no longer trimmed and sweet smelling. It's knee-high. The front yard has grown more than a foot since I knocked on the door.

The sky shifts above me, from deep blue to midnight black and back again, and I keep going, past Mrs. Owens's house. She's still out on her front porch, the broom propped up in the corner where she can no longer reach it. She doesn't need it anymore. The frog is sitting in her lap now, and she's cradling him like a small housecat as she watches me pass.

"Are you going to fix this?" Her eyes are wild with fear. "Are you going to fix anything, Talitha?"

I don't answer her. I just continue walking along the cracked sidewalk and up the cobblestone path to my own house. The front door is open again, and I wander through it, my body numb, my vision blurring. The shadows are swirling around me, but I won't look at them. I'm afraid of what they might do.

And anyhow, I've got other things to worry about. My mother's waiting at the kitchen table. "There you are," she says, as though she's been expecting me, the same as everyone else on this street.

I hesitate in the middle of the room, something smoking on the stovetop. "Is Sophie here?"

"There's no one here." My mother turns to me, her eyes sunken and sallow. "Nobody except you."

"And you."

"You should sit. We should talk."

At once, I know what this is. It's a trick. The neighborhood is trying to trick me. Either that, or my own mother is.

"I don't have time," I say.

"Sure you do." She scoffs. "That's the only thing we have here: time. And a lot of it."

I glance again at the stove. There are four pans now, each one with something inside. Maybe it's strips of bacon like before, or maybe it's something else. Either way, it charring to a blackened crisp.

I shudder, the weight of this place pressing into me as I finally speak the words I've spent years searching for. "Why do you hate me?"

Her eyes turn to steel, and my mother stares back, like this is a question she genuinely has to think about. "I don't hate you," she says, and the acrid smell of burning meat rises through the air.

"That's not how it feels," I say. "It feels like you've blamed me and Sophie for everything."

She slumps back in her chair, looking older than before. "There's no room to say you regret it. You're not even allowed to think it. What kind of person would that make you? What kind of mother?"

A painful moment passes, melancholy settling into the lines on her face.

"There's no way out," she says, and at last, I understand what she means. There hasn't been a way out for her since I was born. She's been trapped here for much longer than she's been a ghost.

Because that's the real riddle of it all, isn't it? Marry the wrong person, and you get a divorce. Choose the wrong profession, and you get another job. There are ways to fix every other mistake in life except this one. Because once you have children, they're the ultimate trap. A gift you can never return.

I heave up a desperate breath. "If you felt that way," I say, "then why did you have Sophie?"

She exhales a defeated laugh. "To make sure it wasn't you." An unfathomable sadness echoes in her voice. "To make sure it was me."

A distant giggle through an open window, and my head snaps toward the sound.

My mother, however, doesn't react. She just keeps sitting at the table, her eyes on me. "You know what you have to do, don't you?" she asks. "You have to stop her."

I stare at her. "Stop who?"

"Enid. She's the one."

Rage rises up the back of my throat. My mother's just like Mrs. Spencer, just like all of them. Of course they blame everything on Enid. She's always been the easy mark. The weird girl, the one they'd rather forget.

"It's not her fault," I start to say, but then I hear it, lilting in through an open window. That familiar lullaby crooned in a crystalline voice.

Sophie. My little sister is somewhere nearby.

"I have to go," I say, and head toward the door, smoke filling the room now. On my way out, I pass by the stove again, and this time, I see what's in the pans. I smell it too. Hundreds of millipedes fried up in Crisco and margarine, burned to bits, their legs falling off like eyelashes, their thin bodies burst open in the middle.

"Dinner's almost ready," my mother says, and I nearly gag up a scream, but I don't stop, stumbling outside and down the street, back to the culvert. Back to where everything happens.

And it's the right choice this time, because Sophie is waiting there.

"Where did you go?" she murmurs. "You were right there in the house, and then you weren't."

"I'm sorry, baby," I say, and scoop her up, holding her close, promising myself I won't ever lose her.

But the moment I pull her into me, I feel it. The way her flesh has gone soft, her body like something impermanent. Something optional.

Sophie is falling apart in my arms all over again.

"But I brought you back here." Panic clenches my throat. "I did what I was supposed to do."

"It's not your fault," she says and squeezes my hand, her fingertips crumbling away.

I'm losing her. Even after all of this, I'm about to lose her anyway.

Below us, the earth has opened up a little farther, the darkness simmering within.

I back up a quiet step, fear spasming inside me. "What's waiting in there?"

"Everything," Sophie says, a strange sort of hopefulness in her. "And it will be ready for us soon."

I look at her. "Ready for what?"

But she doesn't have a chance to answer. Nearby, there's a rustling in the culvert.

"Who is it?" My voice splits in two as I edge closer, still clutching Sophie. But as I peer inside, my eyes adjusting to the darkness, it's not what I expect. No swirl of hungry shadows, no mountain of creeping insects. Instead, it's only Del and Grace, curled up inside, their arms wrapped around each other.

"What the hell are you doing?" I ask, even though I already know the answer. I should have guessed Grace wouldn't go home. She'd go to her boyfriend's house, the two of them sneaking away like horny kids, even in the middle of a suburban apocalypse.

Together, they climb out of the culvert with sheepish looks on their flushed faces.

Grace snaps her tongue at me. "It was good enough for you and Brett, wasn't it?"

At this, Sophie giggles. "Is that true?" she asks, her faded eyes shining for a fleeting moment. "Did you kiss Brett in there?"

"A very long time ago," I say, but then I wonder if it really was a long time in this place. Or if it was only yesterday. I look to Grace and Del. "Where is she? Where's Brett?"

Del shrugs. "Probably the same place she always is. At home."

Of course she is. That's where I found her before.

We climb up the hillside, Sophie still clinging to me, everything about her as fragile as porcelain. The entire neighborhood is emerging from their homes now. They know where we're headed. And they want to come too.

"Help us," they keep saying, their voices an unholy choir.

I hold tight to Sophie, desperate to keep her safe, but her body starts to turn to dust against me.

"Be careful," she whispers, her voice small and slight and pitiful.

"I'm sorry," I say, and together, we keep going, Grace and Del lagging behind us.

Inside Brett's house, her mother moves like a phantom, like something that can't even remember what it ever felt like to be alive.

"Is she home?" I blurt out. "Is Brett here?"

"Everyone's here," her mother murmurs. "Or they will be soon."

She's right. They're behind us, no more than a few steps now. Mrs. Spencer and the twins. Del's parents. Mrs. Owens, her frog resting in her cupped hands. Enid's dad, still gripping his old copy of *Playboy*. Even my own mother.

We keep moving toward the end of the hall. Toward Brett's bedroom.

When we walk inside, Enid's the first thing I see, waiting in the shadows. Waiting for us.

"Hello," she says. Her whole body's gray now, even her wild red hair, and she's tucked back in the corner, looking as if one swift movement and she's liable to crumble into nothing.

She and Sophie are fading. Everything is fading here. They told me I could fix this. That the three of us—me and Brett and Grace—could put this right again.

But we can't do anything. Grace is gawking in the doorway, as hapless as always, but I'm not looking at her. I'm looking at Brett. She's sitting on the bedroom floor, her gaze on the wall.

I kneel next to her. "Talk to me," I say, my hand on her arm, her skin gone cold, but she doesn't move. She can't hear me. She can't hear anything. My best friend is drifting away.

So is Sophie. She squirms out of my arms and disappears into the hallway. For a moment, I hear someone cooing to her. Our mother, welcoming her back. The daughter that was stolen from her.

I won't go after my little sister this time. I'm only watching Brett now.

"Please," I say, but she still doesn't hear me. I turn to Enid. "Do something."

"I can't." She drops backward, and her ashen body starts to merge with the wallpaper. "It's your turn now, Talitha."

But I don't know what to do. I never have.

And nobody else can help me. Brett has gone quiet on the floor, the past seeping into her, so deep I'm afraid she'll never return. Grace is still in the doorway, glancing between us, trying to fathom what's happening. And the rest of the neighborhood is crowding the hall, repeating the same thing, over and over, their whispers rising to a roar.

"It's her, it's her, she's the one to blame," they say, and their eyes are on Enid.

Still in the corner, she flinches at their words, like they're tiny daggers digging into her skin.

I stare at her, dread churning in me. "What do they want?"

"To watch," Enid says, and that's exactly what they're doing, a hallway of spectators pressing forward, jockeying to get the closest seat. We've always been the best entertainment on the whole damn street.

"What do they expect to see?" Grace asks, and I notice suddenly that Del's no longer at her side. He's fallen back with the rest. A useless bystander of our panic, of our grief.

"They want to see what comes next," Enid says. "What comes back."

"What is that supposed to mean?" I ask. "What's coming?"

But Enid only shakes her head. "I'm sorry for bringing you here," she says, and they're suddenly all around us.

The shadows, emerging from every direction, threading through our bodies, stitching up our insides. They're in us, this lost part of ourselves, and I never imagined being invaded by yourself would feel this raw and wrong.

At last, I understand it. Why they needed all of us. To re-create this. The last night. And I know what that means, even before it rises up in the air, choking the hope from our hearts.

A stench like afternoon sweat and WD-40.

He's not a shadow. He's real, conjured like the dead, like a nightmare from beyond. That hulking form. Those calloused hands. Those dull eyes that have barely returned before I realize what he's looking at.

Brett. He's staring right at his stepdaughter.

The darkness dances around us, as his thin lips curl into an ugly grin.

"There's my girl," he rasps, and everything falls apart.

CHAPTER 16

After all these years, I'd forgotten what he looked like, those deep crevices around his eyes, that snarl of his obscene mouth.

This feels like something I should remember. The face of the man we murdered.

The shadows swirl around him, eager and inviting. He shouldn't be here, not like this. Either he should be a ghost like the others, or he should be gone like my father. But he's become something else, something worse.

I twist toward Enid, barely wheezing out the question. "Why?"

She won't look at me. "He wasn't quite dead," she says, and this settles over me slowly, the brutal truth of it. We didn't check his pulse. We just ran. It never occurred to us that we hadn't killed him. That's why he's not quite a phantom like the rest of them. He's not quite anything.

That is, until now. All of us have returned, and it's like a magic spell, like its own form of witchcraft. The same way it took the three of us to bring Enid back at the culvert, it took all of us to bring him back. In spite of ourselves, we've conjured the past into the present, everything merging at once, forcing us to relive it.

Brett is still sitting cross-legged on the floor. This place has hypnotized her, sinking deep into her veins, tearing her away from herself. Away from me.

"Please," I say, clinging to her, desperate to pull her back.

Her eyes finally rise to meet mine. "Too tired," she whispers, and with Grace shrinking into the wall, I realize I'm alone in this.

Yet I'm not alone at all. The others are still right there, my mother and Brett's mother and Mrs. Spencer at the forefront, the rest of the street loitering behind them. They don't move to help us. They don't move at all. They're like wax figures crowding the doorway, blocking our only path out.

Brett's stepdad is leering nearer now, his body returned, his stench filling the room.

"I've missed you," he says, and runs a filthy fingertip along Brett's cheek. She barely flinches, an emptiness blooming in her eyes.

I'm losing her. I'm losing my best friend.

I lunge between them, swatting his liver-spotted hand away from her. "Leave her alone," I seethe, but this only makes him laugh, a grimy sort of cackle like a puking dog.

The light inside the room goes dark blue, the shadows absorbing everything, and I feel it, the way we're on repeat, looping through that last night.

Spring break was over, and we had to go back to school. Grace and I went to Brett's house to pick her up, Enid tagging along, because she had nothing better to do.

"Don't you want to get out someday?" I asked her, but Enid only shook her head.

"I don't get that choice," she told me, and I should have asked her why. I should have tried to understand her, but right then, all that mattered was getting Brett and getting the three of us back to school.

But when we found Brett, she was sitting on the floor of her bedroom, the same way she is now, her eyes down, shame hanging over her like a torn wedding veil, her stepdad looming next to her. We didn't even have to ask her a question before she answered.

"I'm not going back with you," she said, and the words were so plain and so brutal.

I stared at her. "Why not?"

"Because," her stepdad says, his voice echoing suddenly with the past, "that was my money too."

The joint bank account Brett had with her mother, the one for her tuition. My stomach corkscrewed as I realized it was already gone. Her stepdad spent her future like it was no more than petty cash.

Money—it's such a funny thing. The people who have it think every solution in life is so simple. But for those of us who don't, it's not simple at all. Her stepdad could withhold a thousand dollars, and that was the end. Brett would get kicked out of school halfway through the semester, her grades left hanging in the balance, everything in her life unraveling.

Maybe there were other options. Maybe we could have gone to the registrar's office and begged for an emergency loan. Maybe there were ways out of this. But we didn't think of any of that. All I could see as we huddled together in Brett's bedroom was the vile glint in her stepdad's eye, the reason he was doing this. To bring her home.

"That's not fair," Grace says, because it's the same thing she said before. We're replaying this night, mimicking ourselves, like we're no more than marionettes.

Brett's stepdad scoffs, his thin lips peeling back from yellowed teeth. "Nobody said it was fair, honey."

All of this is an echo, each of us in this room cycling through what we did before. Enid cowering in the corner, cool as a cadaver. Grace in the doorway looking gobsmacked.

And me kneeling next to Brett, her gaze gone glassy, her new future unfolding before us. The way she'd go back to working at the diner, greasy hands on her ass, stray tips in her pocket. The way she might never get out now. Because we all know somebody like that, the ones that never escape their hometown, never escape the past.

The beetles are skittering along the walls, their iridescent shells glinting brighter than crown jewels.

Her stepdad eyes me up, the same way he looked at me that night. "You're Talitha, aren't you?" He glances at Brett. "This is the one you like, right?" He moves closer to me, his breath like sour milk. "Maybe I'd like her too."

From the doorway, Brett's mother stirs suddenly. "Stop it, Samuel," she says, and my heart catches, because it's the first time I've ever heard her tell him no.

That didn't happen before. She wasn't even here when he died. Things are shifting, the past coming apart at the seams.

But Brett's stepdad pretends not to notice. "You can head on back to campus, girls," he says to me and Grace. "Brett will be staying here a while."

And that was it. He was walking away. He was done with us. But I wasn't done with him. Just like I'm still not done with him.

It happens in a flash, the same way it did before. A blank-faced porcelain figure on Brett's shelf, the one to celebrate her seventeenth birthday. My hand gripping it tight. A single blow across the back of her stepdad's head, one that sends him staggering.

There's a spot of blood, no bigger than a thumbprint, blooming in his dark hair.

He reaches back and touches it, his fingers sliding over the wound like he can't believe it's real. Then he whirls around, glaring right into me.

"Bitch," he says, and the word rolls off his tongue like it's an old favorite.

In the doorway, the others are crowding closer, all of them

watching us, waiting to see what will happen next. Waiting to see what we did that night.

But I already know, the memory of it like a grim carousel in my mind.

At last, Brett snaps out of it, her eyes going clear, as she rises to her feet.

"Leave her alone," she says, and picks up another figurine, the one for her sixteenth birthday, swinging it at his cheek, slicing open a gash.

Always eager to follow behind the rest of us, Grace takes a shot at him too, landing a blow right to the side of his hideous face. Over and over, the porcelain figures pummeling him, and when they're broken into bits, our hands red with virtue, we just use our fists. He's bigger than us and stronger too, but we've got an advantage: he never expected it. Even now, even on repeat, he still can't believe this is happening. Three little girls with bloodlust in their eyes.

When he finally falls, we stand in a circle around him, as stunned as we were the very first time.

"It was our only choice," I whisper, but even that night, I didn't really believe that. There were probably a lot of other choices. This was just the one we wanted to make.

We gather closer to him, none of us reaching out to touch him, to take his pulse. I close my eyes, remembering how it played out before. This was the moment when Enid told us she'd fix everything. This was the moment we ran.

But Enid doesn't say anything, and neither do we. There's nothing left to hide. The whole neighborhood knows what happened now.

With his limp body on the floor, it's not over. He's not dead, because nothing ever dies here, not now. We've learned that the hard way. He had nothing to do with this place turning into a specter—that was all Enid, her favor to us. But he was swept up in the aftermath, half-dead and half-alive, less than a ghost, less than nothing. Now, thanks to the three of us returning, he's back too. This feels like our birthright and our curse. To keep repeating this night. To stay here forever.

Unless we can figure out how to stop it.

I suddenly remember what Brett told me all those years ago.

It's not the land. It's us, Talitha.

Only that wasn't completely true. It was never our fault, not me or her or even Enid or Grace. It was everybody who wouldn't listen to us, the ones who are still here gawking in the doorway.

The shadows are swirling around us, settling in our veins, pooling beneath our fingertips. This neighborhood beckoned us back because it wants to absorb us. But we never belonged to it. If anything, we only ever belonged with each other, with our families. With the people who were supposed to protect us.

That's when I finally understand it, the truth that it's taken me decades to reconcile. I can't do this alone. I've never been able to do it alone.

The only way we change this is if we do it together.

His body twitching back to life on the floor, Brett's stepdad is rising again, the way men like him will always rise, but I'm not looking at him anymore.

I'm looking at my mother, still lingering in the doorway.

"Help us," I say, and something passes between us.

A truce of sorts, an opportunity. Maybe for the first time in our lives, we understand each other.

Brett's stepdad is struggling to his feet, starting toward Brett, but my mother steps over the threshold into the room.

"That's enough, Samuel," she says, and with her gaze set on the dusty shelves above the dresser, she grasps the nearest figurine.

Gripping it with both hands, she smashes it across his face, the blood splattering like a Pollock painting. Brett and I jump back, pulling Grace with us as we retreat toward the corner. Toward Enid.

"This is it," Enid whispers, and my mother doesn't stop, the whole room shaking around us, the house feeling liable to give way. Hope brimming suddenly in her eyes, Brett's mother follows right behind.

"You had no right," she says to her husband, and unlike my mother, she uses her bare hands, his flesh turning to pudding at her touch.

Mrs. Spencer doesn't want to be left out. She grabs the last figurine on the shelf.

"You should smile more," she says to him, and crushes in his front teeth.

Tittering like a knitting circle, our mothers work together, pulverizing the rest of him into the floor until he has no more pulse, no more heart, no more skin that's recognizable. It's a glorious, gory sight to behold, and I've never seen anything so beautiful.

Meanwhile, the rest of the neighborhood stands back and watches. I can see it on their faces—they're figuring it out now. How the three of us didn't come back to repair this. We came back to destroy it.

And they're ready to do exactly that. They're everywhere at once, pulling apart the hallway, the plaster soft and malleable in their hands. This place has been coming apart for a long time, so it doesn't take much coaxing.

They're moving all over the house now, skittering faster than cockroaches. I hear them out in the dining room, yanking every tacky commemorative plate out of the cabinet, and smashing them one by one on the hardwood floors.

With the walls trembling, Brett, Grace, and I huddle together, shielding each other from the debris. We're not like the others. We're not ghosts, not yet. If this house falls, we fall with it.

Enid sees this, the terror boiling in our eyes, and as always, she knows what to do.

"Hurry now," she says, guiding us through the crumbling rooms, all of us barely making it out onto the front yard before the house tumbles behind us.

Brett turns back, the wreckage of her past at our feet. "About time," she says, her eyes glinting bright.

But the others aren't done yet. They emerge from the rubble, fanning out around the street, headed to all the other homes too, peeling siding off the walls, doors ripped from their hinges as if by the Santa Ana winds.

It's something I never thought I'd see—ghosts tearing down their own haunted houses.

Sophie appears at my side, giving me that gap-toothed grin. "You can help too," she says, grabbing my hand, and we rush into our own house, where together, we tear apart the rec room, one tacky piece of wood paneling at a time, the whole room crumbling around us, all these mementoes crumbling.

When we're finished, we dash upstairs and back onto the street, where there's chaos everywhere. The abandoned houses at the end of the block have already been reduced to rubble along with Del's house. Next door, Mrs. Owens is holding her frog with one hand and ripping her porch to shreds with the other.

"I told you that you didn't belong here," she's hollering, while the whole facade cascades to the ground.

"Don't stop," they call out to one another, as Grace's house falls next, and her mother lets out a whoop that could split the sky in two.

Enid's house is the last to go. She and her father work together, the two of them making circles around the overgrown yard, grinning at each other, and it's the first time I've ever seen them look happy together.

When they're done, everything is crumbling, and I keep waiting for the perimeter all around us to stop shimmering, for the boundary between this street and the rest of the world to disintegrate. But that doesn't happen. The houses on Velkwood Street are gone, the ghost of Brett's stepdad vanquished, but it doesn't seem to matter. When I reach out and touch the border, it's thick as stone. We can't move through it. We're still trapped.

"We need to find a way out," Brett says, her eyes wild, and I know she's right, but I'm not ready, not yet, not until we can take Sophie with us. Not until we can take everything.

We were supposed to fix this. That's why the three of us came here together. But it's not fixed yet, not even close. If anything, it's more broken than before—even the illusion of the past is shattering.

Except Enid doesn't look worried. Smiling, she motions us on. "This way," she says and leads us to the end of the road. To the valley where the culvert is waiting.

The place where everything always happens.

We ease down the hillside, all of them following behind us, a stampede of a neighborhood. The crevice in the earth has opened wider now, and there's no longer darkness crawling within. Instead, there's a blinding light, golden as the sun, brighter than infinity.

This is what they've been waiting on. I thought this was supposed to bring them back. I thought this was supposed to be enough. But when I take Sophie's hand, my fingers pressed into her wrist, I feel it there. The gray coldness of her skin. The way her pulse is gone.

She's not coming back to life. She's finally dying instead.

I search the crowd, the dozen people left from this street. Panic seizing me, I surge forward, my hands fumbling for every wrist—my mother's, Mrs. Spencer's, even Bobby's and Bert's—but one after another, they're all the same. They're slipping away, their heartbeats vanishing along with the neighborhood.

I turn to Enid, a sob caught in my throat. "You said I could fix this."

"And you did," she says with a grin, as I reach out for her, clasping her wrist, remembering how I did this all those years ago when we were kids who coaxed her back from the beyond. Back then, her pulse had slowed to almost nothing.

Now it's completely gone.

I back away. "But you're still a ghost. You're all ghosts."

"Of course we are," she says, and I realize at last, this is what she always meant.

Nothing can change the past. Nothing can bring them back. That's how we were supposed to fix this. By finishing it.

My mother drifts closer to me now, and I expect she'll have some withering comment. Some way to remind me this is all my fault. For standing up for my best friend. For not letting that shadow of a man hurt her again.

But she says something else instead.

"Thank you for coming back for us."

I nod, my hands shaking in front of me. "You're welcome."

The crevice in the earth is opening wider, and the whole neighborhood is crowding closer, desperate for a front-row seat.

But I'm already standing at the precipice, gazing down at what's waiting for us.

"Is it heaven?" I ask.

"No," Enid says with a giggle. "It's far more interesting than that."

With the rubble of our lives disintegrating all around us, this is it, everything brimming in this moment.

"What do we do?" Brett wheezes.

"Don't worry," Enid says. "There's still another way out."

Her eyes flashing, she motions toward the culvert. The rumor was that you could follow it all the way through, that it would take you out of this place, but I never tried it. I was always too afraid.

And part of me is still afraid, especially since I don't want to leave. Not now, not when I'm back with Sophie at last.

Brett gazes at me, despair in her eyes, because I'm not moving, I'm not trying to run. "You know I can't stay here."

I look at her, pain clenching inside me. "And you know I can."

I have a second chance. I can finally be with my little sister.

And I'm not the only one who doesn't want to leave. Grace is standing with her arm looped around Del, her brothers' faces returned to normal, her mom behind them, all of them clustering together, as if posing for a family portrait.

"Come on, you two," Brett says, a mile past frantic, but Grace shakes her head.

"I'm staying," she says, adjusting the engagement ring on her finger. The diamond looks shiny and new again, her skin no longer green against the gold. This is where she belongs, where she always wanted to be, and now that this neighborhood isn't trying to evict her, it's exactly where she'll remain.

The detritus of the neighborhood is turning to ash around us. The insects skitter closer, forming an unbroken circle around the valley, their writhing bodies piling up.

Brett moves toward the culvert, ready to flee this place for good. But before she does, she glances back at me, the weight of the world in her gaze.

"Please, Talitha," she says, but I don't say a word, everything in me hollow and frozen.

And as the sky unravels around us, my silence is more than enough of an answer. Brett's face looks ready to crumble, the pain in her bubbling up, her eyes gone vacant. But she won't let me see that, not here, not ever again. Instead, she turns without another word and disappears into the culvert, escaping to freedom. Escaping me.

Grace has made her choice. So has Brett. Now I have to make mine.

Where does someone truly belong? Is it where you came from or where you're going?

A twinge in my chest, and I gaze at the culvert. Brett is already gone. I left her behind so many times before. Now she's left me, and I don't blame her. I've let her slip away for years.

It feels like this is the only thing we're good at—walking away from each other.

I could stay here. I could join Grace and never grow up, never grow old. Not one more day.

The others are murmuring around us, Grace still clutching Del, Mrs. Owens still clutching her frog. Enid's father is even edging closer, as though after all these years, he finally remembers that he has a daughter. A good one. A girl he should have been proud of.

This is how this neighborhood should have always been—together. They belong with one another.

But after everything, I don't belong with them. I never really did. That's why I made all those plans with Brett. Because there's somewhere else I need to be.

I take Sophie's delicate hand. "I'm sorry," I say, and at this, my little sister goes pale with panic.

"Don't go." She clings to my legs. "You promised me you wouldn't go."

"I know," I say, and it aches inside me, because it turns out I said a lot of things that didn't come true.

Maybe that's the trick of being young. You genuinely believe all the promises you make.

But I know better now. I know I can't stay.

"I'll take care of her," Enid says, and I have no doubt she will, because she already has. She's been the family to Sophie that I couldn't be.

I kneel before my little sister. "I love you," I say, and as she gazes back at me, she understands it.

Sophie wraps her tiny hand around my fingers. "You'll be my ghost now."

I smile at her, my heart hurting so much I can barely breathe. "And you'll be mine."

The insects are creeping closer, the sky drooping above us, and I know beyond reason that it's time.

"Goodbye," I whisper, ruffling Sophie's hair one last time. She wraps her arms around me, pulling me in like she'll never let me go.

Only she does let me go. And I do the same to her.

I move toward the culvert, climbing inside. The grit is thick beneath me, clinging to my jacket and hands, and there's nothing except darkness ahead of me, but I keep going. Something's shifting behind me, the light growing brighter and warmer and more inviting, but I won't look back, not even when my little sister's sweet giggle echoes through the rusted metal.

"Is that it?" I hear her ask. "Is that what we've been waiting for?"

"Yes, little one," Enid says, and even from here, I can tell she's smiling.

I wish I could be with them. I wish so many things. But there isn't time for that now. I keep crawling until I reach the vague light at the other end. Then I tumble out of the culvert, my knees skinned, my body half-broken.

Next to me, Brett is huddled in the dirt, her legs pulled into her chest, her cheeks soaked with grief. She stares at me, disbelief swirling in her eyes.

"Are you real?" she asks finally.

"I hope so," I say, the weight of that place still hanging heavy in my bones.

Together, we look behind us, but there's nothing left to see. Velkwood Street is already gone. Not a hint, not even a whisper it was ever there. Just an empty lot where the whole world used to be.

"Home," I murmur, and for the first time, I'm sure I no longer have one.

CHAPTER 17

The next few days dissolve around us in an instant.

There are news crews and freelance journalists and podcasters who broadcast weekly shows I've never heard of before and will probably never hear of again. Everyone's suddenly fascinated by the Velkwood Vicinity now that it's vanished altogether.

Jack returns too, bringing a clique of blank faces with him. A few fresh researchers along with all the ones from before, still purse-lipped as ever, pretending like they never left. Like they were never afraid.

Brett and I don't put on the same pretense. The two of us are numb, barely speaking, barely doing anything at all. At the diner, Delores tries to ply us with offers of free all-day breakfast platters and bottomless cups of coffee, but we don't take her up on the offer.

"You've got to eat, kids," she says, but we don't even bother to look at her.

Instead, we slump back in the corner booth where we used to sit together, long before the past was chasing us, long before there were ghosts. Meanwhile, all the journalists and podcasters flock around us, peppering us with an endless barrage of questions.

"What did you see? What was it like? Where did it go?"

They ask the same thing a dozen different ways. Sometimes we answer, and sometimes we don't. It doesn't seem to matter either way.

"Are you happy to be back?" they ask, but they're already sure they know the answer to that one.

Of course we're happy. Why wouldn't we be?

This goes on for hours, for what might as well be forever. All the while, they keep calling me by Brett's name and calling her by mine, the two of us interchangeable to them.

"And Grace?" they ask, referring incessantly to their notes, since they can't remember her name at all.

"She's gone," I say without inflection.

A podcaster in the front makes a note. "But why would she choose to stay behind?"

I shrug. "Doesn't everyone want to go home?"

"Then why didn't you stay?" someone asks, and Brett grunts up a small, rueful laugh. This twists inside me, because I know she's laughing at me. At how I almost did exactly that.

And in a way, we do stay here. We don't leave town at all, not to go to the hospital, not to go anywhere. I wonder if we even can. If *I* can. Sophie could never leave. She'd crumble into nothing if we started toward the edge of town. What if I spent too much time over there? What if I already belong to that place, and I just don't know it yet?

"I'm afraid," I whisper, but in the cacophony of voices, nobody hears me, not even Brett.

At night, with the houses on Carter Lane long gone, Brett and I have nowhere to go.

"Don't worry, girls," Delores says, and offers us the cramped room above the diner. The one where Brett and I used to make-believe plans for our future.

The two of us curl up together on a stained mattress without a sheet, Brett's long hair falling over me.

"Do you think Grace is happy?" I ask in the dark, the pale glow of the streetlight leaking in through a smudged window.

"I'm not sure that Grace could ever be happy," Brett says, her face shrouded in shadows, and I think how she's probably right.

But at least in the end, she got what she wanted. Grace got to live in the past forever, crystallized in a dream.

The next day, we live through the same morning and afternoon all over again, strangers asking questions, us barely answering. Afterward, they offer to pay us, meager recompense for what we've been through. I pocket the money, the same thing I do with the payment from Jack. It won't last forever, but nothing ever does.

Brett, however, refuses all of it. "I'm not profiting from that place," she says with a shudder, but we both know it's easy not to take the money when she doesn't even need it.

She lingers in town anyhow. That night, we lie together in bed, a gulf between us, something in Brett gone suddenly cold. Overhead, we see them, a wave of obscure shadows darting back and forth, jagged as knives, ethereal as fog.

"I wish they'd go away," Brett says, but we both silently wonder if they ever will.

We expect the interviews to last for weeks. The tests from the researchers. The general pomp and circumstance. But we're wrong. Just as quickly as they arrived, everyone trickles out of town again, leaving no more than dust in their wake.

Brett and I sit on the crumbling curb in front of the diner as the last media truck pulls away.

"So this is it," she says, her voice tinged with melancholy. Not because she wanted them to linger here, but because she knew they were our excuse for staying, the two of us tucked away in that shoddy room like escaped convicts on the lam.

We visit Velkwood Street one last time, standing together on the empty spot where we grew up. This is where everything happened, and where everything ended, too, our childhood flattened into nothing, bulldozed by ghosts.

All that's left now is gray soil. Not a single blade of grass. No pavement, no culvert, no valley. It's like we never existed at all.

Brett and I walk together, retracing our past, imagining where each house used to be. When we pass the place where Mrs. Owens's porch was, a tiny frog hops past. I watch him, my breath twisted in my chest. He looks at us, his eyes black as infinity. Then he moves on like he never saw us at all.

"What happened here?" Brett asks.

I gaze back at her. "You mean, to the neighborhood?"

She shakes her head. "No," she says, and her eyes shift to me. "To you. Why did you come back? Why didn't you stay with them like Grace did?"

A long moment passes, as she gathers up the courage to speak the rest, the real question she's desperate to ask. "Why didn't you stay the way you always wanted to?"

This is it, the reason why she's gone cold to me. She doesn't think I want to be here.

She doesn't think I want to be with her.

"Because," I say, "I belong out here."

Brett continues walking, kicking up dust. "And why's that?" she asks, not even glancing back.

I struggle to keep up with her. "I think you know."

But I still don't say it. Even after everything, I can't speak it aloud. It feels like I've come so far, only to end up in the exact same place.

We're lingering now on the spot where I used to live. Where the rec room used to be. This is where Brett and I fell asleep together, where everything fell apart. I start to turn away, but my foot catches on something in the dirt. I kneel down and dig for it, my throat closing up as I yank it free.

It's a bright red pony, its hair in knots. Sam, Sophie's favorite toy.

Except it's not the same anymore. It's withered and aged like it's been here for a century. Or maybe just for twenty years. Maybe ever since this place disappeared.

The breeze whips around us, and for a moment, I'm sure I hear her. That crystalline giggle, pure and sweet and finally free.

"She's all right," Brett says. "Enid will make sure of it."

I don't say anything else. We drive back to the diner, the pony on the dashboard. Jack's waiting there for us.

Brett scoffs when she sees him, but then she glances at me, softening a little.

"I'll give you two a minute," she says, and puts the rental in park.

I climb slowly out of the car. Jack's loitering nearby on the sidewalk, and the two of us stare at each other, suddenly feeling like the same strangers we were all those months ago when he found me in my front yard. That feels like a long time ago now. A different girl, a different lifetime.

"I'm sorry," I say.

He raises an eyebrow at me. "For what?"

"Your life's work has vanished into thin air."

He nods. "And your whole life has."

I look back at Brett, as she leans against the car, pretending she's not watching us. "Not all of it," I say.

"So what now?" he asks.

I shake my head. "I'm not sure yet. How about you?"

"There will be plenty of papers to write. And plenty of interviews, too. I can still squeeze a whole life's worth out of it." Then he gives me a pointed look. "Can you?"

"We'll see," I say, and shove my hands into the pockets of my jacket. That's when I feel it there.

Jack's compass necklace. In the chaos of the last few days, I'd forgotten to return it to him.

"This is yours," I say.

My fingers steady, I pass it to him, and we both see it at the same time. It's not bent in the middle anymore. The charm is smooth and shiny, as if brand-new. For the first time in years, the compass points north again.

Jack marvels at it, turning it over and over in his palm. "Proof of ghosts," he whispers.

I smile at him. "I think she'd be proud of you, Jack."

He brightens for an instant. "I hope so," he says, and starts to turn away before glancing back at me. "There was something I didn't mention. Something Sophie said to the other researchers."

I seize up at the mention of her name. "Like what?"

"It was about Brett's stepdad. About how he died."

All at once, I can't breathe, the whole world dangling on piano wire. "And do you believe her?"

A long, strained silence. Then Jack gives me that crooked smile.

"Of course not," he says. "Just the fanciful tale of a fanciful kid."

"Thank you," I say, and with that, he walks away.

I wander back to Brett, and together we watch him go, that beat-up Camry clunking its way down Main Street. "He *is* cute," she says begrudgingly.

I laugh a little. "He is, isn't he?"

Brett gazes at me, her cheeks flushed. "Do you need a ride out of town?"

She knows I do. She knows everything.

"If you wouldn't mind," I say.

Delores waves goodbye from the front window of the diner. "Have fun, girls," she calls out, her voice muffled through the glass, and part of me is convinced she just wants to get rid of us, the two troublemakers in town. But then she flashes us a wide grin, and I realize for the first time that it's genuine.

And I can't help but smile back.

In the driver's seat, Brett turns the wheel, heading the way we always go. South on the state highway. Back toward the burger shack, toward all the places we've been before. Past the dead mall and the dead hospital and the dead dreams we should have shed years ago.

"No," I say suddenly.

We've been driving along that same stretch of highway all our lives, memorizing every signpost, every crack in the asphalt.

Without another word, Brett understands what I mean. She twists the wheel, the tires screeching until we're heading north, away from Velkwood Street, away from everything we've known.

What's left of downtown rushes past the passenger window. I pick up Sophie's pony from the dashboard and hold it close, but I already know I can't keep it for much longer. It's going soft in my grasp. And it's not the only thing that's changing. I can still feel the shadows stirring within me, this remnant from the past.

We haven't quite reached the outskirts of town when Brett does something I don't expect. She asks her question again.

"Why didn't you stay there?"

I don't hesitate this time. "Because of you," I say. "Because I want to be with you."

It's the truth, but it doesn't seem like enough anymore. It seems like it's way too late. I can sense it within me. How the shadows will never leave. How they don't want me to leave, either. We haven't gone beyond the city limits yet, and I don't think I can.

We're on the last street, on the last block, and without even glancing down, I feel it. The pony turns to ash in my hands, crumbling between my fingers like pale grains of sand. The same way I'll crumble.

There's still time for one thing. For what I should have done years ago. Back when we were alone in the culvert or the rec room or anywhere else.

"I love you," I say to Brett, and it's my entire life, my entire past wrapped up in three words.

A small smile appears on her face, the darkness suddenly gone from her gaze. "Thank you," she whispers, and I think how this will have to be enough. This will have to be goodbye.

I close my eyes, waiting to dissolve like a pillar of salt. Waiting for everything to end. For my mother and Brett's stepdad and that neighborhood to win after all.

But then something else happens. We breeze right past the city limits sign, the pavement whirring beneath us, the sky gray up ahead. Soon, the town is disappearing behind us, everything disappearing.

For miles, I keep waiting for it. For everything in me to fall apart. But it never happens. We just drive, the two of us together on this road we've never taken.

"You all right?" Brett asks, her gaze flitting over to me.

"I think so," I say, the ash of Sophie's pony drifting through the air, the color of stardust.

The hours vanish in a flash. In late afternoon, we stop off at one of those tacky roadside attractions in the shape of a giant ice cream cone, the kind of place brimming with greasy cuisine and a freezer stuffed with sugary treats. At a splintered picnic table, we share a basket of french fries and split a twin pop.

"For old time's sake," Brett says, and we laugh together like we used to. Back when we weren't so busy running from phantoms.

We're heading back to the car when I turn to her.

"Can I drive for a while?" I ask, and Brett doesn't hesitate. She tosses me the key, and we slide into the rental.

The weather brightens as we take the highway north, and another highway after that, passing places we've never seen before, places I never even knew existed. Little houses in little neighborhoods where nobody's ever conjured a ghost.

But we aren't so lucky. It's still light out when I notice them. The shadows dancing in the rearview mirror, filling up the back seat like a silent nightmare. Brett sees them too, their restless forms seemingly everywhere at once. They haven't left us. They never will. But maybe they're not supposed to.

And maybe we can live with that.

Brett reaches over and entwines her hand with mine, everything about her warm and golden and real. With a grin, she's holding on tight. She won't let go.

This time, neither will I.

"Where do we go from here?" she asks, the sun on her face, the future in her eyes.

"Anywhere we want," I say, and above us, the sky is clear and bright and full of promise.

ACKNOWLEDGMENTS

Every life is a haunted house in one way or another. I know mine certainly is. This book is an exploration of that, and perhaps the most personal story I've ever written. That's a scary thing to put out into the world, but here we are.

Tremendous thanks to Saga Press for publishing this very haunted and very personal book. In particular, a shout-out to my editor, Joe Monti, for his support of my characters on Velkwood Street and for helping me to get this story to its best possible form. Thank you to Savannah Breckenridge for her work as the marketer on this novel and to Jéla Lewter for everything she does at Saga; both of them have enthusiasm that is positively infectious. Also, I want to say thank you to Lucy Nalen who worked as a publicist on my last book, *Reluctant Immortals*; what a joy to have her in my corner, supporting my writing every step of the way.

I want to give a hearty thanks to my writer friends including Sara Tantlinger and Christa Carmen who are always there to listen to me on the bad days and celebrate with me on the good ones. Also, a big thanks to everyone at HWA Pittsburgh; it's such a wonderful experience to be part of a group that supports one another so much.

Last but in no way least, thank you to my husband, Bill, who is without a doubt my writing's greatest champion and my biggest fan. He's the first reader on all my tales, and he's the one who encourages me to keep going, even when I'm ready to set fire to everything I've ever created. Everyone needs a Bill in their lives.

Writing is an act of magic. It can also be an act of self-discovery and self-preservation. For me, creating *The Haunting of Velkwood* was both. Whoever you are and wherever you may roam, thank you for picking up this book and reading it. It means the world to me.